HANSON

VIEWFINDER

PETER ANDERSON

LIMBERLOST PRESS

2023

VIEWFINDER

To Jeanne, lifelong fellow voyager and

viewfinder extraordinaire.

Whereto next, my love?

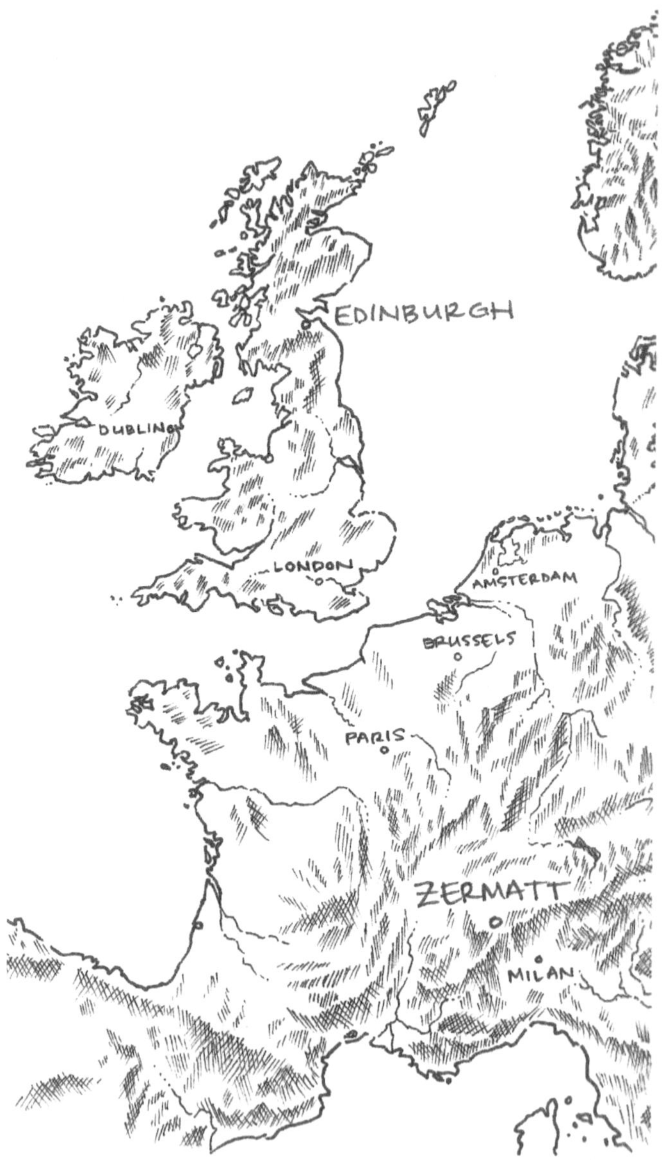

EDINBURGH
DUBLIN
LONDON
AMSTERDAM
BRUSSELS
PARIS
ZERMATT
MILAN

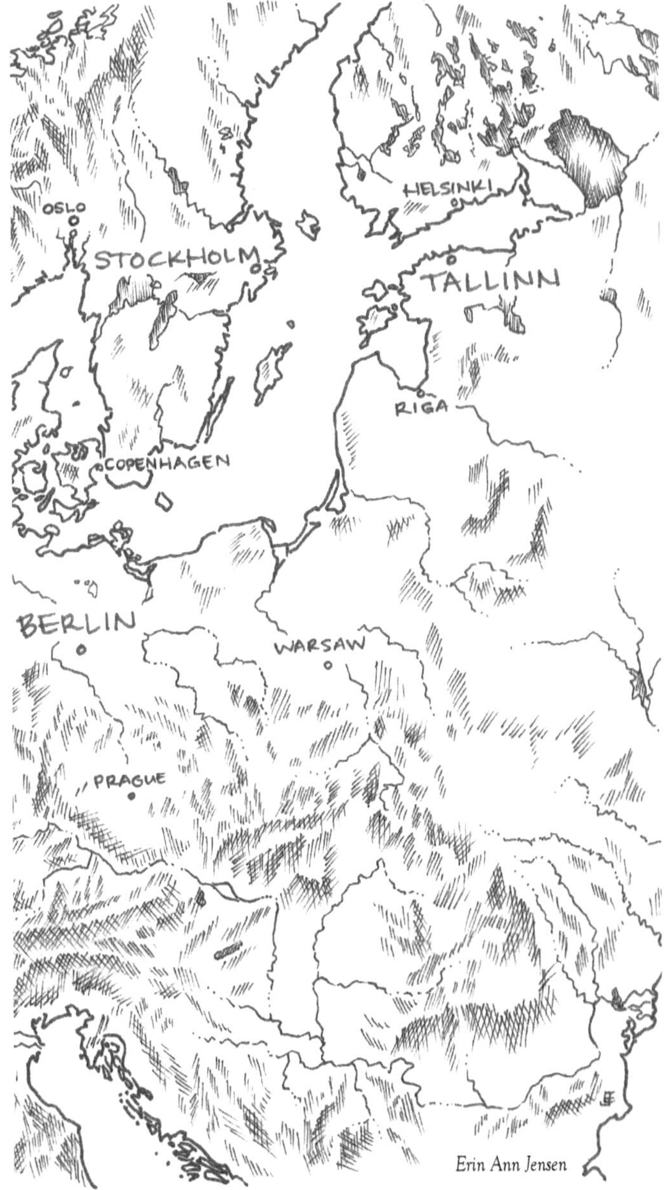

OSLO
STOCKHOLM
HELSINKI
TALLINN
RIGA
COPENHAGEN
BERLIN
WARSAW
PRAGUE
Erin Ann Jensen

*Truly the universe is full of ghosts, not sheeted
churchyard spectres, but the inextinguishable
elements of individual life, which having once been,
can never die, though they blend and change,
and change again forever.*

— H. Rider Haggard

PART ONE

LINE. SHAPE. FORM.

———— **CHAPTER 1** ————

A camera, like any tool for observing, must fit the person who observes. Lucas Block's camera is a Zeiss Ikon Contina. It is as old as he. It has sidestepped relegation to a display of 1950s oddities. The steel camera, leather-wrapped, thus faintly warm to the touch, is solid and heavy for its size. Its lens and delicate *f*-stop and range rings mount the end of a small folding carriage that clicks open on a hinge. The camera nestles his palm.

Lucas lifts his camera to his face, sights through it, places his finger on the shutter release lever and then pauses. He lowers the camera and looks over it. He sights through the viewfinder again, and once more lowers the camera.

His subject is a wall of glass. He stands on a granite curb at an angle to the wall. Between Lucas and the wall, people pass in multiple directions. The reflections of the people, displaying their opposite sides, shine off the glass and converge with their creators and separate from them. The light of the late sun is heavy, snowy and dense. Across broad Ebertstraße, behind Lucas, black-branched trees, barren and wet, cast shadows which scrabble down the glass.

Beyond the wall of glass, more people float along a broad corridor inside the building. These people also cast trailing

1

silhouettes in the slim light which washes over them through the wall of glass onto pale stone behind. A segment of an elegant old building pre-dates the spasm of bombs and bloody soil and rubble. Under glass, the fragment of wall is an exhibit in a museum.

Commuters stride by. All hurry. It is afternoon. The people mostly hasten to dinner and urban seclusion and the little agglomerations of known spaces and forms of homes before the weather closes in again, as it is predicted to do. For some of them, it is easy to imagine, this hoped-for after-work respite is a wish, a vision of life, not life as it may actually be; image and its obverse. The schism shows on endless passing faces. Schism or perhaps just fatigue. The people and their reflections and shadows cross and intersect and melt, a chaos of images.

Berlin, perhaps more than many cities, provides a lucid observer with endless perfect viewfinder moments. Fragments of the past lodge between glassy expanses of the present, the theoretical future. A glance away, a viewer spots a splinter of what used to be, comfortable, tidy spaces where willful, reliable amnesia flourishes. Many locales offer such visual moments; Berlin brims with them. Lucas seeks these places. He sees them.

Lucas raises the camera once more and clicks the shutter.

A long yellow bus rumbles past behind him in the street. A high-low-high-low *Feuerwehr* siren, roughly E and B-flat slices the roar of traffic in Potsdamer Platz. Facades of towering buildings loom, glow and bend away.

Lucas winds the camera until the next frame of film settles into place. In the fifteen minutes he's been watching shifting images in the glass wall, storm cloud has solidified over the city again and renewed wind moves up the wet street, lifting his coattail. He raises the camera, cocks the shutter and clicks one more shot. Then he folds the slender camera closed and drops it into the left inside pocket of his overcoat and buttons the top button and straightens his scarf.

He lifts his bicycle from the rack in which it leans, wipes the wet seat with a bare hand, straddles it and pedals into the bike lane, a marsh of slush laced with bicycle tracks.

At the intersection, when the crosswalk signal changes to green-man-walking, he threads crowds pressing against the burgeoning wind and its overdue freight of new snow. The little triangle of Henriette-Herz Park opens before him and beyond, across Lennéstraße, the Tiergarten.

He cuts through a corner of the park. He crosses a gentle expanse of frozen meadow and along snow-layered mud paths among the trees. Overnight, a hands-breadth fall of snow had crusted the city, breaking the branches of lindens and maples, slowing morning traffic, decorating rooftops, chimneys and cornices.

At sunrise the wind of the cold front collapsed and dead cold settled. Children towed to school by adults skated in their boots along gutters and walkways. Commuters trod the ice, stepping high over ridges of frozen snow rimming streets. Trams shunted shining ice-coated rails.

But by noon the day, if not the ground, had thawed and the vast city, a land of 3,000 lakes and waterways laced among boulevards and neighborhoods, malls and factories, old brick and glassy curtain-walls, slewed into an endless webwork of slushy ponds, shores clotted with leaf mulch. Veils of mist drifted, the leading edge of another wall of weather approaching across the frozen dunes and estuaries, the plane of farmland zinc-plated under winter, from the distant North Sea.

In Tiergarten, Lucas encounters few fellow venturers on the dark paths angling through stands of dripping, tossed forest: A handful of joggers in thermal-wear; people walking dogs, gripping leashes and hunched into their coats and hats; a pair of *Polizei* on horseback, both poking at their phones with cut-finger gloves, their horses glancing, tossing heads and breathing clouds. A low roar of afternoon traffic grows from Straße des 17 Juni. Lucas emerges from the woods across from Brandenburger Tor.

Only one group of tourists stands on the far side of the great gate, photographing. They are Asian, bunched, faces pale in the Saxon winter, bundled in black. They gaze upward, stoic and doubtful. Their tour guide, red flag on a stick, has fallen silent.

They raise their phones to the quadriga high above with its four bronze horses against the wreckage of violent dark sky.

As Lucas crosses under the massive gate, a cyclist coming from the other direction, from the east, suddenly slows and veers across and circles back around him. Lucas stops.

"I thought I might see you coming this way, based on where you said you'd be shooting this afternoon, so I waited. I left messages but your phone's dead, I think," the man says in English to Lucas. He clenches his bare hands under his arms. His face shines damp and reddish.

"Nik, my phone's always dead. I forget to plug it in."

"There's bad news. It's Mama. She died. Somehow. They found her in the river this morning. Eloise is a wreck. I think Heike went over to be with her."

"The river," Lucas says. "What happened?"

"No idea. Eloise just said they found her. Way out past Charlottenburg toward the ship channel. Eloise didn't know anything else. I've been trying to call the cops but I can't get anything."

Lucas and Nik stand astride their bicycles in the shadow of the great arch in the center of the gate in the gloaming. The flagstones slope slightly here, and water moves downhill in a slow, filmy slide. In a few hours, this sheet will be pure ice again.

"Mama," Lucas says. He looks up to the sky.

"I'm sorry," Nik says.

Lucas reaches out and takes Nik's cold hand, which Nik unfolds to him, and shakes it. "I'm glad I saw you. I'm sorry I didn't answer my phone."

Nik is smaller than Lucas. He looks up to him. "It wouldn't have changed anything."

"No, it wouldn't."

The two men briefly hold each other's eyes.

"It's as if we always knew," Lucas says.

"I'm sorry," Nik repeats, looking upward into the taller man's face. "Of us all, you were the closest." They stand together, straddling their bicycles, aimed different directions but adjacent and near each other for a moment. They slowly release their handshake.

"No such thing as fate, is there?" Lucas asks, not of Nik, just of the afternoon. Nik shakes his head. "But sometimes," Lucas says, "something that sure resembles fate blows through."

"She seemed better lately," Nik says, "almost as if she was happy." This is stated more with generosity than conviction.

Lucas says, "The more I see of the world, the less I believe what I see. Especially the fronts people put on."

This comment stops them from speaking for a minute. Along Unter den Linden all the way to the river, traffic undulates softly.

"The opening at Denver is going ahead tonight," Nik says. "I called Frankie. She was still hanging pictures this afternoon." Lucas nods.

Bent over his handlebars and standing on the pedals, Nik rides away under Brandenburger Tor toward the west, where a slash of baroque sunlight has suddenly underlit the clouds, defiantly. The momentary light cuts under the monument, slicing shadows into the wet stone.

Lucas looks upward, to the horses or their shadows or the sky. He reaches and touches his camera in his pocket through his thick woolen coat, but doesn't take it out. He stands alone with his bicycle, one hand on his breast over the bulge of the camera. The Asian tourists have vanished. He waits for a minute, watching the swift changing of the light. Wind skids the pavement and sluices wrinkles in the puddles.

"Mama," he says softly.

—— CHAPTER 2 ——

Overlooking Rosenthaler Platz, Lucas Block's flat occupies much of the top floor of an undistinguished building. The ground level of the building houses a Viennese café and an elegant Indian restaurant, a small organic grocery and the shop of a maker of lenses for optical instruments. A hotel with creaking wood floors and showers down the halls occupies floors one through four. The narrow elevator stops at floor four and Lucas must ascend a dark and squeaky stairway to reach his flat above.

He chose this place on Rosenthaler Platz because it offered a panoramic overlook of the busy intersection below, with its curving tramways aiming multiple directions, the four stairwells descending to the U-Bahn, the endless serpentine rivers of cars and bicycles stopping and starting in rhythm with the shifting of the lights: a pulse. Deep into the evening, the trams rumble past every two or three minutes. Lucas sits on his balcony or watches through his windows for hours, a book sloping in his hand, in peace.

The flat also offered anonymity. At the time he took it, two decades previous, anonymity was paramount to him.

Doubled windows in old frames wrap two walls of the main room, with a pair of French doors opening onto a small balcony holding two chairs and plant pots, now snow-filled. Modern appliances shine in the small open kitchen. The bedroom, too, is slim though long, and he still occasionally knocks shins on the bedframe as he skirts it. But the rooms are large, tall and elegant, in a sparse, ashy Scandinavian fashion, with coved ceilings and woodwork, once painted white, partially-stripped and polished to show its veins.

Hundreds of framed photographs cover the walls of the rooms, a collection of artwork photos and stray snapshots spanning many years, mostly black and white: portraits and figures at rest and in motion, angles and corners, spaces, surfaces and textures, odd juxtapositions, pieces of architecture. Some of the photos were taken by him. Some are antique. Some are signed with short comments addressed to Lucas, either by the subject of the photo or the taker of the photo.

When he rented the flat, a vacant workroom occupied a space in the attic directly above, reachable up a short further flight of cracked and groaning wooden steps. Lucas converted this space into a darkroom for developing film and working on his prints.

Lucas parks his dripping bicycle in an alcove off the narrow lobby of the building. In his flat, he sets his camera and his lifeless phone on the stone counter in his kitchen. He shrugs off his coat, wet-wool scented.

A small pile of his girlfriend Heike's clothing—underpants, camisoles, exercise tights—lies folded neatly on a side table, where she presumably left them for later pickup. Her clothing tends to accumulate over periods of time, but then is occasionally whisked away in her carryall purse back to her own flat, always coming and going.

Lucas pours bottled water into a tumbler and stands in the window looking down into Rosenthaler. Daylight erased, the low cloud ceiling with its portent of snow deadens the city's illumination. Headlights on cars and bicycles trace comet trails along wet pavement. The soft roar of the evening rush reaches him caressingly.

On the face of a building across the intersection, newly-installed, a large, yellowish banner stretches between two floors: a young woman, head fallen forward, dark hair framing her face. Her image is three meters tall. Her posture bespeaks sorrow, or possibly guilt. The banner bears no slogan or insignia. Nor does the building on which the banner hangs offer clues: on the lower floors, a hostel; the upper floor, a language school.

He sips some water. He considers the face of the downcast woman on the huge tapestry-like poster. He opens a French door. Wintry wind seeps around a corner of the building and sweeps cool in the room. His face is still damp from his ride along the river and up from Hackescher.

He closes the door and clicks on the television to see some news: Mounting movements to exit the EU; a gas strike in France; a bus accident in Thüringen; the immigration crisis, protests and anti-protest protests; the slow sag of the GDP; the string of winter storms crossing the continent. This does little to warm the solitude.

It will be best to be with a few friends this evening, given the news he's just received. Anyway, the event at the gallery is a tribute to him.

He showers and shaves, combs his hair carefully. He studies his image in the mirror as if to decide whether anything has changed. Nothing ever changes, or perhaps everything changes but unnoticeably. Per habit, he slowly swivels his face from side to side, examining as much as possible the view of himself from varying angles. He again adjusts his hair, strokes his neck. He applies lotion.

In the kitchen, he rinses his glass and sets it to dry. His phone on the counter, now partially charged, rings. He glances at the number: unidentified. He picks up the phone and says, German-style, "Block."

There is no response for several moments. Lucas says, "Block," once more.

Then a woman's voice says in a voice barely above a whisper, "I've been searching for you." The voice speaks in English.

"Who is this?"

"We'll meet soon." The line disconnects.

It is too late to catch the series of U-Bahn trains necessary to deliver him to Gendarmenmarkt in time to make the opening of the gallery. Lucas had promised Frankie, the owner of the gallery, he would be there punctually to meet guests.

"You're never on time anywhere," she had said.

"I'll set an alarm," he said.

"You don't know how, and anyway your phone is always dead," Frankie had said. "I'm just worried because I want people to be there, and I'm afraid no one will show up. I'm always afraid no one will show up. My life is a perpetual prom date panic."

So Lucas takes a taxi, which is doubtfully quicker than trains, given the opacity of traffic. The driver swerves and swears. He rockets away from lights. But this does little to decrease the duration of the four-kilometer ride through the city.

Frankie's art gallery is called Denver, named after the city in which she was born and of which her father was once mayor before being elected to the Senate. Her father accompanied Kennedy to Berlin. Her mother brought along six-year-old Frankie.

The gallery sits on a curve of a street entering Hausvogteiplatz, down from the Französicher Dom. The gallery's multi-paned door centers between matching windows facing the street.

Two partial arcs of little halogen lights like eyebrows overlook the façade.

In the left window, lettering has been applied to the glass. The lettering spells *ghosts* in an obscure, lower-case typeface with letters a half-meter tall.

—— **CHAPTER 3** ——

In the ivory-walled gallery, a substantial crowd has already gathered. Women in black cocktail dresses circulate with trays and platters balanced on fingertips, champagne flutes, little toasts with French cheeses and slices of prosciutto and chilled kippers and caviar with sour cream. Constellations of lights in fixtures the size of espresso cups inset the high ceiling. On tables, clusters of candles glow in slim glass cylinders. Lucas takes off his coat. Many eyes turn to him.

Heike hurries over.

"I've been trying to reach you."

"I got here as fast as I could. I was shooting late this afternoon."

"To talk about Abbie." Heike never called her Mama, though most friends did because that was what she called herself.

"What do you know?"

"Not much. The police told Eloise this afternoon that they don't see any signs of violence. They're implying she fell in the river."

"Or jumped."

"I was going to add that. She's seemed more on edge recently. More nervous than usual. Eloise said so, too."

"How is Eloise?"

"Okay. Not here. I was afraid she would want to come. I was afraid to leave her home alone. But you know Eloise."

An aged woman and man step up to Lucas and Heike. The woman is sleek and tight. She gleams. She holds out a hand knobbed hard with emeralds and knuckles.

"I've always admired your work," the woman says. "And you're a photographer, too. I had no idea."

The main salon of the gallery is u-shaped, formed by two side walls and a free-standing partition wall at the back. Five large photographs hang under airy light in the main salon, two on each side wall and one on the rear wall facing forward into the room.

Frankie takes Lucas from Heike and guides him through the small crowd. They stop for many introductions. Everyone seems to know him; he knows none of them.

"I call them *ghosts*," Lucas says to the group, gesturing to the photos. "They're image collaborations between a friend and me. She could not be here tonight." He states this first in German and then in English.

"I love how the vague figures are actually more vivid than their backgrounds," a man comments.

"Superlative contrasts," a woman says.

"How did you pick each pair?" another woman asks.

Lucas explains to a group around him that his collaborator, a photo archivist, selected old images of people taken by other photographers at other times and passed them along to him. He does not identify the collaborator by name. It is the woman who has died: Mama.

All the people in the photos are no longer alive, he explains. They wear outdated clothing, bell-bottoms and wide ties, thick-heeled shoes, all shades of grey in the photos. They stand in snapshot poses, some pensive, some lively, glancing around and over their shoulders. Lucas matched the images against his contemporary shots of location artifacts around the city.

"They're double-exposures, triple, quadruple, in other words," he says, "but altered. I printed the old negatives over new ones, but images are pulled back, screened, misty. The horizons vary. The focus varies. The feet of the people float above the ground of their settings just a little. Joined but loosely. Detached. The idea is that people long gone appear in places they may have been, or perhaps wish they had been. People who left too soon. I wanted to feel like both the person and the place are imaginary, out of place in time. Thus, ghosts."

Music plays soft, vaguely jazzy lounge rhythms. Glassware clinks. Conversations drift and swell, some in German, some in English. Frankie has composed a group of thick candles, at least a dozen of them, on a small table. There is no outward indication, but the obvious suggestion is of a shrine to a departed loved-one.

Lucas moves slowly around the room trailing a small group. He signs a few autographs. Eventually Heike steps in, takes him by an arm and leads him away.

"You're being wonderful," she says. "I know this is bothersome for you. Frankie will owe you."

Lucas says, "She would have enjoyed seeing people's reactions."

"Frankie?"

"Mama. I wish she was here. I'm having difficulty understanding what's real tonight."

Heike hugs him. She's tall, in her heels as tall as Lucas, although Lucas is not a towering man. Her dark brown hair with lacings of gray smells of verbena—tense, dense hair cascading to her clavicles, the type of hair bespeaking vagaries of bloodline that some German women seek to tame, but not Heike. When she looks into his face again, she reaches her hands and cups his cheeks. "You look very handsome tonight. You always look handsome. I love this jacket."

"I'm old. People remember me as young. The image they have of me doesn't match the reality of me."

"People see you now and think, wow, he's doing great. Someone over there, the young woman in the blue sweater thing, told me she thinks you look much handsomer now than then."

"That and three Euros will get you a bad coffee," Lucas says, but he glances across the crowd to survey the woman in the blue sweater.

Heike says, "Frankie told me the man in the bowtie is a member of the Bundestag. I think someone ate all of the caviar. People keep bumping into that little table with the big glass thing on it. What a mess that would make." Lucas gives Heike a quick kiss and they move off in separate directions.

Immediately, a woman in a red dress with chrome zippers and high suede boots steps up to him and begins to chat. She is blonde. Her face is placid as if she holds back expression. She is perhaps half Lucas' age. She smells lightly of Diptyque *l'Ombre dans l'Eau.*

She speaks in a low, confidential voice. She watches him with unmoving, unblinking eyes as she talks. Her eyes are the same shade as his, and when he glances at her he feels a twinge of recognition.

"Have we met before?" Lucas asks.

"No," she states. "I came here because I was very interested in seeing what you are doing. With your photos, but also in general." She gestures over her shoulder to the photos. Her arm is stiff. Her eyes never leave his face.

"Mostly, I just keep to myself," Lucas says. He flashes her a smile.

"Your partner on these photos was Abbie Ingvall, right?"

"How did you know that? I didn't think anyone else knew that," Lucas says.

The woman disarms her question with a little wave of her hand and says, "Oh, it's around." Her voice is slightly hoarse.

Nik approaches with three champagne glasses, two empty and one half-empty, the empties splayed by their stems between fingers of his left hand.

"My friend Nik Ng," Lucas says to the woman in the red dress. "Nik is a writer."

Nik's thick, pure white hair is tied back in a ponytail with a sharply-cut end. He wears sharp, black-rimmed eyeglasses. He is much shorter than Lucas and seems to weigh nothing, partly a result of his thinness and partly his electric air. His pale hands and fingers branch from black cuffs. His face, like Lucas,' is chiseled and lined and his teeth flawless.

"My name is Andrea," the woman says.

"You're American?" Nik asks.

She nods.

"Our little crowd," he says gesturing to Lucas and then to Frankie who stands chatting with some patrons not far away, "are all Americans, too. Well, Lucas is sort of a combination. He was born in Germany."

"I know," she says.

"Are you an expat also?" Nik says.

She shakes her head. "Just visiting." She sets her champagne flute on a passing tray and takes a second glass. "You are from Vietnam?" Andrea says to Nik.

"Born there. I grew up in Los Angeles," Nik says. "My name is Khiem. But I go by Nik. Feel free to call me whatever you wish."

"What do you write?" Andrea says.

"Science fiction about Berlin. Past and future. Berlin lends itself to the gothic imagination, of course."

"I'd like to read one of your pieces."

"I'd love for you to read one. When one is eventually published."

"Where did you meet him?" She flicks eyes at Lucas.

"In film school. There was a time when our dreams intermeshed. Lucas soared; I mired."

Lucas stands with them, but is disengaged. He watches the crowd. Another woman moves slowly down the row of photographs. She is young. She is alone. She wears a slim, dark shirt brightly printed with paisley, tight jeans with bright-stitched seams running down the thighs, cut raggedly short above her ankles. A round buckle fastens a wide brown belt. Her boots, likewise, are brown. She wears round, dark-pink-tinted glasses. Above the pink frames, her forehead is smooth but tense. Her hair is blond and long, cut with curved bangs to her expressive eyebrows. An orange nylon parka with a broad and shaggy faux-fur collar is tossed over an arm.

She stops before the photo on the back wall. She stares, frozen. From his angle, Lucas sees only the back of her. But anyone would sense the tension, the stiffness of her neck.

Lucas steps to the young woman.

"What do you think?" he says quietly over her shoulder. She turns slowly to look at him. Her face is travertine. He sees the curve of her jaw, her eyes, dim behind the lurid lenses, wide-set and hurt. An image of Lucas reflects in her eyes. She flinches without moving.

She looks at him for a moment, a mélange of confusions and perhaps anger. Then abruptly she turns and hurries away. Lucas watches as she slips her shoulders into her coat, tossing her blond hair down her back, as she swings through the crowd and quickly through the door and out into the street. She vanishes into the dark beyond the little circle of lights over the sidewalk.

Lucas returns to Nik and Andrea. Andrea has watched Lucas speak to the young woman. Her face is a mask of careful calculation. She says to Lucas, "I was just telling Nik that I loved you in that movie way back when. I was trying to remember when that came out. I was a teenager. You don't look a bit different. You haven't aged."

Lucas says, "Time stands still for those who move. I think it was Confucius who observed that. Someone along those lines."

Nik says, "Confucius. Maybe Tony Robbins."

Andrea says softly, "I was also thinking you must believe in ghosts. Or you must love the idea of ghosts."

Lucas shrugs. "All I know is that the past never vanishes. I've heard that ghosts cannot speak to us until they have drunk blood; they demand the blood of our hearts. We give it to them gladly."

Andrea says, "I believe in ghosts. Real ones. I think they're watching us all the time." Over her glass, her eyes flame.

In the space of sixty seconds, Lucas has observed two pairs of eyes stabbing into him, but from much different angles.

He slowly tilts his glass to finish a sip of soda water. "There isn't much I believe in," he says. "Just images."

He steps away from Nik and Andrea again. He rejoins Frankie at a counter at the far end of the room. Frankie is tallying numbers on her credit card reader.

"We did well tonight," Frankie says. "Thank you."

Heike slips toward them across the room through the remnants of the crowd. She carries her jacket and scarf over one arm and Lucas' coat over the other.

"Let's get out of here soon. I'm starving," she says.

CHAPTER 4

When the last of the guests has left, Frankie, Nik, Heike and Lucas step out onto the street. Frankie locks the door of Denver behind them.

Through the windows, with the lights turned down, the main salon of the gallery now only glows. A litter of empty champagne glasses coruscates on a table near the door, deposited as guests departed and neglected by the temporary staff. On the velvety walls, charcoal in the dimness, loom the large framed photos, old jewels under glass.

During the two hours of the engagement in the gallery, the temperature outside has dropped fifteen degrees, as it is wont to do this time of year on the steep shoulders of latitude. Slush in the streets has set into basaltic ridges. Shoeprints in the ice on the paving stones weave like dinosaur tracks underfoot. Snow has begun again, *adagio.*

Across the cloistered space of Gendarmenmarkt, between the French and German churches and over the ecclesiastic marble gaze of Schiller in his iron cage before the concert hall, oblique, gauzy cones drift and waver under streetlights.

On the corner just down from Denver, Andrea waits alone at the curb, as if for a ride. She glances over her shoulder at the approaching foursome. She has wrapped herself in a heavy overcoat, red matching her dress, and a lilac scarf. Still, her narrow shoulders clench into her frame with the cold. Epaulets of snow have collected on her shoulders. She smokes, tightly. Her hair sparkles with crystals. Her outsized fingernails shine red.

As the group passes, she meets Lucas' smile and smiles back, exhaling a cloud. Lucas stops. He speaks to Andrea.

"Would you like to join us? We're getting something to eat."

Andrea touches out her cigarette stub under a boot toe and merges with the group. They cross the square, skirting the Konzerthaus, and enter Taubenstraße.

As they walk, Andrea reaches across Lucas to shake hands with Heike. Fingers icy and hard, she apparently waited for some time on the street corner.

She grew up in Nebraska but lives in Baltimore, Andrea relates in her rasped voice. She is a forensic accountant, in Berlin for a conference. She offers her card, dark blue with a logo resembling an abacus, to Lucas. She says she came to the gallery with a friend, but the friend left earlier for a date. Lucas tucks the card into a coat pocket.

Frankie walks behind, holding a silvery scarf over her face, mask-like, against the slow but diamantine wind. Heike expresses no overt interest in Andrea, asks no questions. This may be because the surety of footing on the stones of Gendarmenmarkt is doubtful due to the ice, and Heike wears nail-heeled black suede boots matching her velvet cocktail dress.

"I should have changed my shoes," Heike says softly to no one.

"I hope you don't think I was just angling to meet a movie star," Andrea says to Lucas.

"If you see one, let me know," Lucas says.

The restaurant on Taubenstraße is Tuscan. Heavy purple draperies frame steamed windows. Inside, most of the tables are occupied, it being a Friday evening. Waiters swing through with trays of pastas and grilled steaks. Prosecco corks pop. Candles adorn every table and shelf. The proprietor greets Lucas, and guides the group to a rectangular table toward the back.

The four friends sit in a quadrangle, two on each side, Heike next to Lucas and Frankie next to Nik. Andrea sits at one end of the table, between Lucas and Frankie.

Near their table, on a raised dais, a man plays a piano. He is bearded and dressed in a frayed tuxedo. He plays Gershwin very quietly and sips liquor straight from a blue bottle between songs, with a sad, elegant touch and turn of the wrist.

Wine is brought, opened and dispensed. Lucas takes no wine, but raises a glass of water. They all fall quiet, lean on their arms toward the center of the table and touch glasses.

Lucas says, "It hasn't sunk in yet."

Nik says, "I'm numb."

"I wish we could find out what happened."

Heike's face washes quickly with irritation. "Berlin police. Good luck finding out anything."

Lucas relates the news of Mama's death to Andrea.

"Tell me about her," Andrea says quietly.

The four friends contribute fragments of explanation.

"Abbie was the leader of our little salon," Heike says at one point. "I think it's fair to say that each of us had some profound connection with her. She was in Berlin since the late sixties. She knew Bowie. She knew Fassbinder. She knew Christa Wolf and Peter Schneider. She seemed to be everywhere all the time."

"But she wasn't a social animal," Nik says. "She was deeply private. Mercurial."

"Difficult to get to know, but once she locked onto you, you were chained," Frankie says. "She had some sort of power."

The four nod in agreement.

"She came to you when she wanted to," Frankie continues. "She would just appear out of nowhere on your doorstep. She would offer you something—some Schnecken, some wildflowers, a bottle of Federweißer, an antique book. She would watch you very carefully with her one eye."

"She always seemed to know more about you and what you'd been up to lately than you thought you had told her," Nik comments. "Sometimes it could be freaky."

"She called herself Mama. She would never explain why," Lucas says. "But it fit."

The waiter takes orders. The first bottle of wine is depleted, so two more are ordered, some sort of Barolo. Nik tilts his glass to the light and studies the wine's legs.

Though explaining for Andrea, Lucas addresses the group at large as if reviewing the set of circumstances that have led to an inexplicable outcome.

"She sent five photos to me. Just the negatives. She declined to tell me what they were, who the people in the photos were, or why she had selected them. She just said they were people who should be freed from anonymity. She told me they were from a collection she had been working on. She identified nameless people in old photos. She was an archivist for the photo department of the Staatsbibliothek zu Berlin." Lucas sips at his water for a moment.

"They were perfect photos of people from the past standing and looking about them," he continues. "Observing the world. Expressions of wonder and appreciation. They appeared to be from maybe forty years ago. No idea who the photographers were. I think they're just snapshots, but very good ones. They didn't look staged or posed. They looked honest. Transparent. For each of the photos, I could imagine a background. We'd talked about the *ghosts* idea in the past, so Mama knew what I'd been looking for, what I'd been seeking to find. Or maybe she knew it before I did and she led me to it. All I know is that, one day, *ghosts* just bloomed in my mind."

—— **CHAPTER 5** ——

The music has enlarged. A second musician has joined the pianist and plays jazz guitar. The restaurant's velvet acoustics swell as voices rise, wine flows, friends greet friends deep into the onset of the weekend.

The group at the table leans in and takes pieces of bread, passes around liters of sparkling water. Nik pours olive oil and dips his bread.

"That's so American," Frankie says to him.

"I'm so American," Nik says.

Lucas resumes. "I printed each of the photos Mama gave me and set them up around my flat, on tables and walls, on the refrigerator. I imagined what the people might be seeing, or thinking, based on their expressions, their physical moods. Then I went out in Berlin searching. I wasn't so much looking for specific locations as I was searching for forms, spaces, lighting, movement. Senses that seemed to me to match the individuals I was trying to resurrect. But the bottom line, the end product, really all began with Mama. Without her photos, I would never have gotten my idea off the ground. She never got to see the finished products. My big composites. My *ghosts*."

"You knew her—Mama—for a long time," Andrea says.

Lucas notices that she says this in a thin, horizontal voice, more statement than question, but he nods.

"Mama was one of the first people I met in Berlin, so twenty years ago. Heike introduced us. We spent a lot of time together early on. Mama helped me. Sheltered me. Growing back into the language and culture was the first step. I'd been a child in Germany, and later spent my teenage years with my German-speaking aunt and uncle in the U. S., but I needed a lot of reintroduction to the language. I was also naive and childlike in Berlin when I re-arrived. The Berlin of the nineties, post-Wall, when the fruit of creativity dumped into the blender of capitalism. Mama saw something in me, I guess. Just as friends. She wasn't into men, *per se*."

"Which reminds me," Heike says. "I need to check in with Eloise."

Heike stands and takes her phone from a pocket and moves away from the cloud of music and dining room clatter to make the call.

Lucas says, "But Mama was always very prone to upswings and downswings, especially downswings. We all worried about her."

Drink and music circulate for several minutes. When Heike returns to the table a few minutes later, she signals that all is stable with Eloise.

"She doesn't really want to talk right now. She says she wants to meditate tonight. I can understand that."

Food is delivered, platters of *Rigatoni alla Norma* and *Cacio e Pepe* and colorful salads. They share from big oval serving dishes, although Frankie eats only salad.

"Heike is a photographer, also," Lucas says to Andrea. "She's created some wonderful images of old industrial architecture. Things dating back to the war. She's very well regarded."

"Hm. Well-regarded. I don't know about that," Heike says.

"She had a big, beautiful book published by Taschen a few years ago. Photos of derelict bridges and factories, artifacts of bygone industry, with essays written by her ex-husband. Ruminations on ruins. The book won an award. He was a brilliant journalist and writer. We all speak of him in the past tense."

"My husband was a better writer than I was a photographer. I suppose that was at the root of our problems. Some imbalance I couldn't tolerate."

"You are German," Andrea asks across Lucas.

Heike nods. "I'm the odd one in this crowd."

"You're very beautiful," Andrea says.

"Me?" Heike makes a small noise with her lips and waves a hand gently. "It's just the nose. Lucas says I have a senatorial nose. He says things like that."

Nik says, "Heike used to be a model. You can still see by the way she carries herself. Like a tall stack of china cups."

"I don't know if that's a compliment or not," Heike says to Nik. To Andrea, "Nik says things like that. These men, always with their peculiar observations."

The two women talk back and forth across Lucas' plate.

"Are you doing photography now?"

Heike nods again, her mouth now full of spaghetti.

Lucas says, "She has a studio over in Kreuzberg. She's a pro. Unlike me. I'm the amateur."

Heike swallows her pasta, touches her lips with her napkin. She says, "Amateur? You're the one with a show in a gallery. Frankie, how many did you sell tonight?"

Across the table, Frankie looks up from her salad and then digs in her bag for her phone.

Heike continues, "I mostly photograph babies and brides. Sometimes food. I can make currywursts look edible. But Lucas is the artist."

"Your eye must see a composition or an expression that life itself offers you," Lucas says, *"and you must know with intuition when to click the shutter.* It was Cartier-Bresson who said that. Not to be ostentatious."

"Eat your supper," Heike says.

Lucas turns his gaze directly to Andrea as if to make a special point just for her.

"Especially in our modern world of ubiquitous vision, there are seers and there are watchers. In my view, seers know everything but cannot understand any of it. Watchers capture what they can in fleeting moments, but they freely admit they understand nothing. Seers are the mind of humanity. Watchers are the heart."

Andrea swallows. She lifts her glass to her mouth and takes a sip of wine. Her eyes are ice.

"Which are you?" she says.

Lucas' shrug is slow. His gaze falls back to his dinner plate. When his eyes rise back to Andrea's, he says, "I hope only to watch. But in the end, I find I'm forced to see."

"Two," Frankie says. "No, three. We sold three. That British lady with the little dog bought two. When she comes back to pick them up, she may buy another."

"Three out of five. You see what I mean," Heike says. She tosses her hand in a gesture of annoyance, perhaps envisioning her studio's monthly balance sheet.

"I almost stepped on that dog," Nik says.

"Good thing there were no small children," Frankie says.

"It was a pleasant little dog on the surface," Nik says, "but with a vindictive look in the eye. Presumably a Tory."

"I wish people wouldn't bring animals into my gallery," Frankie says. "A few days ago, it was someone with an iguana draped over a shoulder. Big, wild dreadlocks. The person, not the iguana. I thought the lizard was just part of the man's hairdo until it looked out at me with those blank, equatorial eyes. I had just put up the sign on the window that says ghosts. The man asked if I had any to sell."

"Nik is a musician," Lucas says to Andrea. "Guitarist." Nik exudes shyness.

"What do you play?' Andrea asks, turning to Nik.

"A little of everything. Right now, a little classical Spanish. Casals. That sort of thing."

"He was a rock star," Frankie says, prodding Nik with an elbow. "Remember that song *Lightning* which was so big back in the eighties? We all–everyone–rocked out to it. Back when people rocked out. Nik wrote that."

"Please," Nik says. "Noble faded hipster. Look how old I am." Nik places the tips of his fingers along his narrow sternum and slopes a slanted glance of humility into his plate. He is dressed in a black turtleneck, slim black slacks and a black suede jacket. His white hair is tied with a black ribbon. On an index finger he wears a carved black onyx ring.

"Do you have children?" Frankie asks of Andrea. Andrea shakes her head slowly, but her eyes do not lift from her plate. Sudden, unaccountable sadness weights her features, which Frankie apparently interprets as despondency at not having children.

"We're a family-unfettered bunch ourselves," Frankie says quickly in a chipper tone. "All our parents are gone and all of us are child-free, as far as I know." She glances with mild derision at Nik.

"Except for Heike, the rest of you are expatriates?" Andrea says, lifting her gaze to the the group. She clasps her hands over her plate.

Frankie says, "Lucas was born in Germany, but he has an American soul."

Lucas pauses mid-bite. "I'm not sure what you mean by that," he says.

"He's a beautiful human being, but he insists on the illusions of affirmation, vibrancy, amazement and re-birth. Europeans, I find, are a little jaded about those notions."

"At a practical level, choosing to be an expatriate," Lucas says to the table, musing, "places a person in a difficult position, with the difficulty renewed every day. A person is neither here nor there. It's inescapable no matter how well you learn the language and customs, no matter how close-to-local you dress and eat and shop and amuse yourself, no matter how long you've been embedded in your adopted home. And it doesn't matter where in the world you expatriate yourself. One ripple of discontent and everyone is quick to blame the alien. Actually, I stole that last line from *Oedipus at Colonus*."

"You're full of them tonight," Heike says. "Full of something, anyway."

Nik says, "I know what Frankie means when she says impossible. Not about Lucas specifically, about America. When I was young, I wanted to grow old in a society that seemed on a trajectory for continual improvement, a progressive marvel. Fairyland. No place has arrived, but Germany is closer. Strong societies, like strong people, are built of humility and scar tissue. No shortage of that here."

Andrea reaches for bread. Her wrist knocks her half-full wine glass, tossing a lurid splash of red across the linen. A waiter springs with towels.

"I'm so awkward," Andrea says as the waiter reaches over her shoulders to mop at the table. "I guess that's why I've always been alone."

In the evaluative little silence that swallows the table following this remark, Lucas reaches for a wine bottle and refills Andrea's righted glass. "You're among similar souls," he says. "No specific course. Ships on a dark sea. No stars to navigate by."

"Nice, Luke," Nik says, raising his glass. "Right out of Jonathan Livingston Seagull."

"You mock, but you know I'm right," Lucas says.

Nik turns to Andrea again. "One could picture us as four fallen angels, our wax wings sun-singed. We were once spectacular. Now we're just old spectacles."

Frankie tilts her head as if with curiosity. "Speak for yourself," she says.

Nik continues speaking across Frankie to Andrea. "We're isolated in conjunction, a little expat solar system. Mama was our sun. We've all been cast a little adrift, I think. We've lost our center. Lucas was closest to her." He gestures with his glass.

"I'll be okay. It's Eloise I'm worried about," Lucas says.

Nik says, "I've known Lucas forty-some years, but he surprises me every day. Something trying to mend itself in there. A wobbly gyroscope trying to straighten upright again."

Frankie sits squarely, precisely, in the middle of her chair seat. She is directly across from Lucas. She wears very tight white pants with a silver belt, a thin grey sweater and over it a silver vest, zipped to the neck. Her boots are white. Her hair is white. She has tied it up in a mysterious manner, sculptural, with a single silver pin emerging at the top. She wears several large silver rings. She is very tanned. Even seated, she is several inches taller than Nik. She eats with her left hand, fork inverted.

She says partly to Andrea but also partly to the group, "Alone. Together. Adrift. Connected. At least we're all still here." The four once again raise and touch glasses. Andrea lifts her glass, but not in time for the toast.

"Friends are God's apology for relations," Lucas comments.

"How did you meet?" Andrea leans around Lucas to ask Heike.

"Him?" Heike says, pointing a thumb at Lucas. "I used to go to the Berlinische Galerie a lot. This was probably twenty years ago. I saw a man there several times. Nice-looking guy. Always taking notes. He saw me, too, I think. One day we chatted. That's all there was to it."

"You didn't know who he was?"

Heike shrugs, "No, and he never mentioned it. I didn't go to many movies when I was young, you see. American movies were all the rage in West Germany in the eighties, but I was against whatever was all the rage. When I asked Lucas what he did in the past, in the U.S., he just said media stuff, never very specific. I thought he was embarrassed or bored with his job or something. Or maybe there had been some problems, he got fired or something. I didn't want to pry."

Heike swipes at some leftover sauce on her plate with a piece of bread. She continues, "We'd been dating for maybe a month or so. We mostly just went for walks in uncrowded places and talked a lot at first. I noticed some people looking at him one night when we crossed Alexanderplatz. They were pointing at him. I didn't know why, thought maybe they were mistaking him for someone else. Lucas sort of hurried me onward. Then a couple nights later we were sitting together in my flat watching TV, drifting through channels, and a film came on. I was sort of absently watching it for a few minutes and then I looked at Lucas and then back at the TV. I said, 'That guy looks like you.' I watched some more and then I looked at him again. He was just sitting there with a little shy, fallen smile, like a boy who's been caught at something naughty."

"Which movie was it?"

"I don't know. The Jesus thing, I think. The dubbing was very bad. Lucas looked like he was chewing gristle, with someone else's voice coming out."

"His hair is so beautiful. Just like on screen."

"He does have nice hair genes," Heike says. "His hair is—or was—the same shade as yours."

Platters have been emptied. The wine bottles are empty.

Nik says to Frankie, "You ate about a bushel of salad. You must be very regular."

She arches. "As a matter of fact, my digestive health is excellent."

Then she makes a small fist and turns and socks him in the upper arm, lightly, but with enough force to make an audible thwack. Nik slowly rubs his arm.

"It's those big rings she wears," he says, looking across to Lucas. "Like brass knuckles." Frankie has resumed a prim pose on the center of her seat.

Heike says, "You should see these two argue politics." She is apparently saying this to Andrea.

Nik says, "I agree with Frankie that politics, especially in America, is completely fucked up. We just disagree about why. She says it's the right wing. I agree that the right wing is to blame, but I think they are irrepressibly goaded by the left and vice versa. Proetus and Acrisius. Neither side can help itself. This is their nature. She believes politics in America is redeemable, that it can be restored to some sense of sanity. I say no."

Frankie says, "Nik is a nihilist. I have no problem with nihilism in general. All the people I've ever loved are nihilists. They can be very charming, you know. But Nik confuses nihilism with misanthropy. I think people are inherently good. They've just lost their way, largely because they've been led astray. Nik thinks we began astray and will end astray. There is no place except astray."

Nik says, "The worst part is that radicals of both extremes have joined hands. You see it everywhere now. Things fall apart;

the center cannot hold. Devils and angels have exchanged costumes. They all dance at the pyre of civilization."

"Oh my," Andrea says.

"He merges Old and New Testaments," Frankie says. "Synthesis."

"What's synthesis?" Andrea asks.

Nik looks across to Lucas again. "Some sort of hallucinogenic mushroom, I think," he says. Frankie raises a fist as if to thwack Nik anew.

Andrea says, "You all are artists and intellectuals. I'm just an accountant."

Frankie leans to Andrea, "Like Lucas said. Tonight, you're one of us. Don't let this guy annoy you." She glances sideways at Nik.

At this, Nik slips his phone from an inner pocket and stands. He frames Andrea with Lucas on one side of her and Frankie on the other. Lucas leans good-naturedly toward Andrea, on his right. On Lucas' left, Heike leans away to stay out of the photo.

Lucas flashes an electric smile. Lucas, Frankie and Andrea form a vague pyramid, like a family portrait, with Andrea in the center.

Andrea's face is glacial. Her eyes flicker. Her gaze is not cheerful. She stares into the lens. Nik takes the photo of the trio. "Send me that photo, okay?" Heike says to Nik.

Andrea resumes the prior conversation. She says, "But you all ended up living in Berlin somehow. You're creators. You all have profound imaginations, and aren't afraid to display them to the world. That's what brought you all here to Berlin, I bet. Your imaginations."

Lucas says, "Or maybe the ends of roads. All our roads met up here. Roads have a way of needing to suddenly end."

Andrea says lowly, "Oh I see, you mean after that problem about your wife came up."

At this, the table falls silent. In the soft cavern of the restaurant, music and chatter carry on, emphasizing the sudden stillness among the group. Frankie and Nik glance at Lucas' face. Heike studies her empty plate.

On the sidewalk a short while later, the wind has diminished, but the snow has started in earnest again. Parked cars show white shoulders to the streetlights.

Before parting, when Andrea speaks to Lucas, she says, "I'm sorry," as if apologizing for the remark, but her eyes glitter with deep light that belies apology. Lucas, perhaps noticing this, glances at her twice.

Then he shrugs in his overcoat and makes a casual face with outthrust lips as if to signify nonchalance in the face of peril, an expression perhaps practiced before mirrors.

"The way things look is not necessarily the way they exist," he says.

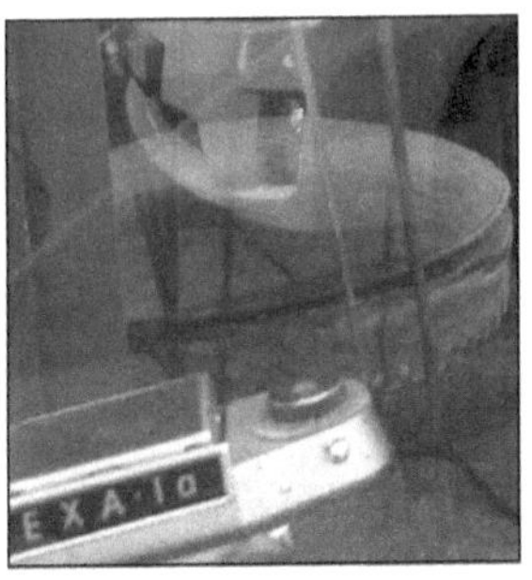

———— **CHAPTER 6** ————

In the morning, Lucas and Heike awake in his Rosenthalerplatz flat. The storm, which rattled windows and clawed at eaves all night, shuffled off just before sunrise. Now, the square is quiet. The usual soft, insistent roar of activity does not float up to them. They lie awake for a while, testing this silence.

She lies curled against him under the down comforter, he in an old pair of long underwear bottoms, she in nothing at all, as is her habit. He has never known her to wear pajamas of any sort. She is notoriously hot. To avoid making him sweat, she sometimes rises at two or three in the morning and dresses and sleeps on the couch or goes to her own flat. But not this morning.

Lucas rattles coffee from the Nespresso machine. Heike pads into the kitchen wearing a bathrobe of his and his slippers. She is inserting her hearing aids. Lucas turns on his phone, which he left to charge when he went to the gallery the night before. He glances through emails.

"Look at this," he says.

Heike comes to his side and reads over his arm.

Lucas,

My friend. I am sorry. I am sorry to drag you into this.
And I am sorry for leaving you. You are a good person.
You didn't deserve to be tricked. You didn't deserve any
of it. They needed you. Please take care of Heike.
The past cannot be undone, but it can be accommodated.

Best always,
Abbie

"When did she send that?" Heike asks. Her eyes are wet. Lucas, too, wipes a tear.

"Just before two yesterday morning. I didn't look at my email at all yesterday."

"What does she mean by tricked?"

"I don't know."

"And what does she mean by dragging you into something?"

"I don't know. It's all very confusing. Almost incoherent. She must have been doing very badly."

Lucas calls Nik. As they're talking, he forwards the email.

Reading it, Nik says, "Wow." The two men are silent for a minute.

"It doesn't sound like Mama at all. When she would fall into one of her terrible moods, she would become more lucid, not less. That makes no sense. She never touched a drop of anything in her life."

Lucas says, "Maybe she was taking anti-depressants finally. There were times we encouraged her. As far as I know, she never even went to a doctor. But if she was, that just would have made her plastic and tractable, not morose."

"Drugs affect different people in different ways."

"It's all very uncertain. I just hate to think this was her last comment. Mama, of all people. The most eloquent of all. Eloise said she just disappeared."

"You know what confuses me? She signed it Abbie. I never once heard her call herself Abbie."

"Maybe the situation. It was, after all, her last statement."

Lucas calls Frankie but her phone just rings.

He sits in an armchair facing the broad windows overlooking the frosted intersection. Trams pass through sporadically. A handful of intrepid pedestrians scorn the ice. He sips at a cup of coffee until it is cold, sets it aside. He calls Frankie again, but still no answer. He leaves a message this time asking her to call.

Heike steps from the shower in a pair of towels into the bedroom. She emerges a short while later dressed in jeans and heavy boots and a thick sweater, a customary outfit. Her hair is still damp. She fiddles with her hearing aids.

"I have an appointment this morning at the studio. I have to be there in thirty minutes. Are you going to be okay?"

"I'll be fine. I have to be," Lucas says into his coffee cup, which sits slightly askew in its saucer on the table in the ashen light coming through the window, in a tone resembling the color of the sky.

——————————— **CHAPTER 7** ———————————

Lucas works in his upstairs darkroom for an hour. He accomplishes little. He moves listlessly, straightens things, glances through some folders. He does not remove the current roll of film from the camera to develop since it is only half-exposed, plus the motivation to see the shots he took yesterday is negligible.

Not long after noon, his phone rings, or specifically it flashes since his ringer is turned off, per usual. But he has it near him on the worktable and sees it light up. Frankie is calling.

"Lucas, something bad has happened. Denver was broken into last night. I got here about ten this morning. The police have been here since then. Someone forced the side door and took some things. Hendrika found it when she arrived before I got here. They took the pictures. Your pictures."

"My pictures," Lucas says after a pause. "Why would anyone want those?"

"They didn't take anything else, as far as I know. There was no money in the building. There never is. But there are other valuables, computers, a few antiques, things like that. But all they took were the pictures. All five of them."

"Let me get this straight. They took the *ghosts* photos."

"Yes."

"They're not small. One-twenty by one-fifty centimeters, something like that. Each one is as big as a mattress. They carried them out."

"Yes."

"They're not light. The glass and the frames."

"I know." Frankie is crying softly on the phone, her voice shaking, her breathing ragged. "Also, someone wrote something horrible on the wall. Someone who came in after the thieves had left."

"Maybe I should come down there."

"Yes," she says.

"Are you alone?"

"Yes. I sent Hendrika home. I was fine until just now. It caught up with me. The police have left. They didn't find anything. They're coming back later to talk to me some more. They said not to open today, not to touch anything until they're through. But they left. I'm just sitting. It's freezing in here. The door was standing open all night, and all this morning while the police were looking at things."

Lucas calls Heike at her studio. She is just beginning her shoot. She answers with tension. A small child's cries can be heard in the background. Lucas relays a brief of what Frankie has told him.

"I'll get to the gallery as soon as I can," Heike says.

CHAPTER 8

Forty-five minutes later, Lucas stands before the front door of Denver gallery. He wears his heavy overcoat, a winter knit cap and a thick scarf. The arc of lights over the façade of the building is off. A handwritten card stating *closed today* has been taped over the elegant little sign listing Denver's regular hours. Frankie's handwriting is narrow and rigid, the way Lucas has seen it in the past when she was writing things that shocked her.

Lucas knocks on the glass. Frankie glances up from behind the counter, startled. She has apparently been rooting through boxes underneath. She hurries around and to the front door. She locks the door behind Lucas as he unwraps his scarf. He hugs her long, hard frame against him. Since she is as tall as he, her cheek rests against his. She shudders.

"Thank you for coming down here. I'm so sorry. I can't tell you how sorry I am. I know I locked up last night. The police said the same thing. They broke the window in the little door on the side of the building, off the hallway. The burglars, I mean."

"Hendrika found it?"

"Yes. She got here at her usual time. She said the side door was just standing open. Broken glass on the floor. I haven't swept it up yet. I raced down here when she called." She looks apologetically down at her clothing, tight jeans and leather boots

40

and a thin, pale green sweater, tasteful as always. Her hair is pulled back in an asymmetrical ponytail. She wears simple amber jewelry. "I'm a wreck," she says.

"Do you have an alarm?"

"No. I used to, but it had so many problems that I had it taken out. It was so sensitive. It would go off when the humidity changed. I was going to replace it but never did. This is such a small place and it's right across the street from the church."

Lucas grins at her.

"The police chided me about that, too."

"But you do have cameras." He points to a small camera mounted on a wall, and then another on the opposite wall. The cameras aim downward over the surfaces on which artworks are displayed. His eyes move from the cameras down to the walls. Only the twin wires which held each picture still dangle in lank coils from their brackets in a slim rail running along the ceiling two meters over their heads. The photos had been suspended away from the wall a few centimeters, floating in pools of light from clusters of fixtures above. The thieves had carefully unclipped the wires from the holders on each frame.

On the left wall, roughly waist-high, a word has been written in black pen on the light paint: *MURDERER*. It is printed. The block letters are large and slightly canted and trail downward to the right.

Frankie stands by Lucas, watching him as he looks at the walls. After a minute, he says idly, "What were you doing behind the counter when I came in?"

Frankie looks startled. "Nothing," she says. "Just storing some of Heike's things." She glances at the counter and back at Lucas.

Lucas looks back to the empty walls and to the scrawled word. He shakes his head slowly.

"I'm sorry," Frankie says.

"They're photos, not original paintings," Lucas says. I have the proofs, and the negatives of the proofs. I can always have new prints made."

"At least they were insured," Frankie says. "I've already called. The insurance people will be over later today. When the police come back to give me their report. The police scare me, though."

Lucas gives her a quick sideways hug.

"It's such an affront," she says, her voice muffled against his shoulder. "It's like being attacked. So personal."

"It's very odd," Lucas says. She looks up at him. "You say they took nothing else."

Frankie nods and shrugs.

"And from the security video," Frankie says, "it was someone else, who came in a couple hours after the burglars took the paintings, who wrote that on the wall. That person was only here a few minutes."

He walks over to the near wall. Where one of the missing photos had been, the label card remains on the wall: *ghost #3*.

Frankie leads him to the little office in the back. He sits at Hendrika's desk piled high with folders and books and portfolios. He clears a path to a computer screen.

"The police already looked at this," Frankie says. "They downloaded a copy of the video."

The security camera application is still open. Lucas scrolls through it. Frankie watches over his shoulder.

"It was earlier. About two AM. There were two people. It looks like a man and a woman."

The images from the two cameras, displayed side by side on the monitor, seem frozen except for occasional blips of light as the headlights of cars pass in the street. The dangling wires cast thin, curling shadows on the walls. Lucas scrolls slowly backward in time.

At one point in the video, around four in the morning, a figure enters the gallery from the rear hallway. It is a woman's figure in a long black coat tied tightly around her waist and reaching her knees. She wears black boots which leave snow on the floor. The coat has a large hood, which completely covers her head. Her face remains obscured from the cameras.

She stands in the empty gallery for a minute. Then she digs with a gloved hand in a pocket and pulls out a pen. She steps to the empty leftward wall and writes.

"Hardly looks like a vandal," Lucas says. "But I guess you never know."

Lucas continues scrolling. The time counter rolls gradually backward. Then suddenly, earlier in the night, a blur of dark motion moves in the room. Dim figures flutter and then are gone. All five photos are instantly back in place on the walls.

"Right there," Frankie says.

Lucas stops scrolling and clicks the play button. The video plays in real time. They watch for a minute.

"You went too far," Frankie says. "It's only twelve-thirty here."

Lucas scrolls forward again until the figures flicker and jerk. He adjusts back and forth and finally allows the video to play at normal speed just as two forms appear on the walls. The forms are shadows cast by two figures in the light of the little lamp on the rear counter. They move slowly. They step into view of one of the cameras. The figures stop. Both slim figures are dressed in black, cartoons of burglars. Due to the angle, their faces are not visible, just their backs.

The two figures move to the pair of photos on the east wall and slowly along it. One of the figures points to a photo, then to another. The pointing figure is slightly shorter than the other. It appears to be a woman based on the physical structure of the person, the posture. The other figure has broader shoulders, bigger hands. Their faces, though uncovered, remain out of view of the camera since it aims at the wall from behind the figures.

Working together, the people swing the photos out on their suspending wires a few inches. They examine the attachments on the backs of the frames. The taller figure digs in a coat pocket with a gloved hand and draws out a pair of pliers, a shiny multi-tool of some sort. They pry at the first photo. One at a time, the wires spring free of the frame. They set the heavy photo on the floor and move to the next.

They turn to the other wall. They step out of view of the first camera and into range of the second, appearing now on the left side of the monitor. They remove the two photos from this wall.

Then the shorter figure points to the photo on the back wall of the u-shaped room. The taller figure shakes his head. It is not clear if he is disagreeing or disbelieving. They remove that photo, the last, from its hanging wires and set it on the floor. The taller figure appears irritated, turning away suddenly. He turns back to the other wall, still angled away from the camera.

The smaller figure joins him. Together, they lift the first photo and carry it toward the black corridor at the rear. Appearing again a minute later, they remove the second. This is repeated until four photos have been carried out.

Frankie says, "There's a camera in the alley. They had a white Skoda van, the police said, but no license plates on it."

Lucas says, "Always and everywhere, we're being watched."

When they return a final time for the fifth photo, the one leaning against the rear wall, the woman turns, her face momentarily angled upward toward the left camera and at the same time vaguely lit by the lamp on the counter. The view is brief and blurred.

Lucas stops the video. He slides it back slowly and then lets it play again as the woman turns and shows her face. Her streaked visage passes across the screen. He stops and rewinds once more. Just as she turns, he stops the video, freezing her image.

"Is there some way to zoom this?" he asks of no one, clicking around in the controls. He finds a zoom slider and enlarges her.

The face is oval, wide-eyed. Her skin is pale between her black knit hat and black knit scarf wrapped high. Lucas scrolls a few frames back and forth. He zooms in and out, seeking the best picture. The woman's face, enlarged, blurs to blocks and pixels. He returns the image to partial enlargement and sits looking at the woman. He studies her.

Someone taps on the glass of the front door of the gallery. Frankie gasps. Then she steps out of the office and into the main salon. She returns a minute later with Nik.

"I came over as soon as I could," Nik is saying to her. "After Lucas called earlier, I fell back asleep. I was out late last night."

"Look at this," Lucas says. He leans back in the chair and points to the still image of the woman's face on the monitor. "This is from the security camera."

"The police already looked at that," Frankie says. "One of the things they said they would be checking today is whether they can identify her from that shot."

Lucas says, "I can identify her." Both Nik and Frankie look at him. "She's *ghost #5*."

———————————— CHAPTER 9 ————————————

In his flat, Lucas shrugs off his coat. He makes coffee. He showers. Dressed afresh, he climbs the stairs from his flat to the darkroom on the top floor, under the rafters.

A heavy black drape hangs inside the door of the darkroom and must be thrust aside to enter the room. Long plastic trays lie in a tidy row along a rough tabletop. Jugs of chemicals, sealed boxes of print paper and rolls of towels rest on shelves beside a crusted work-sink. An enlarger with a crane-like neck and bulbous head, a small light table and a printer on a stand cluster against a far wall.

Hanging from the ceiling timbers, racks of negatives trail curling slips and braids of film like curtains in a Turkish boudoir with weighted clips at their tail ends. A short refrigerator in a corner lodges hundreds of rolls of unexposed film, Ilford HP5 and Kodak Tri-X, mostly in 400-speed, which must be mail-ordered since film is seldom available in camera shops. Two nicked, stained, pre-war wooden filing cabinets stand against a wall, stuffed with manila folders of negatives and prints. Despite a tinny ventilator mounted in a cloaked dormer, a stink of metol, hydroquinone, acetic acid and borax gently suffuses the space.

Lucas stacks the developing trays and slides them aside on the work table. He pulls stacks of folders from a file cabinet and spreads them across the tabletop. He finds the envelopes containing small prints of the *ghosts* photos, including a proof print of *#5*. He studies the image of the girl with a magnifying glass, but the nature of the print washes her in fuzzy light and dims her features. He tries a loupe, but this enlarges elements of her face so much he cannot view its entirety.

He rifles through more folders. He finds a large envelope labeled with his name handwritten in another's cursive. Inside, more envelopes bunch. He slides these out.

Each envelope is labeled with a number, apparently randomly. These negatives formed part of a larger collection. Lucas did not pay attention to these numbers previously. Now he studies them, searching.

Each envelope contains a single negative, all 35mm. They are clipped closely; two still bear their borders and sprocket holes. Lucas draws each wrapped negative from its envelope and lays them in a row on the table. Each negative is wrapped in thin paper, numbered in his handwriting one through five. Lucas opens the wrapper numbered *#5*.

He holds the negative up to the light. There, the image of the young woman glows. She wears a fur-collared coat and a winter hat. Her hands are in her coat pockets. She wears old-fashioned pin-striped pants. In the black and white photo, the pants are light and dark grey, and the coat is pale grey. Her face is brightly lit, which in the negative means deep black with light moons for eyes and black teeth in her lighter smile. She tosses a happy glance across to the camera. She appears to stand on a dock. In the background, an indistinct church rises from a low hill.

Lucas looks again at the thin paper wrapping, almost on-ionskin. He turns it over. On the back, a line of handwriting in small script crosses just under the edge of the paper. When he first received these photos, he glanced at this writing, but it meant nothing, so he passed over it, or in his compositional fever the focus of his interest had been the images themselves.

With the magnifying glass, he studies the handwriting. *She has helped you. Please help her.*

Lucas looks through the other four negative wrappers. Each bears writing in the same small script, but not declarative statements, just names, numbers and cities.

Lucas takes the negative from #5 to the enlarger. He clips it into the rack and begins focusing. Then he goes to the shelves where sealed boxes of print paper lie in stacks. He selects 203 x 254. He turns off the lights and opens the box by feel, slips out a sheet of paper, reseals the box and takes the paper to the enlarger. He locks it into the easel's blades. The he clicks on the enlarger again, sets the timer and clicks it on.

The girl appears and sharpens on the paper.

Lucas quickly fills three plastic trays, two with chemicals from his store of bottles and jugs and one with water. When the enlarger's timer has clicked off, he unclips the paper from the easel and lays the image of the girl gently into the bath of developer. Then he shifts the print to a tray filled with clear water to stop the developer. He slips the print into the tray of fixer. Finally, he rinses it under a slow trickle of cool water in the sink and hangs the shining print to dry.

He gazes at the girl. She seems to look past him, behind him.

He had printed this negative twice before to study her and imagine her against various backgrounds, but he had disposed of those prints when he had begun to compose his composite image. Now, she is back in his studio.

At the gallery, Lucas had printed a screen shot of the security camera video image of the girl's face. The quality of this image is very poor. But now he brings it from the flat, where he had left it on the kitchen counter, to his darkroom and holds it beside the drying print.

Lucas calls Nik.

"It definitely looks like the same girl," he says. "I don't understand. I thought the photos Mama gave me were all from the seventies. Also, there's an odd note on the negative's wrapping paper. She was trying to tell me something. I'm at a loss."

———————— CHAPTER 10 ————————

Lucas' bicycle is a black, older-model Kalkhoff. He leads it again from its cubby under the stairs and out of the lobby past the mailboxes and onto the sidewalks. The wind has stiffened from the north. He pulls on brown leather gloves. Pedestrians veer past huddled into their coats and hats, shopping bags clenched in gloved hands.

He rides slowly with the wind along Rosenthalerstraße, turns west, then crosses the island beside Berliner Dom on Karl-Liebknechtstraße. Traffic roars unceasingly, wet tires singing.

He angles into quieter streets and meanders south toward Gendarmenmarkt, past blocks of offices, under naked charcoal trees and their harmonies of winter wind. The print of the girl is tucked inside his coat, flat against his chest, along with the printed snapshot from the video. Faint curves of spray curve from his tires across the cobbles.

At Denver, he meets Nik and Frankie. Most of the lights in the gallery are still off, but the lamp on the counter glows and Frankie has lit a few of the candles. These impart some warmth to the shadows.

Nik found a leftover bottle of champagne in a refrigerator and has popped the cork and poured glasses for Frankie and

50

himself. He hands a bottle of seltzer water to Lucas and then, glancing over Lucas' shoulder, he pours a glass of champagne for Heike who has just dashed up the pair of steps into the gallery.

"I couldn't find a place to park," she says. "I have to go check my car in a few minutes."

"Are we celebrating something?" Lucas says, cracking open his bottle of water.

"Long, rough, weird twenty-four hours," Nik says. Frankie clicks the deadbolt on the front door and joins the group. The group of four tap drinks. Nik continues, "I remembered a guy I knew a few years ago who works for the Polizei. He's not actually on the force. He does database consulting or something, and one of their clients is the Berlin police. I asked if he could tell me anything about Mama's case. I once saved this guy's life, but that's another story. He couldn't state anything specific, but he looked at the case record and said that its categorization has been changed from likely suicide to potential homicide."

Frankie gasps. "What in the world?"

Heike says, "I just talked to Eloise a half hour ago. She says the police came around to ask another round of questions, like did Abbie have any enemies, did she have any debts, was she in conflict with anyone, had she received any threats lately? That sort of thing. Eloise was very upset. She was better this morning, but right now she's inconsolable. I'm going over there in a while."

"I'll go with you," Lucas says.

"The police came back here, too," Frankie says. "Well, one policeman. He was only here a minute. He said they put the image of the burglar's face, the girl's face, through a process to enhance it digitally, make it clearer, and then they ran it through their system, but didn't find any obvious matches. They also didn't find anything here, earlier. They were wearing gloves, as we could see in the video," she says, looking to Lucas. "And the vehicle they were driving was just an old white van with no license plates. So basically, a dead end. The policeman seemed a little apologetic, but not much. Stiff. My German's not as good as yours, but I get the nuances."

Lucas removes his coat. Nik looks around for chairs, but the room is sparsely furnished. So instead, he sets a candle on the floor and sits on the floor facing the candle and crosses his legs with the mostly empty champagne bottle beside him. Heike decides to do the same and sits on the floor facing Nik. Lucas joins her and after a minute so does Frankie, carefully in her cream-colored pencil-thin pants.

In the center of the room, the four individuals face each other in a squared circle, cardinal points of a compass, leaning together, the flickery candle in its glass flute in the center of the quadrangle.

"I went home to print this," Lucas says. He hands around the photo of the girl, and with it the snapshot from the security video.

"I feel I should know her," Nik says. "I looked so much at the *ghost* photos."

Heike compares the two photos. "The angle is different but they do look the same," she says.

"Tell us again how this came to you," Frankie says. "The photo you used in your composite."

"About six months ago," Lucas says, "Mama relayed to me that she had some photos that might work for my ghosts. I had mentioned my idea to her a while earlier. That night we all had dinner at that fancy place down by the river. When Nik got a little drunk and was hitting on the waitress."

"When doesn't that happen?" Frankie says.

"Now that I think of it, that was the last time I saw Mama in person. She called me a few days later," Lucas continues. "She told me she'd been thinking about it a lot. She said she happened to be working on an archive project that had brought her some interesting photos of people. They appeared to be from a while back, maybe the late seventies, judging by clothing. She had the negatives. They'd been done in black and white, maybe originally in Ektachrome or something and then converted. They had that look."

Lucas sips at his water. Nik lifts the mostly empty champagne bottle and sights through it. He stands and goes to the little office in the back.

Lucas expands to Frankie, "You can print black and white negatives from color film. But it usually gives less than perfect images, which these were. It has to do with the nature of the film. In color film, there's a yellow filter mask between the red and green layers, which gives you a very high density and low contrast on the negative if you try to do it in black and white. But these photos had been over-exposed in the first place, which helped."

There is a muffled pop in the office. Nik returns with a second bottle of champagne and re-seats and pours full glasses for Heike, Frankie and himself.

Outside the front windows of the gallery, a few people pass on the sidewalk. Some of them glance into the darkened gallery and notice the four people sitting on the floor with the candle as if in a seance.

"Mama mailed me the negatives. There was a bundle with five little packages, each with a negative wrapped in paper. That brings up the other interesting thing. Just today, when I dug out this negative again to reprint it, I noticed something written on the paper wrapping for #5 that I hadn't seen before, or hadn't paid attention to. Some writing. It says, *She has helped you. Please help her.* Definitely in Mama's handwriting. You know how she wrote. Like diamond etching."

"She has helped you. Please help her," Heike repeats.

"Referring to the girl in the photo," Frankie says.

"I guess. It looked like a label on the wrapper. Like it had been written specifically to identify that photo."

"Why would the girl want to steal her own photo?"

"No idea. But one thing is obvious. Assuming the girl in the photo is the girl who stole the photo, that image apparently wasn't old. In other words, all the other images were from maybe the late seventies, based on how they looked. Number five looked that old, also. But the girl who stole the photo is no older than the girl in the photo. In other words, that one was a new image. Or it was carefully staged and doctored to look forty years old. The negatives had tiny scratches on them that I had to clean up, like they had been scuffed around in drawers for a half-century. They showed signs of fading."

"Mama told you they were all people who had died," Nik says. The group considers this. They sip champagne.

"Written to you?" Frankie asks. "The note on the wrapper, I mean."

"I don't know."

Nik asks, "Were the other photos labeled like that? With notes on the wrappers?"

"The others didn't have notes on them. Just some dabs of information, names of cities. Addresses, I think."

Frankie says, "In the video, it looks like the burglars have no doubt about four of the pictures. But when they get to #5, they pause and discuss it, like they don't understand or aren't sure. It's weird that they were arguing about the picture of the female burglar herself."

"Nik," Lucas says, "last night when you were talking to Andrea, did you see the blond girl that was looking at the photos? We were standing over there."

"I saw her back. The one in the retro outfit?"

"She was looking at *#5*. I went over and tried to talk to her. It was as if she panicked. She turned and looked at me and then she dashed out. Very odd, but I didn't think much of it. I thought maybe she hated me, or the five-digit prices on the photos. I only glimpsed her face for a moment. But now I would swear that it was the same girl. The girl in the photo. The girl who stole the photo. She was looking at a photo of herself."

"So we have two pictures of her and Lucas saw her in the flesh. If we see her again, we'll know her," Frankie says.

"And this is a pretty good shot," Heike says, holding up the print of the girl from the negative. "She looks happy. As if she's saying, *Come on, follow me*."

"I wonder if that's the same person who came back later and wrote on the wall." Nik says. All four of them turn slowly in unison and look for a moment at the word written on the wall near them: MURDERER.

"Maybe she was very angry about something," Frankie ays quietly.

"Why would she have changed her clothes to come back?" Heike says.

"Anyway, the woman in black doesn't look like the burglar woman," Frankie says. "Different posture. Taller. You can see in the video. She's as tall as I am."

Lucas says softly to no one, "I wonder what she was referring to."

At this, the group sits in silence for a long minute, considering, faces downturned into the candlelight.

Lucas says, again mostly to himself, "I supposed something like this would eventually come up. History has a way of showing up on your doorstep when you don't expect it."

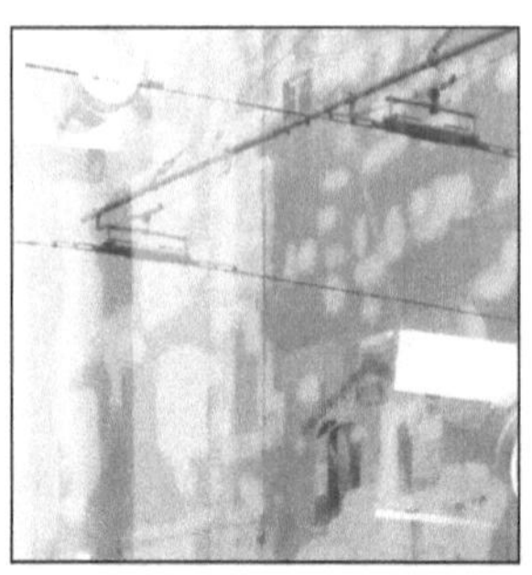

CHAPTER 11

When Lucas leaves Denver gallery, he and Heike stand on the corner for a minute.

"I'm going out to see Eloise," Heike says. Snow has started again, light but swirling. "I was thinking it would probably be best not to crowd her right now. Go home and relax for a while. I'll call you."

"How long?"

"I don't know. However long she wants. If she wants me to stay the night, I will. Last night she was fine, but you know how these things go. Sometimes it takes a day to change from a bad dream into a nightmare."

On his bicycle, Lucas retraces his path up into Mitte. The pavements are still wet. Snow slants into the streets from alleyways. When he arrives at his building, the snow has increased, cloaking the clattering intersection.

Lucas stows his dripping bicycle in the cubby under the stairs and ascends by elevator. When he reaches the fourth floor, he takes the stairs. Just as he reaches the floor occupied by his flat, he notices a slim wedge of light on the hallway wall where it should not be. He stops. A small scuffle of footsteps sounds from above. He cannot pinpoint direction.

He quietly climbs the last few steps to the hallway and turns toward the door of his flat and advances slowly. There is no light in the gap under the door. He stops again. He turns.

Just as he realizes that the light spreading down the wall is coming from the darkroom upstairs, the door of the darkroom opens and a figure, backlit, emerges in a rush. The figure clatters down the little flight to the hallway where Lucas stands. Only now does the descending person see Lucas standing a dozen paces away.

It is a woman. She cries out. She straightens and spins toward the stairs. Now she is partially lit by the snowy grey light coming through a barred window at the top of the stairs to the lower floors, the last of the daylight.

She wears a tight black coat and a colorful ski hat. Blond hair protrudes from under the hat in many directions. She wears a small, green backpack. The woman turns and thumps down the stairs.

Bewildered, Lucas runs upstairs to the open door of his darkroom. He sees little changed except that the row of labeled folders he left on the tabletop earlier in the day, the folders containing the negatives of the *ghosts*, are no longer there. He can hear the thudding footsteps of the woman in the stair-well descending floor by floor.

Lucas runs after her. He skims down the stairs to the fourth floor. The elevator which he took only a minute before still waits there. He jumps in and punches the button for the ground floor. As the elevator slides quietly down, through its walls he can still hear faintly the woman's footsteps as she reaches the bottom floor and bangs open the building's front door.

The elevator opens in the lobby. Lucas sprints into the street. He spins in the whirling, heavy-flaked storm. There, in the slow traffic on Rosenthalerstraße he sees the figure of the woman. She is on a bicycle, weaving through stopped traffic. The tails of her blond hair fly in the wind.

Lucas runs back into the lobby and grabs his bicycle from the cubby behind the stairs. He leaps onto it and cranks into the snowy evening.

He cannot see the woman at first, but then spots her distinctive hat and hair, the green backpack, in a crowd of other bicycles bunched at the corner of Orienburgerstraße. Streams of cars press past, wipers snapping and taillights blazing; two trams rumble in opposing directions.

The woman pushes forward against the light, between two cars. She cuts behind the further tram and rides across the sidewalk into Hackeschermarkt. Lucas careens into the traffic behind her. He wobbles among pedestrians and past stalls, holdovers from holiday markets, brightly lit. Pedestrians are snow-shouldered. A scent of *glühwein* swirls.

The two riders, the woman with her backpack and the man in his overcoat, ride frantically through the arches under the S-Bahn, swerving between two more trams, one stopped and one moving and dinging its bell, and onto the gentle arc of the bridge to Museum Island. Lucas sprints, but he cannot close the distance, his breathing ragged. Snowflakes sting his eyes. The surface of the bridge over the Spree is slippery, having frozen ahead of the streets. His tires slew about in the slush. The river shines black.

They race past the bullet-pocked pillars before the gardens of the National Gallery and Pergamon and between the hulks of the Altes and Neues Museums. Snow curves among the columns and over the gleaming gardens.

She stays a full block or more ahead, and gains a slight advantage when Lucas is slowed crossing Friedrichstraße. She swerves at an intersection and stands on her pedals for Behrenstraße. When he reaches the corner, he realizes that she has just crossed the street and ridden into the Memorial for the

Murdered Jews of Europe, and he realizes that night has fully fallen amid the flurries.

Bicycles are not allowed in the memorial, but there is no one around to enforce the rules or even glance askance. She took this path either to elude him or as a shortcut. He rides after her and enters the memorial. It is nearly vacant owing to the weather. Lucas dives into a passage and rides slowly, scanning left and right. Blocks of concrete rise around him. They shelter him from the wind, although snow drifts and settles. All is dark and quiet among the stelae. The roar of the city suddenly grows calm and distant.

The columns shadow their canyons, except for every fourth alley which is vaguely upward-lit by fixtures in the pavement. Video cameras mounted on slim poles gaze down into some of the dark, wet corridors. Spaces between the vertical stones barely accommodate handlebars. Lucas must concentrate on accurate maneuvering while searching each alley for a glimpse of the woman on her bike.

The path on which he rides inclines for a distance and then crests and descends in a slight swale. The stones tower here. He searches each crossing path, row after row after row, undulating. The site is vast. He changes direction several times. He may hear voices. He may hear the wheels of another bicycle, but this could be echoes of his own. He becomes disoriented, straightens his route and rides for the far end, whichever end that may be.

Just as he emerges from the forest of columns, he sees a figure on a bicycle darting from a pathway far down the row, a long block away. That cyclist aims across the street, curves away into the crush of headlights and disappears into the night and the snow in the direction of Potsdamerplatz.

Lucas stands for several minutes at the mouth of the passageway from which he emerged. The stelae here are shorter, hip-height. He leans against the last one in the row, breathing deeply.

─────── **CHAPTER 12** ───────

Lucas awakes from rough dreams. His pillow sops with sweat. He is alone. The bedroom is cold, though wind no longer chafes the windows. He lies thinking, organizing. He rubs at a slight headache behind his temples.

Heike stayed with Eloise until late. Then she drove to her own flat since it was closer, and she has a reserved parking space there. She and Lucas talked on the phone until after midnight.

"Don't chase anybody," she said. "Let the police do that."

"I should have locked the door," Lucas said. "I should have locked my files. I should have taken the negatives with me."

"How could you have known?" she said.

After a while, he rises and makes coffee and sips it slowly sitting in his armchair overlooking the square. The headache dissolves with the warmth. He dresses and goes to the street and buys two croissants and a Sunday *New York Times* and, though several days old, a copy of *Die Zeit*.

He returns to his flat and sheds the clothing he donned to venture downstairs. The Nespresso machine vibrates anew. He settles again into the armchair under a blanket before the closed French doors. A sea of pearl grey sky hangs over Rosenthaler Platz. Across the square, the downcast face of the girl on the gigantic poster hangs dimly. He sits and reflects.

60

Why would someone steal the photos and then try, awkwardly and ineffectually, since he has other copies, to clean up by taking the negatives from which the photos had sprung? Obvious answer: They didn't want the photos to be seen. Who would want this? The most likely candidates would be the subjects of the photos. But Lucas knows neither who those people were nor what they could be hiding from.

It is late afternoon when the group of four again comes together. They meet at Lucas' flat. Outside, Berlin shimmers and clanks in the cold. Inside the flat, Brazilian music plays. Heike, in the kitchen, moves about preparing croquettes, one of Eloise's favorites. She is returning there later. Against the winter outside, she wears jeans and a thick green turtleneck.

Nik and Frankie sit together on a leather couch sipping cocktails and cracking pistachios. Frankie wears one of her all-white outfits: sleek white sweater and skin-tight white jeans, like a sheaf of snow. Beside her, Nik wears all black, per usual.

Lucas sits on a stool at the counter with a glass of iced tea in a cut tumbler. He says, "The story about Mama made the news this afternoon. They didn't identify her yet because they're looking for her family. But I don't think she has any. Still, I say let them look."

Nik says, "Mama. The photos from the gallery. Your negatives. Someone doesn't want to be found."

Frankie says, "I'm frightened. We have no idea what's going on, but it's too close. I hired a security guard to sit in the gallery all night. In case they come back."

Heike says across the counter from the kitchen, "Lucas, you really must report the darkroom theft to the police. It may help Abbie. And I'm worried about you. It's no longer just an isolated thing."

Nik says, "I wish we knew what Mama had to do with it."

They all turn in a single, tense motion when a knock sounds at the door. Lucas rises from his stool. The door, located in a small alcove off the main room, cannot be seen from the main room.

Lucas opens the door. There stands the blond girl.

She's tightly wrapped in the orange canvas parka with the fur collar she carried at the gallery, though she wears no hat this evening. Her face shines red, perhaps with wind and cold, her hair whipped. She gazes at Lucas. She trembles visibly.

She raises a gloved hand and offers Lucas a large manila envelope, opened. He takes it slowly. He glances down at it, opens it. It contains what appears to be all the folders of negatives. He looks back up at the girl.

"I'm sorry," she says in German. She is rigid. Unmoving, unblinking, she begins to cry.

"Come in and talk," Lucas says.

When they step into the room, Nik, Frankie and Heike watch. Frankie gasps. A samba sashays heatedly from the stereo.

Then Nik says, "Hello, *ghost #5*."

—— CHAPTER 13 ——

Lucas and the blond girl stand side by side. She is angled toward Nik and Frankie sitting on the sofa opposite her with their drinks. Heike, behind the kitchen counter, has put down her spatula.

Lucas, holding the envelope, faces the girl. The girl looks at the people and around the room at the walls of photographs, then back to Lucas.

"My name is Hannah," the girl says. Her voice is very quiet against the music. "Hannah Müller. My grandmother told me to come to you."

"Who is your grandmother?" Lucas says.

"Abbie Ingvall."

Lucas evaluates her, and says, "You have her eyes. Mama's."

The girl's head slowly lowers and she puts her face in her palms. They let her stand for a minute. Nik rises, goes to the stereo and turns off the music.

In the sudden quiet, Lucas guides the girl forward. He turns an armchair for her and she slowly sits. Her knobby knees clamp together, her muscular, bicyclist thighs. She wears high-waisted, tight, thick-weave pants mottled blue and grey and the brown boots she wore in the gallery. The belled cuffs of the pants are ragged and mud-splashed. When she looks up at the group again, her face is wet. She pulls off her tan leather gloves and wipes her eyes with her fingertips. Lucas sits on a low wooden stool facing the girl.

Gesturing to each in turn, he says, "These are my friends Nik, Frankie, and Heike. Frankie owns Denver gallery where some of my photos were displayed. They were stolen. Did you take them?"

The girl slowly nods.

"And then you took these negatives."

She nods again. "But I'm also going to return the photos," she says. "We didn't damage them. I think it was a mistake. I don't know."

Another long pause ensues, toward the end of which the girl collects an expansive breath and then sighs.

"Why don't you start at the beginning." Lucas states this.

For a minute, the girl seems to be searching. Then she says, "Abbie came to Berlin from Helsinki in 1965, I think. She said she was very radical then. She hung around with a lot of radical people, too. She was a communist. They called her Mama because she was a little older and a lot smarter than most of them. At least that's my opinion.

"Before long, she went into the East side of the city. You could do that. A lot of Ossies tried to come west, and they were prevented by the Wall and the guards. But very few Wessies tried to go east. When they did, usually no one stopped them. We learned this in school. Abbie went east through Checkpoint Charlie.

"A few years later, she had my mother. Abbie said she didn't know who the father was. But she named her daughter Ulrike after a radical friend of hers, Ulrike Meinhof."

Lucas nods. He turns to Nik and Frankie.

"Ulrike Meinhof was a devout communist in the sixties who later formed the Red Brigades. The Baader-Meinhoff gang, they were called. She died in prison in the mid-seventies."

Hannah nods. "Abbie told me Ulrike was their hero. But Abbie didn't keep her child. My mother was adopted by some people in Leipzig. My mother never met her mother."

At this Frankie sets down her glass and crosses her legs. She folds her arms.

Hannah continues. "But my mother ran away from home when she was twelve or thirteen and came back to Berlin."

"Where is your mother now?"

"She's dead. She died a couple of years ago. I hadn't spoken to her in a long time. I've been on my own. I think she did her best for me for a while, but then everything caught up with her."

Nik says, "Hannah, how old are you?"

"Almost nineteen."

"You're eighteen. Where do you live?"

"My friend has a flat. In Lichtenberg. He lets me stay there."

The room is warm. Hannah unzips her orange parka, revealing a Guatemalan woven vest over a white t-shirt, her waif-like torso and lengthy marble arms.

"Is your boyfriend the person who helped you take the photos?" Lucas says. "We have a video of the two of you," he adds.

Hannah nods. She combs back her hair with a hand. "But he's not my boyfriend. And it was my idea. I was afraid for Abbie. I talked him into it."

Lucas says. "How do you know Abbie was your grandmother?"

"She told me. It was when I was still in school. One day I came out of the building and there was an old woman waiting on the street. She seemed ancient. She had scars on one side of her face from burns. An eyepatch. As I came by, she said, 'You're

Hannah, aren't you?' Then she said, 'I could tell by the way you look.' She told me she was my grandmother. Just told me outright. She was like that."

Lucas nods.

"We talked for a while and she asked if we could get together to chat. We met for coffee or something a few days later. At first, I was doubtful, but I listened. As she talked, I decided she was telling me the truth. Not only did she know a lot about my mother, but I could just feel it. A connection. There was something about her that seemed familiar. Comfortable. She told me she had searched for me because she found out her daughter—my mother—had died. She was worried for me. I don't think Abbie was the mothering type. I guess none of the women in my family are. But she took me under her wing. She didn't seem to want anything. She just wanted to get to know me. I've never met anyone who was friendly to me who didn't want something from me."

Lucas leans back on his stool and says, "Hannah, what sort of schnitzel was Mama's favorite?"

Hannah wrinkles her brow and rolls her eyes at Lucas, at the test question. "She didn't eat schnitzel. She always said it was the food of the bourgeoisie. She said sausage was more to her taste, the food of the proletariat."

Lucas nods again and smiles at her for the first time. "We're definitely talking about the same person."

Hannah resumes. "But you see, at the time I met Abbie, I was just about to drop out of school, which I did a few weeks later. Abbie wasn't happy about that. She saw value in education. She was once a history teacher, she told me. But I had met some people. I love what they're doing. They're planning to bring changes to the world. Germany has become so fat and complacent and defensive. Everything is about money, about getting rich. The government watches us and controls us.

My friends have plans for disruption. The system needs to be broken so it can be fixed correctly and improved. The system sees everything, but it's blind. It's immoral. It crushes people. It needs to be crushed."

Nik smiles slightly and looks down at the floor. Next to him, Frankie, feeling his change of posture, glances at him.

From behind the counter, Heike says, "Hannah, what did Abbie tell you about her background in the seventies?"

Lucas fills in, "We all knew her well. She was very leftist. But she never said anything about radicals."

"She didn't tell me much, either," Hannah says. "She didn't seem to want to discuss it. But when I told her about my friends and their plans, she seemed very unhappy. She said she completely understood. But she said dreams were one thing, tactics were another. She said she had learned this the hard way. She was trying to help me. She didn't say anything, and I haven't been able to find out much at the library, but she gave me the impression that she had seen a lot of action in her day. Little hints. Some pretty ugly stuff. She never told me how she got the scars."

Lucas says, "Let's jump forward. Why did you take the photos?"

"Abbie—I can only call her that, not Grandma or something —Abbie had seemed very down the last few weeks. I mean, she was often down. She had bad spells. But recently she seemed extra dark. I wanted to help her. I asked how I could. She told me a little about you. She said you had a photo exhibit opening at a gallery soon. I didn't know why she was telling me this. Then she asked me to go see the exhibit. She asked me to do it for her. So I went. I didn't understand what I was looking at. But then I saw the photo of me. Where did that come from?"

"Mama gave me that photo," Lucas says. "She gave me all the photos of people. I added the backgrounds."

"She must have taken that photo sometime when we were out together. I don't remember when. It might have been the time we went to the zoo. Or maybe just some time we were out walking around. She liked to take photos occasionally. She worked with photos in her job at the library, you know. She was cute about taking pictures. She said she liked the way I dress. I don't remember the clothes I had on in that photo, but I go through a lot of old clothes. She said I dress the way everyone did when she was young. I look pretty happy in that photo. When I was around Abbie, I was usually happy. The happiest I've ever been."

At this, Hannah puts her face back in her hands. Her elbows rest on her knees. She sits like this for a full minute, and the others give her this pause. Presently she shudders and raises her face. Frankie has reached for her purse and drawn out a packet of tissues and she offers them to Hannah, who takes two and wipes her eyes.

"I got an email from her the night she died," Hannah says, "which was weird because she never emailed me before. She seldom emails anyone. Her email said, *Go to Lucas. He will help you.* I assumed Lucas meant you."

"What time?" Lucas says.

"What time what?"

"What time did she send the email?"

"I don't know. Middle of the night." She digs in a coat pocket for her phone.

"Never mind," Lucas says. "She sent me an email, too, about two in the morning. She must have sent both about the same time. That might explain why she signed it Abbie. That's how you knew her, and she was thinking of you."

Hannah resumes. "But when I saw the photos at the gallery that night with mine among them, I immediately thought it was her old radical friends. I thought maybe someone was trying to expose them. The photos looked old. I didn't understand. I thought maybe Abbie was trying to warn me of something. I thought maybe you or someone was tricking me. I didn't know why I would be involved. It felt like a hallucination. I panicked. I thought maybe people were coming after me. More importantly, I thought maybe someone was after Abbie. She didn't want her past to come out. She always said it was no one else's business what an old lady did years ago."

Lucas says, "So you came back and took the photos that night."

Hannah nods. "It was the only thing I could think of to do to protect her. Get rid of the photos. We walked around the place for a while checking for cameras and things. That was about midnight. We saw the cameras in the gallery, but they were pointed at the walls where the photos were, so we thought we could stay out of sight. Then we went and borrowed a vehicle from a friend of my friend's. We came back later and my friend just broke the window with a hammer and we went in. There was no alarm. We had decided if we saw or heard an alarm we'd just run."

Lucas says, "Did you come back again? Around four? And write something on the wall inside the gallery?"

Hannah looks bewildered. "No. When we got the pictures we just left there as fast as we could. We went to the flat and unloaded them. We didn't leave."

Hannah's voice is slightly hoarse. Her German is a youthful, lowered-tone Berlin dialect. She speaks quickly. Heike takes a glass from a cabinet and fills it from a pitcher of Lucas' iced tea. She hands it to Lucas who hands it to Hannah who sips it.

When she lowers the glass, she says quietly, her eyes on no one, "Are you going to have me arrested?"

Lucas says, "The photographs are in your flat now?"

"In the bedroom. All five of them. Leaning against the wall."

"Can you bring them back to the gallery?"

"Tomorrow first thing. And I'll pay for the window." She offers this to Frankie.

"How did you find out that Mama had died?" Lucas says.

"The police contacted me today," Hannah says. "They called me. I panicked again when the person on the phone said he was a police detective. I'd become a thief overnight. But he said that he needed to talk to me about Abbie Ingvall. He seemed nice on the phone. He asked if we could meet at a station in Wilmersdorf. I went there. I was terrified. But I needed to know. I needed to help Abbie if I could. The detective asked me some questions about Abbie. Then he told me that she had died. I almost collapsed on the spot. He told me they thought I was the next of kin. Then he said they thought she had committed suicide, but they were still examining some videos. She had been talking to someone on a bridge over the river not long before she probably died."

"When did they tell you this?" Lucas asks.

"Maybe two hours ago. I walked around for a while. I couldn't believe what was happening. I had to talk to someone. But I don't know anyone except some kids, my friends. And Abbie. But then I remembered she had said to talk to you. I went back to the flat and got the negatives of the photos and brought them here."

"There was a news story about her earlier today saying that said the police were not sure how she had died."

Hannah nods. "They told me there was no sign of violence. But they wanted to check."

Lucas turns to Nik and speaks in English. "Can you contact that friend of yours again and see if there's anything new in the system? I don't know if the police will tell us anything if we just call them."

"You don't believe me?" Hannah asks, obviously understanding.

"I would like to find out, if we can, what the police know. It may change what we do. You see, Mama was right. I am going to try to help you."

Heike puts out bread and olives for the group; she wraps croquettes for Eloise in a flowered towel and places them in a basket. Nik stands and moves to the other end of the room and works with his phone. When he returns, he says, "Maybe we'll find out something later."

Nik then goes to the counter and pours new whiskey cocktails for himself and Frankie. He turns to Hannah. "Would you like a drink?" She nods. He mixes one for her and hands it to her and she flicks a quick smile.

Nik sits on the couch and says to her, "You're very stylish."

She smiles briefly again, gamin-like. "I haunt flea markets. Nothing I'm wearing cost more than three Euros. I like to dress the way they did back when people really felt things strongly, when things had meaning. My grandmother's time." She looks Nik up and down for the first time, his black silk shirt and textured cravat, his square tortoiseshell glasses, his cuff-links, his thick-soled but polished black boots. "You're stylish, too," she says.

"You said you think you can help," Frankie says softly to Lucas.

The manila folder sits upright on the floor against the stool. Lucas lifts the folder and sets it on a low table. He draws out the contents and leafs through the folders, opening each and examining the negatives in their wrappers. He lays the five of them on the table in a row. He turns each one over so the writing on the back of the wrapper faces up.

"Let's begin with these," Lucas says.

CHAPTER 14

Lucas opens each wrapper and holds the negative up to the light. He sets aside the photo of Hannah, leaving four. He draws lines across a sheet of paper, dividing it into four equal spaces, and numbers the spaces one through four. He copies the information from each wrapper in one of the spaces.

"*Ghost #1*" he says, "is the woman with the hat. *Ghost #2* is the man with the seabag. *Ghost #3* is the woman in the rain-coat. *Ghost #4* is the man with the dog. The information on each of the wrappers is clearly an address. None of the people in these photos was more than twenty-five when the photos were taken. They were all young. So they may still be around. The writing on the wrappers is new. It's Mama's handwriting. My guess is that she found the addresses for the people in the photos. But I didn't know what they meant and didn't pause to ask." Lucas looks up from the table to Nik and Frankie on the couch and Heike in the kitchen.

"I want to go find these people and ask what they can tell me about why Mama might have given me their photos," he says. "Mama saved my life. When I came to Berlin twenty years ago, I was ready to die. I came here to die. She didn't let me. She brought me back. But now I've let her slip through my fingers.

She died, and I didn't help her. I didn't return what she gave to me. When she sent me the photos a couple of months ago, I think she was asking me for something. I didn't realize it, just like I didn't pay attention to the writing on the negative wrappers. I was too concerned with images. I didn't ask what lay behind."

Heike removes her apron and comes from the kitchen to the couch. She sits next to Nik, leans forward and places both hands on Lucas' leg. Frankie leans in, also, and Nik puts his hand on her shoulder. In this manner, the four friends face each other, close. A long moment passes.

"We will do anything we can to help you," Nik says. Frankie nods vigorous agreement. Heike smiles at him and nods also.

Lucas looks to each of them in turn. His mouth and eyes are level, solemn. "It would help," he says slowly, "to find these people promptly. If Mama's death is in any way connected to them, their willingness to talk may be evanescent. I would be grateful for your help."

"Let's go, then," Nik says. He reaches for the sheet of paper and studies it. "These addresses are all over the place. Tallinn. Zermatt. Stockholm. Edinburgh. What are we going to do with them?"

Lucas says, "I've been thinking about it. I think it would be best to visit each person and try to talk to them. Put a human face on it. Explain what's happened and ask for their help. I also think we should try to get a photo of each person, if possible."

Heike nods. "I see. Sort of connecting the dots that Abbie was trying to connect. Completing the picture."

Lucas takes the sheet of paper back from Nik and, using the edge of the table, tears it into four strips, each bearing a single name and address.

"Nik, you take *ghost #4: Man With Dog.*" He hands that strip to Nik. "Frankie, you take *ghost #1: Woman In Hat.* Heike, you take *ghost #2: Man With Seabag*. I'll take *ghost #3: Woman In Raincoat*. I'll make good prints of each of their photos for you. I'll get each of us tickets right now and we can leave tomorrow. Probably be back in a day or so. Heike, do you need to be in the studio the next couple of days?"

Heike shakes her head. "This is important. For Abbie."

"Frankie, do you need to be at the gallery?"

Frankie shakes her head. "Hendrika runs things herself."

"So we're good to go, then."

"You didn't ask me if I'm busy," Nik says.

"Are you busy?"

"No."

Frankie is looking at the address on the slip of paper. She picks up the negative for *#1* and squints at it. She says, "What if these people are old criminals or something? They could be dangerous."

Lucas says, "I've been thinking about that, too. If they were connected to Mama way back in the seventies, they may want to talk to us about her now, especially when they learn that she's died. Or they may slam their doors in our faces."

Hannah sits vertically, stiffly on the seat, gazing at them, into their circle. Her oval face is pale. Her blue eyes blink slowly under her bangs.

Lucas turns to her. He reaches his left hand. She looks at his hand and then slowly lifts her hand and takes his.

"I would like to include you in this," Lucas says, "because Mama was your grandmother and because you need to be included. But there are two conditions. First, you need to return the photographs to Frankie like you said you would. Second, you should go back and finish school. It's what your grandmother would have wanted."

They all sit like this for a minute, an awkward, half-closed ring around the small table with the row of film negatives and papers. Eventually, Hannah says in a squeak, "Okay."

Lucas says, "I will help you, as Mama asked me to. And we need your help."

"What can I do?"

Lucas says, "You're coming with me."

The group sits a while in silence. Each face belies a person lost in a private tumult.

Then Lucas adds, "Mama kept secrets from me. I don't know why. I was always honest with her. I think I've always been honest with everyone. But clearly there is much that I don't understand. Secrets withheld are a form of slow torture, both for the person who doesn't know but suspects, and for the person who knows but hides the truth."

PART TWO

THREE TESTIMONIES

CHAPTER 15

Nik Ng — #1

My older brother Bao died when my family lived in Vietnam. I was eight. He was fifteen. He was my entire world. I killed him.

Indirectly. I caused him to lose his life.

A truckful of Viet Cong soldiers came to our village at the edge of the forests fifteen kilometers north of Hái Duong. My parents told me to stay inside, to let no one see that our house had boys in it. They sent Bao to hide in the grain bin.

The soldiers moved about our village knocking on doors, asking questions. From some of the houses they took young men. I remember the crying and yelling echoing through our leafy little subtropical village between the fields and the forests. A small chorus of young men were set to singing patriotic songs by the soldiers. Dogs barked.

My excitement exceeded my capacity for restraint. I slipped out. I stood in the dirt street watching. Eventually one of the soldiers who was rounding up conscripts came to me. He gazed down at me with no expression. But when I asked if I could join them, he rolled his head back and laughed, a sudden crack in the quiet. He told me I was too young and too small.

I told him my brother Bao was big enough.

The soldiers asked me where Bao was. I pointed to the grain bins.

To this day, I cannot say whether I said and did this out of pride or resentment. For at the time, my love and admiration for my brother were shot through with a sense of rivalry. He was always first, always fastest, always best. My parents seemed to favor him since he was the first son. They praised him. He teased me sometimes, and he had done so cruelly that morning, calling me "lefty." I felt, compared to him, a shadow, an invisible slip of a boy.

My brother Bao: glimpses of him ahead of me, his back, his muscles showing through his thin shirt as he ran; his shining laugh; his way of poking me with chopsticks when we were eating; the time he stepped between me and two boys throwing pebbles, scared them away, led me home by the hand; the way he always seemed sure of things even when he wasn't, when he couldn't have been. His shining dark eyes, wet and superior and frightened.

Bao looked back at me with those eyes as the soldiers led him away to the cluster of trucks. They gave him a green canvas jacket of the type the soldiers wore, although it was too large for his frail frame. They put a netted helmet on his head with its straps dangling. They gave him a gun with no ammunition. It was large and heavy. He held it tightly. I still sometimes see his long, white fingers wrapping that gunstock and gunbarrel.

His face was mysterious, unfathomable.
My mother and father sobbed.

He looked at me the way Lucas looked at me
when the police led him off to jail.

I never saw my brother again. We never
learned with specificity what happened to him,
but a month later the village received word that
all the boys taken that day were dead.

Not long afterward I was sent to live with my
grandparents in Los Angeles. I never realized at the
time what an immensely dangerous and expensive
undertaking it was to ship me away, how hard it
was for my parents, how many in our village pitched
in to arrange transport for me and pay for my
passage. I just did what I was told. I walked about
like a specter, hollow and transparent. After they
told us that Bao was dead, I don't think I spoke
for months, even after I was in America.

And then soon my parents were gone, too.
I had been told they would soon be joining me in
America. But more soldiers, this time the ARVN,
came to our village. My parents disappeared.

I was orphaned at about the same time and
in roughly the same manner as Lucas. His parents
were killed by a bomb planted in a car in a small
town outside Berlin. He was ten years old. The boy
was packed up and spirited away to live with old
relatives in the U.S. My war was hot; his was cold.
But we were both casualties. Lucas and I share this
procession. The vanished faces. Skulls buried in the
thin, stony topsoil of childhood memories.

* * *

At Tegel, I waited for the airline to announce the boarding of my flight to Edinburgh. It was a two-hopper through Brussels which portended a half-day airport slog. At least this gave me ample time for reviewing, trying to think this thing through, meandering.

I saw Frankie dashing for her plane at the airport. She went by in the concourse with a wave of her hand and an incomprehensible shout over her shoulder, my precise and perfectly-tuned friend uncharacteristically running late.

My plane hoisted out of Tegel and across snowy, barren farmscapes laced with occasional shining rivers and railroads. Up at the ungodly hour of eight in the morning, I dozed until we bumped down into the northeast suburbs of Brussels.

It must be understood from the outset: For me, Lucas took the place of the big brother I lost in Vietnam. After we met and became close in college, Lucas seemed to take on the role in my psyche of my vanished brother. I needed someone in that role. I still do.

This, too, must be made clear: I would not have set off on a search like the one I was undertaking on behalf of anyone else. I don't typically chase down strangers in foreign countries and ask to take their photos.

The task didn't seem Herculean, though. I had a name and an address and a photo. Go to the house and knock on the door. Ask for the person. Show them the photo. Tell them we're finishing some research in Berlin undertaken by Abbie Ingvall. Ask if they can provide some background on the photo. Ask if I can take their picture.

I could do this, I decided. For Lucas. Because I had to.

It's more complicated than just love. If only it was just love.

Lucas: the broad back ahead of me as we cruised into studios and theaters at UCLA, in film school when we were still kids, so fixated on how good we looked as we walked around, smiling at people. The way he still walks, when he thinks people are watching, the same easily self-conscious way, decades later. His laugh. The tender way he glances at Heike as if they're locked in a perpetual moment of having just saved each other. The way he drifts hunch-shouldered sometimes, lost in worries. The way he swims in recollection I wish I could extirpate. The way he flashes on like the movie star he is occasionally, but then switches off and looks at me in embarrassment like we're all cohorts in an amusing but sophomoric joke.

He is a powerfully self-assured man cracked through with fragile veins of dread and uncertainty, at constant risk of shattering. He is sensitive to sounds and colors and scintillas of feeling. He notices forms and lines and shadows that everyone else misses. He treads quietly fascinated through forests of details. His presence brightens rooms, and sometimes darkens them. He is more superstitious than he lets on.

There is something irresistible about Lucas.

Irresistibility irks.

He still drives me beyond crazy sometimes. Not with things he does or says, though he can be momentarily critical and sarcastic and superior. Just his existence. He is so much larger than I, in every way. His accomplishments. His fame. His money. His looks. Even I, who know every gritty detail of the man's crises and failings—I who have been with him through his worst moments—find myself rubbed raw by him. I sometimes cannot excuse him or make room for him.

In those moments, I leave. I go find something else to do. I toddle about with women half my age or younger, embarrassing myself and, I suppose, the women. These young women usually grab their phones as soon as we've finished in bed to see if anyone has texted while they were distracted.

I wander about Europe. I dive back into music and start ever-failing projects. I attempt to write. I escape from Lucas.

Then, before long, it all returns. I cannot live without him. I am nothing without him. I love him and resent him, which I suppose is a dynamic of many relationships.

Descending into Edinburgh, I saw through the window the city's rocky shoulders rising iced like cakes. The path to Arthur's Seat stitched its way up the crag, a line of blood red engraved onto the icy slopes. My driver took the usual route past the zoo to the low saddle, where the palace sprawls and crossed on Bridge Street.

I checked into the Balmoral. Lucas had loaned me a credit card.

***

Frankie and I go way back. We met at UCLA, I think in our sophomore year. She had run west from her suffocating family, all that old Colorado mining money, her father the great Senator, her mother once the chair of Planned Parenthood, their magnificent place in Georgetown where she took me one time a year or so after we met. She bought my plane ticket. I think that was the first thing she ever gave me, and I was embarrassed, but what was I to do? I had no money. I was desperate to be with her. She said I was protection from her family, a slap at them, I suppose. A tiny, long-haired, wildly-dressed, Asian musician fake boyfriend.

We made up pet names for each other. We held hands a lot. We slept in the same bedroom, although I slept on the couch.

I was in love with Frankie, or at least the image of Frankie: tall, blonde, athletic, Nordic goddess. This playful, malicious posing for her

parents was both delectation and agony for me.
Frankie was in love with Lucas. Back in L.A.,
Lucas was in love with his visions of the future,
and probably of himself. Everywhere Lucas has
ever lived, there have been lots of mirrors. Mirrors
and photographs.

Frankie was a year older than I. When we
met at a party, we hit it off. We saw each other
around campus and at parties and concerts.
She was funny and exciting. I was in awe of her.
She was in a sorority. I'd see her coming across
Wilson Plaza, often in the company of other statu-
esque women. She'd see me and wave and call out
to me. She seemed excited to see me. She would
tell her friends about my guitar-playing, the bands
I was in. I can't tell you how that helped a person
like me, lonesome and broken on the inside, through
those first couple of years away from my grandparents' home.

I don't make friends easily. I seem to drive
people away, which is generally fine with me.
In my entire life, I can count my close friends on
one hand. Lucas and Frankie were always top
of the short list.

Then one night, at my invitation, Frankie
came to see a play I was in at Freud Playhouse.
It was some sort of post-modern adaptation of
Rhinoceros. Lucas was also in the play.

Lucas and I were both taking upper level
classes in TFT—Theater/Film/Television.
We were tight. We cruised the beaches together.
We drove up and down the coast together.

We talked art, film, music, politics, childhoods, ambitions and, of course, women.

We shared a fascination with our own looks. He was a god; I, a demigod. Most men find themselves to be better looking than others perceive them. Lucas and I were right.

But with Lucas in the presence of other people, especially women, I always felt like a clowning and gamboling little figurine, a doll with angular cheekbones and almond eyes. Women would stare at him. He'd smile back with that set of teeth, those cobalt eyes and dense eyelashes. I'd ramble on with inane jokes and offers to make liquor runs, if I could borrow someone's car.

My premier asset, when I was 21 years old, was that I was the best friend of Lucas Bloch (he still spelled it the family way then). That may still be true almost 40 years later.

I'd spent a year keeping my two friends delicately separated—Lucas on one side and Frankie on the other. I'd managed to skirt them around each other. Lucas seemed a threat. I wanted Frankie to myself.

But I wanted her to see me in that play. I fantasized that Frankie, seeing me in costumes under lights, delivering lines that drew rolls of laughter from the audience, would suddenly find some value in me that hadn't emerged to her yet. I was aware that by coming to the play she'd see Lucas. He played the lead, Bérenger. The last remaining human after everyone else has turned into rhinos and the world has disintegrated.

Afterward, backstage, my face smeared and sweaty under pancake, in the clamor and back-slapping, Frankie grabbed my arm with excitement and, gesturing with a tilt of her blonde head toward Lucas, said, "Who's that guy?" Frankie with that hungry look in her eyes.

Lucas and Frankie were connected that last year in college. I strode about, slamming through finals, in silent misery. But before long, Lucas moved on to others. The world was his oyster, and all the women pearls. We'd spoken of this many times in the past. He certainly had an eye for the curve of an ass and ear for the brilliance of a laugh. But those were just entry points for Lucas. He always formed his characteristically careful and deliberate relationships with one woman at a time, and those relationships were powerful and had depth of feeling about them. But they were sequential.

In those days, his relationships compensated for brevity with intensity.

Frankie was devastated when he broke it off, but she hung around with me, and because I was around Lucas a lot, she was around him, too. She never lost that hungry look. This was the beginning of our strange trilogy.

I had an odd, numb feeling toward her after she ran to Lucas. But I couldn't let go. After they broke up, she and I sat in coffee shops and talked about lots of nothing. I twisted paper napkins into knots. I wondered if she was thinking about Lucas. She fastidiously never brought him up.

Time passed. Baccalaureates, we all headed restlessly out into the world. Lucas started getting little jobs—odds and ends in local productions, occasional commercials, eventually a temporary role on a soap opera. I auditioned and was hired to play lead for an up-and-coming band. They had good bookings all over southern California. They had a record deal. I had suddenly and briefly a little money of my own.

Frankie skied with the U. S. Team for a while, but she fell out of that. Frankie's competitive, but loses enthusiasm quickly. Each of us in our own ways quite talented, and each of us riven with weaknesses.

She came into her inheritance. She promptly dove into one of her crazy, short-lived business ideas —she funded a dazzling French restauranteur twice her age who, like her, was a former ski racer.

Frankie and I spent one night together during this period. This happened a couple months after she and Lucas split.

In bed, Frankie was an amplification of who she is the rest of the time, sort of agile and purring and full of little exclamations, and very powerful. I thought she might crack my spine. Apart from the predictable awkwardness, upon which we both remarked in advance, of sleeping with one's friend, the only other oddity was that, it must be admitted, Frankie is quite a bit taller than I am. Her feet reached the end of the mattress in the bedroom of her slick, modern apartment almost devoid of furniture; mine, not so much.

In the morning, I asked in a haze if, since we were already such good friends, she thought we would make a good couple. It was a cool, barren, echoey room. Lying on her side under the sheet and facing away from me toward the vast windows, a long, draped deity, Frankie said laconically and with the attempt at levity that seeks to overwrite sorrow, "Maybe if you stood on Lucas' shoulders."

CHAPTER 16

Nik Ng — #2

I killed some time in my hotel room. In the way that a song can get stuck in your head, I found myself returning to the post-college period I had for so long kept out of mind. The comment that Lucas had made the evening before—about secrets—kept renewing the tune like dropping coins in the juke-box and punching the same number over and over.

***

I didn't see Frankie or Lucas for months afterward.
 Lucas apparently started to re-warm to
Frankie in this interlude. I eventually heard from
her that they were dating again. Then I heard
that she had moved in with him.
 I needed to be back around them, my only
real friends, a visceral longing for a lonely boy.
I called and we met for drinks. I withstood being
the third wheel. I went to parties at their place.
I was popular with their circle. My music was on
the radio a lot at that time.

Lucas was athletic in a utilitarian sort of way. He logged his running miles. He ate carefully. Every movement, every article of clothing, every consumed item, was chosen with an end in mind. His looks were his religion. His body had come into its manhood, and along with it, the job offers he was receiving.

Despite his beauty and outward health, at that time, Lucas was often deeply drunk.

He was a regal, controlled, elegant drunk. One seldom saw him take a sip of anything, but glassful after glassful disappeared. The recycling bins behind the house, for a curious-minded kitchen-interloper, overflowed empty bottles. He became lucid and humorous when he was drunk. He moved judiciously. He made eloquent pronouncements and flashy-eyed jokes. He maintained careful control of his hands.

There always seemed to be a crowd around him now; people followed him like a tail follows a comet.

Then Frankie was gone. I dropped by Lucas' house one day and she was no longer living there. She called me a couple weeks later.

"I had to go," she said. "I was holding him down. I can't do that." She started to cry on the phone "I'm pregnant, Nik," she said. "I'm pregnant with Lucas' baby. I can't tell him. It would ruin him. His career is just beginning. He would marry me. He doesn't need a wife and child now. He wouldn't be good at that at all. None of us would, would we? None of us are parent material. I don't know what I'm going to do."

Almost a year passed during which she never returned my calls. She had disappeared somewhere. When we did eventually talk, I asked her about the baby, but she told me with ferocity never to bring it up again. I never have.

Her departure from Lucas happened just when he had gotten his first significant job, his breakthrough, a role as a young, violent fishmonger in a Scorsese film. It was a noteworthy part; he was seen.

It was also the same moment that he met Katherine Bridger.

Lucas was agog. He focused on her in that penetrating, excoriating way of his. I was dubiously happy for him—maybe a trifle jealous. Long before Frankie's comment in her apartment bedroom, I had stored away a little coal of resentment burning somewhere down inside, scarring my guts. That's my nature. I always have a coal burning, burning, eating away.

Lucas' career took off. Over the next few years, he was in at least ten films. I lost count. He started to get directing gigs.

My band had a hit song, our one and only, and with it came good money for me. That was the last money I ever earned. This unfortunate reality is unsurprising to me. I have no value except an ability to fake my way through.

About two years after they met, Lucas and Katherine married. Along with about thirty other people, Frankie and I attended the small wedding on the cliffside overlooking the valley near the sprawling, Algarve-style house Lucas had bought high in Topanga Canyon. We sat together in the front row. Frankie held my hand.

A Buddhist monk spoke. There was a llama,
for no discernible reason. Security guards patrolled
for paparazzi. Chefs roasted things, and woodsmoke
drifted like a thin scarf through the trees and out
over the bluff. Cuban music played into the night.

* * *

In my hotel room, I stood before the mirror and checked my look. I donned my overcoat. The address I had been given by Lucas was for a house in St. Giles Street.

I hiked up Princes Street past the Scott Monument and cut across the valley on the Mound over the train tracks past the National Gallery. I circled back down Royal Mile past the cathedral. Wind scoured the corners of buildings and my face. Scant pedestrians clipped about; a few moved heads-down into the wind toward the castle. No one dawdled on the cobbles. The Heart of Midlothian in the paving stones near the cathedral gleamed with ice.

I found the house, its front door notched between a small hotel and a cigar shop just below the Mile. Standing outside, I unbuttoned my coat and withdrew the print of the photo Lucas had given me, folded in half to fit my pocket. To it I had stapled the slip of paper with the address.

I stepped to the door and knocked on a varnished black panel. After a minute, I pressed the brass buzzer button. No response. Two or three more rings and knocks went unanswered. In a café around the corner, I took a small window table to wait. I ordered coffee. I may have suffered a moment of annoyance at Lucas. There was no reason to believe that any of the people living at the addresses would be home, that they would know anything about the photos, that what they knew would shed any light on anything. Lucas tends to believe that everything is purposively connected, though the connections may not be apparent to us, and furthermore that everything will work out in the end.

* * *

Lucas didn't kill his wife. At least, I don't think so. Everyone was drunk the night it happened. Empty bottles glowed in the blue light all around the pool.

It happened three years after they had married. In that time, Lucas had been offered the role of Judas. With it, he'd won an Academy Award. This achievement seemed to come at a high cost. Accolades can break a person if they come too soon in life, if they come at a person with fragile internal architecture, if they come unbearably easily. Sensitive and talented people should be wary of compliments.

The more successful he became, the more nervous. He spoke to me of perpetually walking on eggs. Of living on borrowed time. Of fooling everyone, and of the terror of being found out and caught and paraded in disgrace, as in a nightmare.

Lucas and I shared that nightmare. But where I would cope with it by locking everyone out, by withdrawing into myself, Lucas drank.

He began to black out. He misplaced whole days. He missed work. People talked. He lost some roles that he desperately wanted. Functional drunk though he had been, he began to lose his grip. He wasn't yet thirty-five.

He treated Katherine extremely well most of the time. But sometimes, when drunk, he accosted her with critique and caustic belittling.

I felt misplaced around her. One of the legion of blade-eyed, high-featured young brunettes that stalk Hollywood, Katherine had small parts in a few films in her early twenties. These came to her quickly, but she never seemed able to cling to the lifeboat. She drifted, and Lucas pulled her along with him. She was catlike. A quiet, polite and disciplined person, she seldom fractured. When she did, it was like watching a human melt into a glittery mass of twisted, crumpled wire. I witnessed Katherine break down a couple of times. Each time, it was because of Lucas.

She was at least Lucas' intellectual equal. He told me he felt he had married up. He worshipped her, and yet strode angrily past her. He superseded her, as he did everyone. At times, and with increasing frequency, she irritated and disappointed him, as we all seemed to do.

That night twenty-five years ago, Lucas and Katherine had argued at the pool. There may have been others around earlier, but now all was quiet. Only the four of us remained. Our conversations had died with the evening. Lucas had become very silent. He stared off into the trees, at the dying haze from the ocean.

Then he turned to Katherine, who sat on a chair not far from him. She wore a dark green sundress. She was barefoot. She had tilted her sunglasses up on her head an hour earlier, where they still sat though the sun had vanished into the sea.

Lucas said to her, as if explaining some comments exchanged earlier, "The reason I get this way is because you're so unhappy, Katherine. How is a person supposed to withstand that?"

Lucas, Katherine, Frankie and I sat in the quiet for a minute. Then Katherine stood and walked toward the house. Lucas wiped his face with his hands. He stood and followed her.

I caught Frankie's eye as she glanced across the blue-tiled and blue-lit pool, the flicker of evaluation, a ratcheting of private memories, her glint of interest in the seams of their marriage, rootlets in the cracks of boulders, schadenfreude.

Frankie and I stayed down by the blue pool until after midnight. It had grown chilly, and Frankie came over and lay down on my deck chair close against me and spread a blanket over both of us. We chatted about nothing. We smirked, spun little ironies, amused each other. We finished another bottle.

We heard their voices drifting from the patio near the house. The tone seemed softer, no longer brittle, though the words could not be made out. They eventually moved away together along the path toward the bluff.

Frankie and I rose from the deck chair. She kept the blanket wrapped around her long form, like a medieval cloak. She paused to fiddle with her sandals as I walked ahead along the path through the trees toward the bluff. Thus, I was ahead of her when I came into the little clearing on the brink of the bluff.

I alone saw what happened.

Two figures stood at the edge of the cliff, which sloped downward from the grass on sandy rock to the threshold of darkness. Lucas and Katherine, clenched and stiff, faced each other in silence.

There was no moon, but the light of the vast city hung from the proscenium of the humid overcast and lay a tender, auburn hue across the world.

She gestured slowly with one arm. Her arm fell to her side. She turned her back to him. She hunched her shoulders against his presence behind her.

In doing so, she stepped forward. Her left foot slipped. She squatted slightly as her foot skidded on the gritty sandstone.

Lucas abruptly reached for her. His hands groped at the air where her shoulders had been a moment before. If he had been less drunk, I'm sure he would not have missed his grip.

She staggered little quick steps. She jerked against her own momentum. She sank backward and grasped at nothing. Then she vanished just beyond Lucas' wavering hands.

I heard her hit the rocks at the bottom of the cliff. She didn't cry out on the way down. There was only the impact in the dark. I'm sure Lucas heard it also, even in his state. I could see it in his expression when he turned to me, as I ran up to him.

Lucas didn't speak. I came close to him and he gazed directly at me. I placed my hands on his shaking arms and pulled him away from the edge. His eyes were something I've never seen on a human before.

"Don't leave me," he whispered. "Don't leave me."

The police brought up Katherine Bridger's body at dawn. Peachy light spread across the hills, but in the canyons all was still purple. Sirens had

come and gone all night. The police took
Lucas away.

Seated at the dining table in the house, the
police inquired about what I had seen. I said the
light was dim and that I had not been close enough
to see precisely.

They asked if Lucas had pushed his wife.

You see, in that moment I felt like a little boy
who had just found a way forward, a slip of light
beyond a partially opened and cruelly barricaded
door. I didn't understand why I said what I said.
I know now I never will understand. I felt exactly
as I had felt when the soldiers asked me where my
brother Bao was hiding.

I nodded and said, "It looked that way to me."

The papers burst lurid. Television howled and
tittered. I locked myself in my apartment and didn't
come out for days. I didn't respond to the endless
storm of requests for interviews, the ringing phone,
the knocks on the door.

Lucas raised no defense. He was out on bail
for a while, and we spoke once after he came out
of detox. He said he couldn't remember what had
happened. He said he may have pushed her. He
couldn't be sure. The police assuredly had told him
that I'd evinced similar doubt.

Lucas said he would have preferred to die in
her place.

The state's case had been weak. They had only
my vague eyewitness testimony. But Lucas insisted
on hanging himself.

Brushing his lawyers aside, he immediately pleaded guilty to involuntary manslaughter. His comments to the magistrate: "I was drunk. She was drunk. We were too close to the edge. I remember shaking her by the shoulders. Then she was gone. If it hadn't been for me, she would still be here."

Because there was no trial, there was only a brief sentencing hearing six months after her death. Frankie and I went to the courthouse. We sat together in the front row the way we had sat at Lucas' and Katherine's wedding. The lawyers and the judge spoke quietly among themselves. Then they led Lucas in front of us toward a side door.

Passing, he turned to look at me. He looked at me the same way my brother had looked at me.

CHAPTER 17

Nik Ng – #3

I am frozen in time. We tread heavily in childhood. As time passes, our steps lighten. But we learn little skills of speaking, acting, and possessing in ways that remind us we're connected to a past we cannot shake–talismans of youth.

I will never be anything but what I was as a child in an unnamed village in Vietnam. I will never be anything but what I was that night in Topanga Canyon.

An hour had passed in the café. I ordered more coffee. I checked texts. Frankie was on a train for Zermatt, complaining about traveling. I looked up the number of a woman I knew who lived in Edinburgh, but put my phone away without calling.

I would wait until the workday had ended to go back and try the house again. But I would give this project no further time or effort beyond that.

***

Lucas emerged from Cal State Prison in Lancaster after six months. He had lost a little weight, though he had little to give. He had stayed fit. He had grown a trim beard, which had turned slightly grey. He was sober, and would be forever. His face, however, belied a haunted and broken man.

I had done that to him. Sometimes I seem to do things happen that sink into me slowly, and as the horror of what I've done or allowed to happen begins to unfold, I fight and fight with a battery of self-justifications. If I didn't, I would simply die. Denial is, to me, like drawing breath.

Lucas quietly disappeared from public view. His house had been sold. He called to tell me he was leaving town.

"I have to start over, Nik," he said. "I have to go back to the beginning. Berlin is where the nightmare started. That's where I began to die."

Two years passed. I knocked around town lonesome and lost. I withdrew. I quit my band. I'd lost the ability and the desire to socialize, to maneuver among women. I couldn't play music. I'd taken up writing, which I'd always thought I would like to try, but was dismayed at how difficult it was, how long it took to get anything down, and how inevitably disappointed I felt in the product—like learning an arduous and temperamental instrument, say, the pedal-steel guitar, or the harp.

I had not imagined I would feel this way about Lucas' absence. I was startled to learn that Frankie felt the same.

"I've considered moving to Berlin for a while," she said to me one evening in a nightclub. "There's

nothing for me here. I hate this town now."
We stood there together at the bar for a long
minute. Then she added, "Maybe he needs us."

It turned out that I went to Berlin before
Frankie.

I stayed in a good hotel near Ku'Damm
for a while and then took a flat deeper in Mitte.
I was going through the last of my money rapid-
ly. But I knew Frankie and her bottomless bank
account would be along at some point.

For several weeks, I put off letting Lucas know
I was in town. I was concerned about his reaction.
What if he didn't want me near him, and what
was I doing in this dark and steely place, and what
was I trying to accomplish?

When I did eventually call him, he was over-
joyed. He soon introduced me to Abbie Ingvall and
to Heike, both of whom he had met not long after
arriving in Berlin.

Abbie—Mama, she called herself—took me
in as she apparently had taken in Lucas. Slight,
bent, wounded, powerful old woman, she exuded
command. She controlled every room, every
situation, even though she only spoke briefly
and cryptically. Her single eye flashed about.
When she looked at me, I felt impaled.

When I met her, at Lucas' invitation not long
after I came to Berlin, I immediately sensed something going on, some hidden imbalance of power.
It's like walking fresh into a room and feeling a
tension, a dynamic, that no one who's been in
the room for a while is aware of. Heike seemed

mesmerized by Mama. Perhaps stemming from Heike, Lucas was likewise enthralled. They both told me of the wonders of Mama's historical work, her connections around Berlin, snapshots of her history.

Before long, I realized I felt the same about Mama as they did. She built up my strength.

I confided things in her. One evening, shortly after Frankie had moved to Berlin and joined our group again, I sat on a sofa with Mama away from the rest of the group for a long conversation, tête-à-tête. She asked me many questions about Frankie.

Mama seemed to want to excavate Frankie. I'd had a few too many cocktails. I started talking to Mama and didn't soon stop. This was part of the magic she possessed, sitting there quietly with a smile on her half-mouth, partially distorted by her old disfigurement so she seemed always to be smiling and scowling at the same moment, looking intermittently down at her cane clasped in her hands, at the rug and then up at my face, nodding in agreement with my observations.

I described our little group's past together. I described Frankie's time with Lucas. I found myself confiding in Mama that Frankie was with us the night Lucas' wife died. I even told her about Frankie's pregnancy. Mama drew information slowly and inexorably from me. She was charming and seemingly safe. So confidential.

Each thing she asked or said seemed to open more doors. It was like having layers of hard old *paint slowly and gently stripped away until my skeleton shone through transparent skin. Talking to her, I felt naked, cleansed to elements. This was not an unpleasant sensation.*

In her muted, confiding way, Mama asked me to keep an eye on Frankie. She made a little joke about me being her second eye for her. She said it was for the sake of peace in the family. She said she wanted to help Lucas, Heike and Frankie. She said she sensed awkwardness and would like to mediate, but could only do so effectively if she learned more about Frankie and her movements, habits and contacts. I promised I would. It seemed the fair and helpful thing to do.

* * *

The café off Royal Mile had grown noisier and chaotic with the afternoon crowd.

I slid the photo that Lucas nicknamed *Man With Dog* from my coat pocket and examined it again.

A man stands sideways to the camera. His head is turned toward the viewer. He looks surprised and pleased. His hair is black and longish. He has a beard. It's a warm day, evidently — he is in shirtsleeves, a striped, tapered shirt tucked into pin-striped jeans with a vaguely Soviet appearance. On his feet, unbranded sneakers. A dog stands on the ground ahead of him. It is a large dog, shades of grey in the black and white photo. It has stout shoulders and haunches.

The man holds the dog by a leash. The dog turns away from the camera. It gazes urgently into the near distance, and its face is slightly blurred. It pulls against the leash. Its fur rises.

The man's grip is tight on the leash. His sleeve is rolled, and the muscles and tendons of his arm and wrist stand out. Both man and dog appear excited, ready to move, pausing only for the click of the shutter.

After I finished my tea, I rose and retraced my path up the street against the wind to the front door of the house. I rang the bell again.

This time I heard a vague sound of footsteps clumping on stairs. After a moment, the lock turned and the door opened a foot or so. A woman stood in the gap.

She was middle-aged. Despite elements of past prettiness, at that instant she projected mostly fatigue. She wore an unbuttoned parka over a tweed suit. She held a briefcase indicating she had just arrived from work. Her glasses were slightly fogged in the warmth of the foyer.

"Forgive me for interrupting your evening," I said. "My name is Nik Ng. I am trying to fill in some spaces in historical research that a colleague had undertaken before she passed away recently. Your address, though not your name, was cited in connection with an old photograph. I wonder if I may speak to you for just a minute and show you the photo."

I am a slight, dapper, older man. I have a clean, disarming gaze. I look a little exotic. In my experience, strangers don't find me intimidating. In an instant I wondered how each of the others would fare in this first moment of meeting someone, when trust must be established in an eyeblink, at least insofar as would allow a few minutes of conversation. Lucas seems honest to people, and he has an ice-breaker smile. Frankie has the skill of pretending to be confused and outgoing. Heike looks like she might tear an arm off someone, but in a warm, friendly sort of way.

The woman in the doorway sized me up. She told me her name: Camille Larsen. She opened the door for me. I stepped into the foyer. It smelled lightly of flowers. Varnished stairs rose ahead. An antique painting hung on one wall; on the opposite, a small gilt-framed mirror.

"Thank you," I said. "I promise I'll only take a moment of your time." I drew the photo from my pocket and held it out to her with the address slip still stapled to it.

I said, "This photo is from an archive of photos in a library in Berlin. The address, which appears to be yours, was associated with the photo, but we don't know how or why. Do you know who the person in the photo is?"

The woman was brunette. Her hair was streaked and cut short. She wore dots of earrings and wire-rimmed glasses. Her eyes were dark, maybe greenish-brown.

She held the photo for a long time, possibly a minute. She lowered the photo slowly. I was momentarily watching the photo in her hands. When I looked back at her face, tears had appeared in her eyes. She looked at me. She spoke for the first time. She spoke in English, but with a strong German accent.

"The person in the photo is Rainer Weiss. He was my father," Camille said.

A short while later, I stood hunched in my overcoat on the cold paving stones of the Heart of Midlothian, my scarf snapping in the wind. Bells rang from the tower of the cathedral suggesting either calamity or an evening service.

My heart raced with what I'd been told by Camille. But added to that was a fresh understanding, born of the string of events of the past twenty-four hours, the terrible historical reverie in which I'd spent the day, things said, things unsaid, and maybe all whipped by the scourge of icy cold wind down that stony ridge of street.

In that moment, I made a decision.

We stood together, Camille Larsen and I, in her foyer at the bottom of the stairs, for twenty minutes. Camille told me of her father's suicide. She described the day it happened, where she was and what she was told, the clothing she was wearing. She told me about her father's instability and his persecution by the Stasi in Berlin. She told me fragments of her childhood of hiding and lying, the trauma that only East Berliners remember and that never dissipates. She told me about Abbie Ingvall's involvement, the role she played in her father's death when she, Camille, was still a girl.

An origin story, though I was aswim in the effort to determine what beginning it marked.

Later that evening, trying to summon understanding of my sudden electrified state of mind, I called Frankie. She was sitting in a restaurant in Zermatt. I heard chatter and silverware in the background. She seemed very monotonic and quiet, somehow out of breath.

"I've been lying, Nik. It's not the lies themselves, or the act of lying. It's who I've been lying to. Something's happening. My feet are slipping."

And at that moment, at the end of this interminably long day of reflection and discordant memory, with the bells of some nearby church tolling distantly, I understood that I, too, needed to speak. To save myself.

I had lied to and about Frankie Des Plaines, the wild, wonderful friend who had rescued me repeatedly for so many years. I had lied to and about Lucas Block. The brother who had taken the place of my brother.

CHAPTER 18

Frankie Des Plaines — #1

*I was in love with Lucas that night in Topanga
Canyon. I still am.*

*When I came around the corner of the path,
I saw Lucas standing with Nik at the edge of the
bluff in the moonlight. Nik was holding Lucas' arms.
Lucas was gripping him. As I watched, Nik pulled
Lucas forward a step or two away from the bluff.
Lucas could hardly walk. He stumbled.*

*There was a very faint breeze. There had been
rains. The smell of blooming verbena drifted all
night. I noticed it strongly just then.*

*I think I was unsure if I was disturbing a pri-
vate moment: something intimate that I'd happened
upon. I was quite drunk; we all were. Lucas stood
still. Then he slowly turned and looked at me. Not at
me. Through me. He was very pale, and this wasn't
just an effect of the lighting.*

*In that instant, I felt a profound sense of déjà
vu. It hit me like a hammer. It was a feeling of*

*almost unbearably strong love colliding like cars
on a dark highway with the loss of that love.
It was a feeling of knowing something that you
have no business knowing.*

* * *

What I relate happened thirty-five years ago. I admit this first because it's true and second because I think it has something to do with the bigger picture of the whole episode we'd undertaken on Lucas' behalf.

Nik and I talked about it on the phone last night. We talked until one in the morning. That's awfully late for me, although Nik never goes to bed before sunrise.

But he called me because, I think, he was wondering how I was feeling about this project. We started chatting and it went on. We backtracked. We got deep.

At one point, Nik said, "I have a bad feeling about this enterprise. But I'll do it for Lucas. I owe him."

All I could think of to say was, "Maybe it's time for things to come into the light."

In other words, though speaking to each other, we were each talking to ourselves. Mama's death and our aging and the passage of time and the look on Lucas' face converged within and between us. Nik and I shakily opened like dusty, cracking old books. I've seldom spoken like this with anyone, least of all with Nik. Though I love the guy dearly, he's terribly withdrawn and internal.

My accountant once inquired in deep seriousness whether I was being blackmailed. This was because I had instructed her to send Nik Ng money every month, a handsome amount, deposited discreetly. This is one of the elements of connective tissue between Nik and me. I have more money than I know what to do with, money I never earned. I need someone to care for. Nik needs to be cared for.

Clearly, Nik had doubts about the mission Lucas had given us. The conversation started with me being enthusiastic for it and he being skeptical that it would contribute anything to our understanding of Abbie's situation or Lucas' well-being. But by the time we got off the phone, the positions had reversed. He was feeling ambitious and I was feeling scared.

Over the years I've known him, my feelings for Lucas have waxed and waned. There are times when I don't feel much of anything for him anymore, and times when he downright annoys me. Then I don't see him or speak to him for a few weeks or a month or two, but suddenly when we re-encounter each other it's almost like it once was. For me, anyway. I get chattering and then I get sarcastic and feel like having a cigarette, and then I feel sad later. He sends me raw little photos of odd shoes in shop windows and malformed shadows. I reply with cartoon clip art.

I don't think I have any idea what love feels like. I'm a silver-haired woman with a big, fat pearl of protection grown inside me around a little irritant grain that could be love.

Correction: White-haired, not silver haired. White is powerful. Silver is just old.

On the plane, I took out a notebook and made a plan. This consisted of writing out several versions of what I would say to the person I encountered when I went to the address Lucas had given me. For some reason, I dreaded that conversation. I was almost hoping first that I would not find anyone at the address and second, if I did find someone, that they would not speak to me.

My ticket was only to Zürich since it would have taken all day to get to as far as Bern by plane. It's three hours or so from Zürich to Zermatt on the train through Bern.

I raced in Zermatt a few times, though it was never a big stop on the FIS circuit.

I knew Lucas gave me the Zermatt assignment because it's a ski town and he knew I would know my way around. I'd mentioned missing skiing lately. The winter had been hard in Berlin, and at the sight of snow falling and snow on the ground, my visceral urge is to drift back to dreams of skiing. Berlin, city of the vibrantly living dead, can seem especially funereal in winter. I'd brought some ski clothing. If I could get through the little research project quickly, I thought I might stay a couple of days, rent gear, ski over the pass to Cervinia, go to a spa.

On the train, I slept for a while and then texted Lucas. He didn't reply, but that's not unusual. He often doesn't see texts or emails immediately, sometimes not for days. Phone scorn. Anyway, he was on his way to Tallinn with that girl Hannah.

I saw the way Heike glanced at Lucas when he said he was taking Hannah with him, especially since it would be an over-night trip. But Heike is nothing if not calmly trusting. She has what I call fierce serenity. She's been through a lot.

Her tales of growing up on a communal farm outside Cologne—can you imagine, a teenage girl who looks like Heike among all those men in overalls? Her mother saw Deutschmarks in her daughter's looks. She took her to Berlin and dug up some two-bit talent agent who got her a first job posing for butter ads. The farm girl with a churn. Heike tells the story in that quiet, quick, sardonic way she has.

Anyway, Lucas is not the sort of man to dally, and especially not with a girl a third his age. But Hannah's lanky and very pretty, and every man has thresholds. I did wonder what that rather feral girl would get into her head when she had him to herself for a few days, especially if she learned that Lucas is famous and wealthy in addition to beautiful and wise.

I love the way I feel when I'm moving from the valleys up through the foothills and into the arms of the mountains again, the way one does crossing Switzerland, especially on a sunny day like this one.

***

Long ago, I had many mountain haunts in Colorado, afternoons up from Denver to Loveland and Arapahoe Basin for training, weekends racing in Steamboat and Aspen and Vail when it was still rather new. Station wagons full of my type of kids—strong and happy and gorgeous. Mountains of ski gear. The energy of young people in the seventies.

A decade earlier, I had traveled back and forth to Germany a lot, usually with my mother but sometimes on my own. My father was no longer in the Senate at that point, but was based in West Berlin in the legation. He had been friends with JFK. It was all very exciting. My parents, lapsed Catholics and children of wealth and power, never had to work for money, but my dad pounded at politics all his life, and my mother steered non-profits, primarily Planned Parenthood, ironic for a Catholic. She had great ambitions for me. Obviously, I let her down. The chair of Planned Parenthood and her daughter's very unplanned parenthood.

I was accepted to several Ivy League schools. Instead, I chose UCLA. It seemed far from Colorado. UCLA's ski teams trained at Mammoth and competed against other warm-country teams that shouldn't do well against the mountain schools in Colorado, New Hampshire and so forth. But I stood out and was noticed.

My junior year, I did so well in the national championship that I was asked to train with the U.S. team.

I majored in German with a minor in Art History, again partly to spite my parents. My father was a lawyer and my mother a doctor. Even with that degree, I never came around to speaking German as well as others who have spent as much time in Germany as I have. I speak in stilted phrases. I can't shake my heavy American accent. Lucas and Nik are both effortless in the language. But it was Lucas' first language. Nik's just good at talking, so long as the subject isn't him.

CHAPTER 19

Frankie Des Plaines — #2

The train came into Bern station. A few people disembarked and others boarded, and then we silently left the station in the reverse direction. Sitting in a four-place group seat, I had been facing forward, but was now facing backward as we curved away through the hills.

A woman who had boarded in Bern took one of the seats facing me. We nodded good morning, and before long she began talking. Her name was Sonya. She was traveling to Visp to visit her mother.

I asked about her mother. This elicited a small torrent of contradictions—responsibility and bitterness, love and self-criticism, cheerful memories and blank despair—as questions about mothers commonly do. She asked where I lived. She asked me how I liked Berlin and what I did there. She inquired what sorts of things I exhibited in my gallery.

"At the moment we have an exhibit of photos."

"Is the photographer well-known?"

"In a way, but not for his photography. In a former life he was a movie actor."

"What is his name?"

"Lucas Block."

She looked thoughtful. "The name's familiar. Not sure I remember if I've seen him."

"He was in films back in the eighties and nineties. His most famous role was in a film called *Betrayal*. It was an artsy film about the passion of the Christ. Rather controversial when it came out. Lucas played the part of Judas. He won an Academy Award. The film won medals at Cannes and Sundance."

"I do remember," she said. "I remember there were protests at theaters by religious people."

She asked more about Lucas, about other movies he had been in.

I listed a few of them for her. There was a spy picture, or rather two of them, the decent first and then a lousy sequel. There was a comedy about a woman whose husband dies and then comes back to life and causes mischief. There was a remake of an old Hemingway story set in Africa. There was a drama about a man whose daughter disappears in India and he goes there to find her. A dozen others. Then came *Betrayal*.

"His career was reaching its zenith, but he changed course," I said.

Perhaps I shouldn't have mentioned this last point. Sonya thought about it for a moment and then said, "Now I remember. Wasn't there some scandal involving Lucas Block? Something to do with how his wife died."

I nodded.

"Did you know him then?"

I nodded again. My face must have belied something more than I had intended, or hoped.

***

*Nik and I were there. We were steps away, still in
the darkness along the path through the trees. At least
I was in the trees. Nik was some distance ahead of
me on the path. I didn't see it happen, but he did. We
were involved. We were part of the evening and the
atmosphere and the unfolding of events, which
we didn't understand at the time and still don't.
God knows I was connected to Lucas. It was as if
whatever happened to him was happening to me.*

*And the guilt I felt then and still do—it's as if
I willed Katherine over the edge.*

***

I sat in sad reflection for a while on the gently-rocking train slipping along the snowy banks of the tumbling chartreuse river, chalets and old log farm houses with heavy caps of snow passing, a few cars and trucks keeping pace with the train on shining roads which occasionally swept under and paralleled the tracks, with the peaks rising over everything in the sun.

Nothing had changed, I was thinking. Lucas' destiny was entangled with mine, and with Nik's. And we wanted it that way. Nik sometimes denies this. But Nik doesn't understand how I feel.

***

I had Lucas' baby. Nik knows this. I told him at the time. But no one else knows the whole story.

Lucas and I were together as partners for a short while. Four months and four days, to be precise. I think he loved me; at least, I thought so. We'd been such close friends for several years prior, running around to parties and happenings, his small crowd of friends so beautiful, bright, fun and funny and all going places.

I'd met Nik first at UCLA. I was probably twenty-one and Nik was twenty. He just turned sixty. You think he's preoccupied with how he looks now. You should have seen him then. We all were, though.

Nik was in film school and was doing a few auditions, but not pursuing it hard. He was already a brilliant guitarist, and aimed at the music business.

I knew he was sweet on me, and I liked him very much, but I was uncomfortable about the appearance of us together, to be honest. Nik's eight inches shorter than I am. Also, like me, he's lazy and vain. A wonderful friend, but I could never be with someone like that.

He invited me to see a play that he was in. Lucas was also in the play. What an astounding man Lucas was. His physical and personal presence on the stage was astonishing. I was mesmerized for two solid hours. Nik had never mentioned him, but after the play I learned that Nik and Lucas were best friends and had been for years.

Lucas and I knocked around together for a while that last year of college. Our relationship was companionable and heavily physical. I was magnif-

icently in love. But I think he was aiming higher than me. I had nothing to offer him. Objectively, we had little common ground. And if there's one thing I cannot withstand, it's the sensation of being a millstone around someone's neck. We parted.

We all left college. I was still skiing with the U. S. Team, but I didn't make the cut for the Olympics the following year. I drifted away from skiing, disconsolate.

About a year later, after he'd ambled through a string of other women, I saw Lucas in a bookstore in Burbank one afternoon. He looked at me and seemed to see me differently for the first time. We ran back to each other, or more precisely I ran to him. I ran at him. But only for four months and four days.

I suppose a lot of people would heavily criticize me for not doing a better job of letting Lucas go. For carrying a torch. For not moving on. For persisting in the single biggest mistake modern women should not make.

But there was also the baby. I left Lucas because I learned I was pregnant. I'm not the first woman to protect a man from fatherhood, to lift that weight off his shoulders. Lucas' career was skyrocketing. He would have been a terrible father. At least I thought so at the time. He was not nurturing. He was very young, and quite a drinker.

It's not as if I'm really mother material, either. I love children. Rather, I love the idea of children. They fascinate me, but more as empirical studies, objets d'art, than as real items. What bothers me more isn't the Sisyphean tedium of raising a child,

it's the infinity of a child's presence in one's life—
not the work itself, but the inescapable contract.
Infinity is an unendurable weight. As I watched
my mother die, I observed her, in her last days,
fretting about the well-being of her children and
simultaneously complaining about them, their
problems and misdemeanors, the gaps in their
wholeness. A tunnel with no light ahead, even
unto death.

This attitude harshly shaded my vision at
that young age, with all that southern-California
movie-star splendor surrounding me. I didn't want
to lose all of that to a baby carriage. But I thought,
to deal with any of the problem, I had to let go of
Lucas. For a while, at least.

I went back to Colorado. I sat with my
mother. I cried for days. Then I went skiing for a
few weeks and afterward rented an apartment in
Boulder. I did yoga. I worked at a job—the only job
I've ever had—in a health foods store. And after a
while, I had a baby.

My parents were both Kennedy-esque
Catholics. I went to Catholic school briefly as a
child, but I hadn't been to Mass since I was a
teenager. Nevertheless, Catholic Social Services
helped me. My mother arranged it all, at my
request. Everything was discreet and high-social-
order tasteful.

I never met the people who became the parents
of my baby. I was told they were good souls and very
lonely for a child. They had adequate means. They
lived in a comfortable house somewhere in Nebraska.

I only possessed my baby, a little girl, for a day. She was healthy. She weighed a little over seven pounds. She had dark blue eyes, like Lucas.

I think I'm speaking here only to other women who have parted with children. Other people can never truly understand. Empathy doesn't rip out your heart.

CHAPTER 20

Frankie Des Plaines — #3

In Zermatt, I rode in an open, electric taxi with chains on the wheels, sort of a communal shuttlebus, to my hotel at the upper edge of town. The cone of the Matterhorn still loomed in the purple sky up the valley.

I shared the taxi with a shaggy young French couple with snowboards. The girl commented to the boy that Zermatt has a reputation somewhere between Gstaad and Davos as a destination for rich, old people. *Personnes âgées riches.* Then they glanced at me and fell silent.

My hotel was an over-the-top place with turreted towers atop the town's spine. After I freshened up, I came back down to the lobby and spoke to the concierge. She was a small, sharply-coiffed young woman in a thin sweater and corduroy jacket with the hotel logo over one pocket and tall boots over her jeans. Her fingernails were painted black, and her makeup was incisive. She spoke flawless English with a delicate wash of accent.

I showed her the address on the slip of paper which Lucas had carefully stapled to the print of the photo. I asked the concierge if she could show me on a map where the address was located. She examined the slip.

Then, one of those cute small-town coincidences occurred. The concierge said, "Oh, that's my neighbor Thérèse. She lives a couple houses down from me. She's a friend of mine. I look after her dogs sometimes. Do you know her?"

I shook my head. "I'd like to meet her to ask a couple of questions about this old photograph. We're researching it."

She looked more closely at the photo. "Thérèse has this same photo framed on the wall of her house, I think. It looks familiar. It's in a batch of family photos, old relatives and things."

She looked up at me with slight puzzlement and suspicion, an expression both small-town and big-city.

"You were just going to go to her house and knock on the door?"

I nodded.

"She's not there. She works evenings. The dogs would go crazy." She studied me for a moment. "I like the way you do your hair up," she said. "It looks dramatic and beautiful."

"I don't wish to be intrusive, of course. I'd just like to ask her a question or two."

"You said you're a researcher?"

I dodged the question. "The photo was in the Berlin Staatsbibliotek archive. We're trying to identify the person."

The concierge reached for her phone. "Allow me to assist." She scrolled through her directory. She found a number and dialed it. We both waited as the phone rang. She looked up at me again for a moment. Then her eyes diverted as someone answered.

"Hi," the concierge said into the phone. She spoke in German, turning slightly away from me. "I'm at work. I'm sorry to bother you. I have a guest here at the hotel who says she would like to meet you. She's from Berlin. She has an old photo from a museum that may be of someone from your family. She is trying to identify the person in the photo."

There followed a pause. Then the concierge said into the phone, "I don't know." She turned to me and asked, "What's your name?" After I replied, she said to the person on the other end, "Her name is Frankie Des Plaines."

Another long silence ensued. She glanced up at me in a quick survey. "She seems fine," she whispered into the phone, perhaps hoping I didn't speak German. One more long pause. Then the concierge said to me in English, "Thérèse will be happy to speak with you, but she cannot tonight. Can she meet you somewhere tomorrow morning?"

I dined in a restaurant recommended by the concierge, an old building with a stone first floor and grey, hand-hewn log walls above. Monumental piles of shoveled snow surrounded it. One entered through a snow canyon. Candles flickered in the windows. It hung on the side of the tiny river sluice tossing and foaming through town. The concierge said it was the best place for vegetarian fare in town, although most of the clientele seemed to be having raclette and fondue.

My ratatouille was quite good. I asked for a bottle of pinot gris, also.

I called Nik. He was still in Edinburgh. He had met his person. He seemed both urgent and thunderstruck. He spoke of lying, which confused and frightened me. He wouldn't respond to my attempts at probing. Nik, you realize, talks a lot, and speaks eloquently and amusingly, but mostly about superficial matters. He shies immediately from deeper entry. I hung up feeling very lonesome.

Nik and I—we've spent our lives propping each other up, making the way we are okay. You see how best friends can be, subtly and unintentionally each other's worst detriments. Lots of marriages look like this. Eternity.

The young French snowboarder couple came into the restaurant and sat at a table across the dining room. They saw me. The girl waved shyly. The girl's comment came back to me: rich old people. Made me think about the four of us in Berlin, our little quadrangle. No one cares about us, nor should they. First, we're rich, thus unworthy of sympathy. Second, we're old, which is to say, meaningless. Unworthy and meaningless. Hell of a way to feel eating a good ratatouille.

Abbie Ingvall was old, too, though not rich. Odd, creaky, disfigured lesbian lady with thick glasses amid her stacks of books. I respected her. Or perhaps it would be more accurate to say that I sensed she possessed great, roiling whirlwinds of despair at her center, although neither I nor, I think, anyone else knew the source of those storms.

****

I moved to Berlin a few months after Nik.
He stood on the threshold of my flat to greet
me the morning I arrived from the airport.
The following evening, at an artist's party in
Kreuzberg, I was reunited with Lucas and met
his new girlfriend, Heike.

    That night, an emotional one for me be-
cause it was clear that Heike was better for Lu-
cas than any woman he'd ever possessed before,
I also met Abbie. The guys called her Mama, a
nickname she seemed to prefer. I could never call
her that. Mama carried too many implications
for me.

    She seemed adorable and fascinating.
Like one of those ancient, mystical creatures

from the Dark Crystal. I could see why Nik had chattered on about her all the way over in the taxi. She charmed me as she had charmed him.

Abbie and I conversed a lot that night. She seemed interested in me. She seemed to know or sense a lot about the prior connections between Lucas and me, perhaps due to the way I looked at Lucas across the room or the way I spoke of him. She noticed the evaluative way I looked at Heike, standing by him, the two of them—a god and a goddess.

That night, Abbie asked me many questions about Lucas. I found myself talking to her about him, and I liked it. Abbie seemed the right person to talk to, and maybe I'd never had anyone else to talk to about Lucas. She probed, but very gently, almost tenderly. She absorbed everything.

I felt protective of Lucas and his past, but I also felt comfortable with Abbie. I felt like she also sought to protect him. A comrade.

Beginning that night, Abbie encouraged me to get to know Heike. She said we would be good for each other. She commented that we're physically similar—I guess because we're both almost six feet tall. Heike and I did, in fact, become close friends over the following months. We shopped together. We played tennis. We went to Paris to visit museums and to Prague for concerts.

Over the months afterward, Abbie seemed acutely interested in my friendship with Heike. I had become a source of information about Heike. She suggested I fill her in on details of Heike's

*activities, her comments about Lucas and the move-
ments of their relationship. She asked me to keep
her informed of Heike's doings, in other words.*

*I asked Heike about this. She shrugged
and said, "Abbie consumes secrets as other people
consume food." Nothing further, but I had the
impression Heike knew more than she was saying.*

***

Over my half-eaten dinner, a cold wineglass in my hand,
I thought about Abbie's death. She could fall into depths of
depression. My mother used to get like this. My mother drifted
on Zoloft and Prozac. Abbie seemed instead to ride her down-
turns like a train cascading off a trestle into a gorge.

But there was something odd about it. The mysterious little
notes she had written to Lucas and to Hannah. *Please help her*
and *He will help you.* The clues on the wrappers of the negatives.
And then the tripwire of her death. She must have known it
would send Lucas over some precipice. I resented her for that.

I wondered about my own death for a minute. It's not
uncommon for me to do this. It happens each time my long,
pointless and emptied life comes into focus. At least I don't
intend to first jump off a bridge into an ice-cold river or second
cause a lot of turmoil for others.

You see what sort of mood I'd fallen into. I don't know
why. Though long, it hadn't been an arduous travel day, and
I'd already solved half the challenge I came here to tackle. But I
realized I was no longer interested in taking a couple days to go
skiing. I just wanted out of there. I wanted to be back in Berlin in
my big, comfortable flat. I resolved to meet this woman Thérèse
in the morning, ask her about the photo, take her picture and

get out of Zermatt on a midday train. Leave it to the French snowboarders and the rich old people.

In my hotel room, I changed into pajamas and lay on the expansive, fluffy bed. The room was too warm. After a while, I rose and went to the French doors and opened them and stepped out onto the varnished wooden balcony in my bare feet. The sky had cleared. I leaned on the carved wooden balustrade.

The moon, almost full, hung over the valley to the south. Every crag and fissure, crevasse and snowfield, of the mountains stood out. At the head of the valley, the Matterhorn glowed.

I suddenly thought of nights in the Rockies when I was a teenager with my friends, music playing softly from a car eight-track, sky of stars, the snow shining. This was not a joyful recollection—not because of the past, but because of the present. I felt hollow standing there on the balcony in the cold, so alone. So old.

At an early waypoint in your life, the past is a limited assemblage of still-vivid memories. Your successes are luminous. Your failures comprise a small, manageable collection, still in the realm of helpful life lessons. The future outweighs all with promise.

Then, the seesaw slowly, grindingly, tilts.

At a later waypoint, your past is a long trail of glacially eroding images, unnoticed successes and uncountable failures massive and trivial, the good and the bad merged into nothing but a burden, a vast river, Marley's chains dragging along behind you.

The future is a bleak nothingness.

——— **CHAPTER 21** ———

Frankie Des Plaines — #4

In the morning, the town lay cupped in its steep-walled valley solid under the cold. A few skiers were out already, clomping slowly freighted with gear over their shoulders up the icy street toward the base of the Furi gondola. Scraping rasped the quiet as shovelers cleared snow from overstrained chalet roofs.

I located the café where the concierge had told me Thérèse would meet me. At a table against a mahogany-paneled wall, a woman sat alone watching the doorway; a blonde, aging smoothly, one could tell at a glance, dressed in a black parka and jeans and a yellow silk scarf.

The concierge had apparently described me to Thérèse. She removed her black-rimmed glasses and rose from her table as I approached.

"Thérèse Hillyard," she said, extending a hand.

"Frankie Des Plaines," I said. I took off my gloves and we shook hands and sat.

"Thank you for meeting with me," I said. "It's very kind of you to take the time."

"After Kiki's description of the photo and your request, I was intrigued."

128

From my purse I drew the photo we had come to call *Woman With Hat* and unfolded it for her.

In the photo, a woman poses for the camera. She stands squarely with her hands on her hips. The sun is bright. Her face scallops with shadows. She wears a sundress in a pale print with clenched frills around the shoulder straps; on her head, worn at a slant, a sweeping, broad-brimmed fedora. In the black and white photo, the hat is light grey, perhaps some pastel color. The woman is pretty. She seems amused, but maybe distracted. She smiles with only one side of her mouth.

Thérèse accepted the photo and studied it for a moment. She nodded. She lay the photo on the table between us.

"Kiki told me it was the same photo I have on my wall. It's the only photo I have of her. This is my aunt. My mother's sister. Her name was Marie Kiel. She died long ago. How did you come by this photo?"

I said, "It was among a collection in an archive in Berlin. An associate and friend of ours was working on a project to identify people in old photographs. We don't have a lot of detail about what she was working on. Our friend died last week. We're trying to complete a last few identifications on her behalf."

"I suppose that makes sense," she said. "My aunt died in Berlin about thirty-five years ago. In the Eastern sector."

In the seconds that followed this comment, a sensation of *déjà vu* descended upon me. Some sort of memory short circuit, a quick closed loop of the immediate and remote pasts. Usually it's triggered by a momentary sound, a passing glimpse of an object or scene, a smell. This *déjà vu* moment unfolded obliquely, slowly and chillingly. I suddenly felt like I had seen this movie, that I somehow knew what she was talking about.

It was the same wave of sensation I'd felt when I saw Lucas standing on the edge of the bluff in the moonlight.

"How did she die?" I asked.

Thérèse picked up her glasses and slid them onto her face as if to see me more clearly. Behind the lenses, her green eyes glittered.

"She committed suicide," she said. "My aunt took her own life. But make no mistake. It was the Stasi who killed her. My mother, my aunt's little sister, said that it had been whispered that a specific operator had decided my aunt was an enemy of the state. She had driven my aunt into the ground. I remember her name. I will never forget it. That operator was named Abbie Ingvall."

Just before nightfall on the train descending the long valley and out into the wintry farmland toward Visp, I kept snapping between what Thérèse had told me and what Nik had said the night before. He had been talking about lying. About how it was time to end the lying. I didn't know what lying he was referring to. But I knew my own.

Oddly, I wasn't surprised when Thérèse dropped the bombshell about Abbie. Yet it took many hours for the information to even begin to sink in. But eventually it did, like a lead weight. The train window had receded into sliding reflections and blurs of lights near and far. I stopped seeing anything out there. I had a momentary vision of myself standing at the shore of a vast, ice-cold lake, up to the thighs in still water, an inexorable force pulling me forward, beckoning.

The nets of lies, half-truths and secrets that Abbie had told Lucas and kept from Lucas swarmed in that black water along with my own. Tangled with her, I felt drawn in over my head, over my outreaching hands.

It was that evening on the train that I identified my only way out of such depths. My only life-ring. I could not allow Lucas to go his whole life without knowing that he had a child.

The unfairness of that situation overwhelmed me. It took my breath. I cried for a minute, and I seldom cry. A woman in a nearby seat handed me a tissue.

I had planned to take that secret with me to the grave. But somehow now, interment suddenly seemed imminent. It seemed upon me.

Abbie had never revealed her truth to Lucas. I would do so.

CHAPTER 22

Heike Eberhardt — #1

The day my twin brother died, rain fell incessantly. All across the hills and clumpy forests surrounding Nürburg, dense veils of mist clung to the pastures and shrouded the church spires and the bones of the castle on its narrow hill. The rain didn't pour and slash, it drifted quietly, a phantom of itself. A grieving rain, my grandmother used to call it. The lightness of the rain was one of the reasons they decided to let the racing continue that day.

Matthias, my brother, traded off with his driving partner in the long-tailed Porsche 936 they were piloting for Martini Racing. They were testing suspensions and tires and brakes and gearboxes through the rolling hills and curves at Nürburgring in preparation for Le Mans.

Matthias and his colleague were young drivers hoping for spots on big teams. Matthias had worked his way up. For the previous two years, he had secured an escalating series of jobs as

test driver and alternate, eventually catching
the eyes of big teams like Martini. There was
talk of him driving at Le Mans or Spa.

Matthias and I were twenty years old.
He was about my height, maybe a centimeter taller.
My mother used to call us peas in a pod, but when
we wrestled, he always won, even in our adolescence
when I was stronger than he. He had a fire about
him that burst out in head-to-head competition.

I suppose I had that fire, too, but it glowed
out otherwise. That's the fire the photographers said
they saw in my face, my body, through the camera.

I had returned from my home in Paris for a
brief visit to my family and for some meetings in
Berlin. At the time, I was living with two other
girls in a vast flat in an old building just off Rue
Monge, the edge of Saint-Germain. A photo of me
in a black evening dress, no jewelry, hair loose,
barefooted and holding my shoes by their heel
straps, one foot on the edge of a fountain as if
I was about to step into it, had come out the
week previous on the cover of British Vogue.
I had just signed a contract with Elle for two
more shoots that summer. I had signed a contract
to front a campaign for a laundry soap company
because I possessed, as my agent put it, an
indomitable air.

Matthias teased me about it all incessantly,
which I loved. We sat in the kitchen of the old
farmhouse and peeled vegetables and laughed.
He remembered bits from our childhoods—little
stories of foolishness and deviltry—that I'd forgotten.

*He was my counterweight, my external
memory. That focus of his, that casual brilliance,
that concentration. He called me stork-legs.
He gazed at me across the table with incandescent
pride when he flipped through my latest magazines,
not because of how they made me look, not because
I was his sister, but because I was part of him.
Easy, natural pride—the good kind.*

*That night at dinner, the conversation was
of the weather. It had rained for days, and more
was predicted. My mother fretted. She asked if
they would delay the racing. She said to Matthias,
"Why couldn't you have taken up a safer sport?"*

*I saw the look on his face. I shouted at her,
"Mom, it's been his passion since he was a boy.
He's worked so hard. Why would you say something
like that, especially when tomorrow is such a big
day for him?"*

*My mother looked at the two of us sitting at
the table exuding that fire I spoke of, the fire she
had engendered. She lowered her head, mollified.
The way my mother looked just at that moment,
like so much else from those hurtling days, became
variables in the permanently unsolvable equations
of my life.*

*I drove to Nürburg the next day, and my
father came with me. We met Matthias at a café
in the town for lunch, and then he took us to the
track and showed us around.*

*Matthias crashed late in the afternoon.
They said his car came off the ground for a while.
He flew. The old Nürburgring track was notorious
for dangerous rises and rough pavements then,*

though Matthias frequently mentioned that they
had cleaned up, smoothed and cushioned the
Green Hell through the mountains, as it used to
be called.

With the wetness of the track that day, the
test drivers had all been cautioned to ease off on
their speed, to begin their decelerations earlier
coming into corners, to follow and pass with
wider margins, to flatten their turns. Matthias
had related all of this to me, leaning close, as he
walked beside me in the garages and the paddock.
If it had been an actual race day, I wouldn't have
been permitted there. But people recognized me
and ushered me in and drifted around Matthias
and me, taking photos.

Outside on the track, a few feet away,
cars howled past. They screamed. It was so loud
I should have held my hands over my ears, but
this girl always loved the wildest rock concerts in
Paris and London, a joyful barrage of the most
impressive noises; the hearing aids I wear now
could have been foretold, and possibly forestalled,
but for the high-decibel thrills of my youth.

The cars sliced huge arcs of silver rain-
spray into the sky behind them. Their headlights
glistened off the roadway as they came under the
bridge and circled past the pit areas.

Matthias pulled up the zippers on his racing
suit as crew hand-wheeled his car from the garage
into the misty afternoon. The car was white with
red stripes and large black number 16s painted
in yellow circles on its flanks. The car was long

and rippled, a thoroughbred. It looked a little like
Matthias, I thought for a moment as he clambered
into the cockpit.

Before he pulled on his helmet, I stepped up
beside the car and leaned to him. I gave him a kiss
on the cheek.

"This is what it's all about," I said to him.
I've often wondered if I was making that comment
to myself.

He said to me, shouting over the din of passing
cars and cars warming up in the pits, "If we don't
run, we're just ghosts of what might have been."

He grinned at me. I don't know if he heard
that somewhere or if it was original. Matthias
wasn't prone to aphorisms. I prefer to think he
was lifted on wings that day.

I left the clamor of the garage and walked
past the grandstands and the closed vendor shops
and up a low rise to the east. The grass was slick
and shining. I remember I was wearing rubber boots
and tight pants and a belted coat. It was an old,
frayed raincoat of my grandfather's that I loved.

The screaming of the cars came softly to me
through the mist, the low shriek of rain tires on
wet pavement. I stood on a low knoll, turned and
scanned the curve of the track for the white car with
the big red stripes, the number 16.

I remember so vividly the way my father looked
as he came running up the hill to me. It had just
started to sprinkle lightly again. I had been wondering if I should return to the pit area. Then my father
came running, his limping lope, an old injury dating

from the war, with one arm held bent and one swinging straight, his face lifted toward me, shining wet.

He stopped in front of me, groping for breath. I remember thinking for a moment how bony he was. I remember a deep internal flinch from what was to come. He didn't say anything for several seconds. I didn't either. The reason for his running hovered like a hammer.

"On the far side," my father finally said through his gasps. "On the corner they call Aremberg. I looked everywhere for you. I just saw you out here. They said it's Matthias."

He looked around as if trying to determine where we were. Around us, nothing but sloping, wet pasture. Water streamed down us.

The screaming from the raceway was gradually dying away as the cars all slowed. Red lights flashed in the mist. "They said he just broke a track record," my father added. He said it as if he was remembering something from long ago.

In the days following, I blamed my mother for Matthias' death. I told her this. I felt it. She blamed my father, and maybe me. Soon, none of us spoke. A house of slashing silences. I fled back to Paris. My father left my mother a year later. I seldom saw either of them again.

It only occurred to me later that my mother had devoted her entire being to me and to Matthias. This left her hollowed out and desiccated. She was like one of those sacrificial creatures who feeds her children off the flesh of her own body until

she withers away to nothing just as the children flee.
I never realized this was happening when I was
young, when I was a teenager. Later, it was part of
the unbreachable wall I erected between us.

My mother was a beautiful woman early on,
more so than I, in some ways. Her hair, her eyes,
her carriage. She was never a flapping, bespectacled
bird like I was at fifteen, at least so far as I can tell
from photographs. But the first time I visited after
Matthias was gone, I was startled at her appearance
—gaunt and sunken, smoked out with her black-
market Russian Belomorkanal cigarettes.
She wasn't yet sixty. The age I am now.

She shielded Matthias and me from small-
town life, the farm existence she had inherited
from her family, except for the brief period she
escaped to Berlin, a re-found origin, a little secret
life she had shared only with me. When I was a
teenager, on several occasions, my mother held me
by the shoulders and said to me, "Heike, with your
looks and your brains, you can go far. Don't make
the mistakes I made."

* * *

All of this came to me again as I flew from Berlin to Stockholm.
The plane I was on spiraled inward to Arlanda airport. I hate air
travel. And this trip was just an hour and a half. The whole way,
I watched the little farms and lakes flow by below, thinking of
what had been and what was to come.

How odd it is that your life seems blocked out into brief,
foreign segments like rooms in a vast gallery of photos, little

clusters of images in an exhibit. You drift through the museum of yourself. You gaze at yourself, you take yourself in. You appear again and again, everywhere apparitions of yourself.

It exhausts you, wandering through those exhibits. You seek moments of pleasure, but mostly gather wearying, emptying reminders of all the steps you've taken, all the stairs you've climbed. The aches and unslept nights gather around you like disciples around a death bed.

You're just a girl from a small town in the country, and then a job comes your way magically. Then another and another. You're sucked into a storm of attention and activity. Suddenly, everybody wants you. Everybody is reaching for you. Everything seems so exciting, so real, the longed-for reality that it seems you always imagined waiting for you.

When I was a little girl, I read fairy tales, and I cried. I sobbed with desire to be special, to become a princess. My mother comforted me. She said it would happen for me, if I wanted it enough. I did.

CHAPTER 23

Heike Eberhardt — #2

One morning in the farmhouse, my mother announced that she was taking me to Berlin to meet some people. I was just about to turn eighteen. Matthias had left our small-town school, our prison, he and I called it, to drive for a regional racing consortium, mostly small sports cars and rally cars. Perhaps because of Matthias' sudden jolting move, my mother had begun researching opportunities for me.

We traveled to Berlin on the train, which emptied into Berlin Hauptbahnhof. We stayed in an ancient, enormous, echoing hotel, a survivor of carpet bombing. I remember the way the hotel smelled, the echoing corridors heavy with dust.

How excited and determined I was, standing before the long, undulating mirror in the room trying on my entire suite of clothing and much of my mother's. She sat on the bed and smoked and watched me and told me about her life in Berlin, before the war, decades ago. The scenes of her stories always seemed, to me, black and white and grey.

About town, she commented to me in whispers, pointing to streets as we rode the trams, about fleeing back to the farm in the final days of the war, when the factory where she worked in Oberschöneweide had been reduced to ruins and chunks of scorched concrete hanging by shredded strands of reinforcement steel.

I think this experience is why I have always been drawn to desolate factories, their shadows and dead grip. I photograph them. I feel them. I am fascinated by the evidence of life past. I am driven to remember things I have no business remembering.

My mother told me of her neighborhood just off Oranienstraße. Her block burned under the bombs. All her friends dead. The city she described, masses of wandering, silent, empty-eyed people car-rying ragged bags and bits of sausage and potatoes along trails in the rubble, filled my head as we moved through late-70's Berlin. I longed to capture the old light of things.

We located the offices of the modeling agency with whom she had corresponded. This was the secret, the subject of her research. She had sent ahead thick portfolios of snapshots of me, some taken by a photographer in the little town, Bad Laasphe, near which we lived, some taken by my mother.

I stood before a white screen, in front of curtains, beside a lounge chair, as they circled and photographed me. I wore the jeans and flowered shirt I had brought, the dress my mother bought me at KaDeWe the day before with her last forty

Deutschmarks, and clothing the agency people
handed me from racks in the studio.

They told me to turn, to smile, to frown, to look
over my shoulder and tilt my head and put a little
more curve in my spine, to flip my hair.

Two weeks later, the day after our 18th birthday, the big, heavy Bakelite phone rang on the counter
in my mother's kitchen in the farmhouse. Matthias
was traveling with his racing team as mechanic and
alternate driver. My father, like usual, was mostly
not home.

The phone, like the kitchen, reeked of frying
meats and frying leeks and frying onions and of the
farmhands who stood around at the end of the day
waiting for dinner, the silent ones and the loud ones
who patted me and joked as I carried dishes among
them. I didn't mind that sort of thing then. It was
part of the excitement of what was to be, part of
the world ahead.

Observing these kitchen incidents with the
farmhands, my mother would say sharply, "Lars (or
Georg, or Jakob, or Oskar), she has better things
in her future than your bed and your bad breath."
I knew my mother's barbs were aimed at me more
than the farmhands.

The woman on the phone that evening said
she had a job for me. She said the shoot would be for
some stills for billboards. The client was a small dairy
chain looking for a new face. She asked to talk to my
mother. I handed the phone to her, in shock.

I was a millionaire by the time I was twenty.
Every cent is long gone now, though. A skyrocket.

*I was on the covers of magazines. I had a job
on a popular TV game show for a few months.
I modeled for Halston, Saint Laurent, von Fursten-
berg, Westwood, Chanel. I worked with Guy Bourdin
and Jeanloup Sieff. With Gilles Bensimon and
Helmut Newton.*

*There was a period I could step into any news-
stand in Europe, pull a fashion or lifestyle magazine
off the rack, leaf through it and stand a good chance
of seeing a photo of myself. My agent in Paris left
long messages on my old cassette answering machine
daily, always fretfully excited. I traveled constantly.
This lasted four years. Then I walked away.
I let them all down. Especially my mother.*

* * *

I was already ragged emotionally when I boarded the plane for
Stockholm. I felt the world closing in. I sensed we shouldn't be
trying to find these people in the photos, opening these tombs.

Eloise, Abbie's partner, called me that morning as I was
hurrying to my plane. She told me something important.
I should have called Lucas right then, or I should say I could
have called him. But I was running for my plane, and in any case,
I was not ready to talk to Lucas about it.

I didn't call him after I landed in Stockholm, either.

None of the four of us had suggested asking Eloise what
she knew about the photos. Perhaps the others didn't think of
it, or thought it inappropriate given that she had just lost Abbie.
I thought of it but didn't say anything.

I had texted Eloise on my way to the airport to tell her
what we were doing, that Lucas, Nik, Frankie and I were each

setting off to different places to try to find the four people in the photographs that Abbie had given us. This triggered something in Eloise. The news that she relayed to me when she called wasn't, I admit, a complete surprise. But suddenly I foresaw how my interview with the subject of the photo would turn out.

In Stockholm, I took the train from Varlanda into Central Station. The city buzzed about, busy and bright and very cold. I weighed finding a place to stay before I went looking for the person in the photograph. Lucas wanted to make a reservation for me at some fancy hotel by the harbor, but I declined. I needed a spot more suitable to me. I needed a place to think. I didn't need bellmen.

The old City Hall building, where they hold the Nobel ceremony, hunched blood-red to the west. With that fortress-like body and tall neck of tower rising from one corner, it always looked to me like a giant nesting bird at the edge of the water, a heavy fowl of rusty brick.

I slung my duffel over a shoulder and headed from the station on foot southeast toward the harbor. Buskers along the bridge abutments played old tunes. Afternoon hawkers offered chocolate coconut balls and, though Christmas was long past, *smør bullar* in paper cones. A handful of winter tourists meandered.

I'd already looked up the location of the address on the photo. It was near Gamla Stan, down from the palace and the armory. I walked quickly against the chill along the harbor. Midday approached, and people strolling in pairs and small groups thickened as I came to the little round with the statue of Gustavus Adolphus and turned onto Norrbro. Below the bridge, the water gleamed like polished metal.

On the island, the house sat in a row on a narrow street past an arched stone passageway, some sort of little bridge, off Västerlånggattan. Its lower windows wore ancient, riveted iron shutters, painted gentle green and clamped shut. All the buildings in this area were five stories tall, each successive floor decreasing in height. The address indicated a flat on the second floor above street level.

I stood outside for a long time. I had nowhere to go and nothing to do. The tidy little alleyway was almost silent. I shifted my duffel and looked around. I thought about Lucas. I thought about this mission, and how the others had reacted to the idea. I thought about the years I had known these people. I thought about Mama and Eloise.

All of this tumbled in my mind. I was suffused with dread of impending loss. From out on pedestrian Västerlånggattan came the occasional sound of voices, laughter, footfalls. The alleyway was quiet as a chapel.

Here's what Eloise told me that morning, before I boarded the plane from Berlin to Stockholm: Two days before the gallery opening, a note had been delivered to Mama and Eloise's house, the last in a string of notes Mama had received over the prior four weeks. The notes were unsigned. There had been three notes previously: *I know what you did,* and *You will be revealed,* and *Actions demand retribution.*

The fourth and final note to Mama, more of a letter, arrived two nights before the gallery opening. It stated that the time had come for Mama to tell Lucas Block the truth. The letter stated that the photos Mama gave to Lucas, the photos appearing in the gallery exhibit, were a gimmick aimed at Mama's private self-exoneration. In handwriting on hotel stationery, the letter stated calmly that the writer would sooner see Mama dead than see her continue to duck and evade and lead people on. Finally, the letter stated that an article would be coming out pointing a finger at Mama.

Then Eloise added something that was not in the letter. She told me that, many years earlier, Mama had killed Lucas' parents.

I didn't know this until Eloise told me this morning.

Or maybe I did suspect something terrible underlying Mama's friendship with Lucas. She had always been so kind toward him, so protective, that the image of her hurting him was not to be believed. But I knew there was ice at her core.

That someone so kind and generous should be so secretive about her past, so unwilling to talk, had always sounded a little warning bell with me. I could understand her refusal to describe how she had been injured. But, for instance, she wouldn't mention what she had done for a living for the decades she lived in Berlin except in the vaguest of terms.

Many Berliners have difficult pasts. It's a city of broken things twisted and bolted back together. But people who profess to love their friends usually share their difficulties, don't they?

When Mama assigned me to find out what I could about Lucas, to get close to him, she said she knew terrible things about the family's past and just wanted Lucas to be safe. She didn't explain how she knew these things. I believed her, though. She was, after all, protecting me at the time. I was at that moment a broken thing, also.

Standing in the alley in Stockholm seemed somehow suddenly suffocating. I slung my duffel across the other shoulder and headed along cobbled streets to Stortorget and down a side way to some hotels. I checked into a small room. I dropped my bag on the bed and lay down beside it. The awfulness of my enterprise descended.

I began to cry. This lasted ten or fifteen minutes. Then I rose, washed my face and made coffee.

I rolled back through the previous two days: Mama's wrenching suicide, followed by the crashing appearance of the girl Hannah into our midst, breaking open the shell of Mama's past, and subsequently Lucas' sudden desire—predictably emotional and urgent, per Lucas' usual—to solve the riddles of the identities of the four ghosts in the photographs. I gently prodded the idea, like a sleeping beast, that Mama had killed Lucas' parents. They had been blown up with a bomb, for God's sake. And I thought about the apparent fact that Lucas didn't know anything about Mama's role.

I sat in a long time in my small hotel room in Stockholm with the afternoon sun coming between the curtains I had shoved apart hoping for a bit of brightness, hunched on the side of a low, creaking bed holding my now-cooled coffee cup in both hands. The weight of the past forty-eight hours crushed me.

After an hour, I returned to the little street under the arch off Västerlånggattan. Shadows crawled across the alleys and squares. The sky was purple; lights were on everywhere, spilling yellow through the charcoal streets. I checked my watch: 16:24. If the subject of my inquiry worked normal Nordic hours, he or she may be coming home soon.

At the address that had been carefully inscribed on the negative envelope, no lights were on. It was a narrow house with a black-painted door, a brass mail slot, a ceramic pot by the granite step devoid of flowers.

I slipped a hand into my pocket and withdrew the photo that Lucas had printed for me. I turned this way and that trying to find better light. Finally, I resorted to the light on my phone. I studied the black and white photo again, though it had already become very familiar. A friend.

A man, apparently a sailor, stands on a planked dock near a heavy bollard, sturdy and stable, one leg turned outward. He wears baggy pants, a thick peacoat with all four horn buttons fastened, the collar turned up. His hands are in his coat pockets. At his neck, the neckline of a thick sweater shows. The man wears a British-style sailor cap on his head. He has narrow features and, clear even in the grey-lit photo, bright eyes. He gazes directly at the camera. He is almost expressionless. He has a small mustache. Beside him, a fraying seaman's duffle bag stands on end, upright and carelessly rigid, like the sailor, beside the bollard.

From the street a hundred paces away echoed voices. They grew clearer as walkers approached the little stone archway, then receded after they had passed.

I felt suddenly in the condition of being an observer pausing for a moment in a world always slightly out of reach, out of my engagement. Snatches of conversations drifted to me in the quiet alley, the stuff of friends walking home on a Tuesday evening—movies, dates, illnesses, co-workers, families. Laughter. Names called aloud. A child crying and its mother speaking to it. In the little alley, a small flock of black birds dipped through and flew miraculously under the stone arch. For a moment, I heard their wings. They made no other sound. They evaporated into the burgeoning night.

Then a solitary man turned the corner. He approached me, or rather he approached the narrow slip of alley in which I stood. He carried a slim, tanned leather attaché. He walked with his head down, not disconsolately, but rather as one naturally walks on cobbled streets in dim light.

When he glanced up, he saw me standing there. He took me in—a woman alone as if waiting for someone, hands in the pockets of her coat. I don't think he was alarmed. But he moved a half pace to his right as if to allow more space between us. He nodded to me.

He stepped past me and then stopped. He stood before the black-painted door. He dug in a pocket for keys.

I stepped forward toward him. He heard my boot on the cobblestones, turned and looked at me. Though hatless and wearing a tidy grey wool overcoat over a jacket and tie, he was the image of the man in the photo. His eyes were blue and distant.

For a fraction of a second, it seemed to me that he was expecting me. I stopped a few paces from him. Our breaths hung in the chilling evening air.

I said in English, "Excuse me. My name is Heike Eberhardt. I believe you may be a person I've been trying to find. I wonder if I may ask you a question about an old photo that has come into my possession."

He said nothing. I slipped the photo from the pocket of my coat and held it to him. "Is this a photo of you?" I asked, though I knew it was not.

He continued to look at my face for a minute, then down at my hand holding out the photo. He took the photo slowly from my hand, raised it a little to catch faint light flowing under the arch from Västerlånggattan. He looked down at it, as if into it. His hair, I noticed, was very thin on top. His scalp had a creamy, soft tone.

A minute passed. He shook his head slowly and looked up again. "I have a copy of this photo," he said. "It's one of the only photos I have of my father."

I asked if he could spare a few minutes to help me with a task. I explained that I was trying to determine the identity of the person in the photo to assist a colleague. I stated that the colleague had died recently. She'd left unfinished work. I meandered on for a minute about the colleague working with archival photos in Berlin, and this photo having been one of the last batch she was working on.

Through this, he listened to me without moving, still holding the photo in his pale bare hand, but watching my face. When I stopped talking. He looked down at the stones for a moment and then shrugged. His expression wasn't cold. He glanced at his front door.

"Not here," he said. He handed the photo back to me and turned. He said to me, "There's a café around the corner."

CHAPTER 24

Heike Eberhardt — #3

We sat a table near the windows. We shook hands. He told me his name was Erich Goldschmidt. His father, the man in the photo, was named Gunther Goldschmidt. We ordered glasses of wine. It was a glassy, noisy little café with a long ebony bar and high tables.

Erich and I conversed. We touched only briefly on the usual trivialities. He seemed about my age in look and turn of phrase. His eyes watched me unwavering. His eyes were abnormally steady, as if he'd only recently learned to see things and was practicing. The mustache suited him.

We switched from English to German. It was our shared native language. His voice was small and dry. I had the impression he mostly spoke in offices, private meetings. He leaned in toward me and I toward him. Our glasses rested just beyond the fingertips of our hands, a few inches apart on the table. Some tangibly close enclosure, an old, easy sense of familiarity, clasped us both.

Our conversation went something like this:

Me: "Tell me about your father."

He spoke breathlessly at first. His sentences reflected the level to which he trusted me, I think. He usually spoke eloquently and elegantly, I learned later.

Erich: "He was a sailor. He was in the Volksmarine most of my childhood and youth, the old navy of the GDR. Many adventures.

"For example, he was involved in the scuffle with Poland over control of the Baltic coastline, fallout from Molotov-Ribbentrop. Shots were fired. He told me about this when I was a child.

"He was seldom home. He sent money and occasionally little notes and gifts. My mother talked about him occasionally, but always recollections about the period when they were first together. Little framed vignettes. She repeated these stories as if she were teaching me prayers. I have only clipped memories of him, visually. Snapshots. Like the one you have.

"The Volksmarine was dissolved in October, 1990. That momentous month. But my father had died long before that. He committed suicide in 1981. With his old service revolver. In a hotel in the harbor district of Rostock. They returned him to us in Berlin to be buried.

"I remember standing by his grave holding my mother's hand. Springtime in Weißensee, the Jewish cemetery, all the trees blooming, and she whispering to me, 'I just don't understand why they did it.' I could not comprehend why she would say that."

Me: "Why, do you think?"

Erich: "Why did she say that?"

Me (tiptoeing past boundaries): "No, why did he kill himself?"

Erich: "He had been at home in Berlin with my mother and me for a while prior. He had just been discharged from the Volksmarine. He didn't explain how or why. Impassive. As if everything was normal, understood, as it should be. My mother and I both trod water.

"That winter was the longest stint in which he was present in my life. I was eighteen and had just started at Friedrich Wilhelm University. I studied accounting. I manage funds for people."

With this comment, Erich made a slow, apologetic expression and asymmetric posture of his hands. The movements seemed accustomed. This small admission seemed to open a valve, as if his profession, what he did every day, was connective tissue to everything that had come before, everything that composed him. He spoke at greater length.

Erich: "My father always had a tendency toward long periods of gloominess. He would become vacant and silent. He would sit by himself, apart from us. My mother would be by turns frightened by him and angry with him. Nothing penetrated.

"He went for long, solitary walks with his slow sailor's gait, his horn-buttoned overcoat and woolen watchcap, sometimes for entire days. We lived in Mitte, my mother and I, in a new communist flat on Ziegelstraße not far from the river. I remember whitewash and low ceilings and uneven plaster over concrete walls. The way the toilet flushed, as if choking. I would lie awake at night aware of these things, listening. Glow from streetlights; people arguing upstairs.

"That winter, the winter of his brief return, when he spoke to us over dinner, he talked in his low voice of politics. The problems with the communists. The need for reform and liberation. He warned us never to speak of what he said. There was a cheap chandelier over the dining table. I remember the shadow his finger made on his face when he raised it, pointing to the ceiling, to the sky. He told me privately, 'You are very smart. When you are older, you will understand. A person must fight or give up. I fear giving up. But sometimes we have no choice.' He presented this to me like an explanation and apology.

"Sometimes he and my mother whispered together in the hallway. She would collapse into tears. He would comfort her, holding her with his arms awkwardly aslant, as if he'd never held anyone, or dreamed of it, looking over her shoulder out the window into the night, like he was waiting for something.

"He went often to meetings in the evening at places never revealed to my mother or me. He sometimes didn't return until dawn.

"I went to my classes with my satchel of books on the trams in the snowy fog. This went on for months during the winter of 1981. It seemed an especially dark and frigid season, accustomed though we were to life in Berlin. You may remember it.

"Then one day he vanished. I came into the kitchen in the morning and his big, grey seabag, vessel of pathetic pockets and old agonies, as he described it, was gone. My mother sat at the kitchen table. She had finished crying; she just sat. Some letters lay on the table in front of her, which she quickly folded.

"My father had gone back north to the coast, apparently to take a job with a shipping company in Rostock. This was what she told me. He never came back, and we never heard from him again.

"We received word of his death two months later. My mother only lived two years beyond that. She died of stomach cancer. The subject of my father didn't come up during that final period. So, in essence, they both disappeared, inexplicably, before I took my college exams. They left nothing behind but me. That was the best they could do."

The café had grown noisier and crowded. A man with a guitar had taken the stool on a small stage and was playing South

American songs. It being Tuesday, the clientele were mostly young, urban Swedes, stylish and slim-waisted and deferential, but chatty.

Me: "Have you ever heard the name Abbie Ingvall?"

Erich's gaze turned outward to the darkening street, the legions of passing bicycles. He blinked his blue eyes. He sat for a long time as if searching for something.

Erich: "They called her Mama. I would have forgotten, but you're the second person in two weeks to ask me about her."

Most of the time, I am not a loquacious person. Perhaps taciturn would not be an apt description—I'm not disengaged or aloof—but I'm a lesser- and lower-spoken individual. In person, on the phone, online, everywhere. In a crowded room, my voice will generally not emerge.

But at this moment, a dam broke. I talked. The week of terrible stress overflowed my defenses. I opened up to this man. His honesty beckoned, and the caverns of old hurts inside his quiet, diminutive self. It helped that he sat very still and watched my eyes. He listened. I only speak to people who listen.

I began, of course, by asking him about the other person who had visited him. He told me it was a woman who called herself Andrea. Blonde, middle-aged, business-dressed. She had come to him with the same photo and asked the same question: Did he know the man in the photo? They had not spoken long. Before she left, she had also asked if he had ever heard of Abbie Ingvall. It took him a while to recollect, he told me. Andrea had said, "You will soon hear from Abbie Ingvall again."

Maybe that was the exchange that opened the floodgates for me. I told Erich about Lucas. Erich knew of him, as does most everyone of our generation. I described how we had met, the truth this time. I had never told anyone the truth before.

***

155

It was no accident when I ran into Lucas at the photography museum in Berlin that day. Abbie knew Lucas was in Berlin. There had been comments in the gossip columns. He was spotted around town, and for a while that was a noticed thing. His presence made Abbie nervous. He unsettled her. I didn't know why.

Abbie had taken me in when I returned from abroad, shell-shocked and panicked and still in many ways a little girl. I spent a few years knocking about in a void. With what I had left of my little fortune, I had purchased my mother's farm to rid her of the mortgage. I had moved her into a facility. I re-sold the property and lost a lot of money. Some investments that I'd made in London on the advice of friends also went bad.

I had barely thirty years under my belt, a rudimentary and small-town education, a family destroyed and scattered like a bombed-out factory, a truckload of guilt and uncertainty and downright fear. I wandered Berlin, avoiding social situations, hiding. I was broken.

I'd had what probably would have been called a nervous breakdown, if I'd described it to a professional. But the only person I felt I could talk to was Mama.

Of everything I'd encountered in my brief, naïve sojourn through the modeling business, the one thing that stuck was a love of photography. I'd been around some famous and brilliant photographers, of course. I expressed an interest in seeing the world from their point of view. When I wasn't posing and frowning, they taught me bits and pieces.

I acquired a camera. I took snapshots around Berlin. I started by photographing people, but before long—this is stark evidence of my personality—I found I was mostly interested in the shapes and forms of buildings, especially old, broken, abandoned buildings.

I met Mama via a fellow photographer. Mama was a storehouse of forgotten, derelict photographic history about my terrifying city.

Mama gave me a safe place. Most every day, I visited, and we sat on a sofa by the front window of her flat and talked about everything.

I couldn't tell precisely how old she was, and she never said. She had been badly burned in a fire some years earlier. One side of her face was disfigured, as was her left arm and hand. She had only one eye, on her left. She wore an eyepatch over the right. But the glasses she wore were from before she had been injured, and still had both lenses. The lenses were thick. She wore the glasses over the eyepatch. They amplified her blazing eye on one side and the patch on the other. Her nose was crooked. Her hair was white and had thinned greatly. Patches of oystershell scalp shone through. But the part of her that was still intact indicated that she had once been an attractive woman.

She was a lesbian. She lived with her partner Eloise, who was younger than Mama. I came to know Eloise well. She and I were both country girls from small towns.

Mama saved me. I loved her for that.

Mama worked as a photo archivist. She knew immense amounts about documentary photography

and its history. She also knew, it seemed, everyone
worth knowing around Berlin in the photography
field. She taught me and helped me find work.
She seemed to evaluate me and then send me gently
back into the great tides, like a launch from a ship.

In this way, several years passed. I had a
home, a new life. I got married and then divorced
over a period of a few years. I lived for my work.

Then one day Mama asked me to do a favor
for her. She asked me to find and meet Lucas Block
and try to get close to him. Mama asked me to try
to discover why he was in Berlin. She asked me to
keep an eye on him.

I accepted this assignment because I felt
I owed much to Mama. In the several years I'd
known her, she'd never asked me for anything before.
Also, I was intrigued by this Lucas Block person.
I studied photos of him. He had a face which
seemed partly boy-child and partly a power which
could separate seas.

I learned that Lucas was interested in
photography, as I was. Having been on the front
end of the lens for a long time, he, as I had done,
had become fascinated with the view from behind.
I learned that he was spending much time at the
Berlinische Galerie.

Although they're mostly in the Museum für
Fotographie now, at that time the Galerie had a few
Helmut Newton works, including a rather famous
one of me. Huge, aggressive, nude photographs of
young women, a collection of images he made over
several years. One cannot distinguish whether they
are realisms or fantasies. They are powerful and

graphic. Helmut's work was always sexually
charged, but these photos pushed boundaries.
They splashed the pages of artsy magazines
and became instantly recognizable, famous and
scandalous at the time. They amplified Helmut
Newton's notoriety.

And I in all my unclothed glory was one
of his more famous subjects, maybe because of
my pose and angle, the way he had asked me to
stand. He caught something in me that not only
turned heads, as any photo of a naked woman
will do, but held. He captured gravity. Fire.

I knew Lucas would see the Newton photos
at the museum. I trailed him there one day and
presented myself to him in a quiet gallery. I was
right; he recognized me. He has an eye for faces
and forms. We talked photography. We went
out for coffee. We began seeing each other.
We became attached. I soon loved him as
I'd never loved anyone before.

The point is, I lied to him. I've been lying
to him for a decade.

I did, however, begin to build a barricade
around Lucas against Mama. My reports to her
about him and his activities became vague and
innocuous. It was true that he didn't seem to
know of her. He didn't seem to be in Berlin for
any reason other than to hide in the shadowy
old world of his family.

Eventually, I introduced him to Mama.
They hit it off. Her distrust melted. She seemed
to pick up the task from me of protecting him.
To us, he wasn't a celebrity. He was a hurt little

boy who had lost everything – his parents,
his wife, in some respects his life. We absorbed
him, Mama and I.

To me, the American movie star aspect of
him—rich, beautiful, popular—vanished. None of
that ever meant anything to me. I just wanted
him, his touch, his vision, his gentleness, the
way he sees things clearly and intimately and
lovingly, like through a viewfinder.

—— CHAPTER 25 ——

Heike Eberhardt — #4

Erich responded, "He sounds like a nice man."

I responded, "He is. But he's complicated. Sometimes frustrating."

Lucas is friendly, a good conversationalist, but very quiet. His eyes avert quickly when he speaks to people. He carries hidden pain. He has inner intensity. He is a picture of scorched pride and guilt—internal anguish layered over with a calm bon-vivant shell. There is a thread of guilt that runs through him from his family's background to the death of his wife.

I explained to Erich that, with Lucas, I entered a period of joy like I'd never experienced. I'd never known happiness before. It was as if I'd been lifted out of the morass of life, cleaned up and set about ticking like a restored clock. Our life together seemed unbreakable. I had forgotten the morass.

Now it was all going to come tumbling down around me.

I told Erich about Lucas' parents. They were murdered. A bomb was planted in their car. They died on a drive in the countryside on their way to Magdeburg. Lucas was at school in East Berlin at the time. He was only ten.

During the war, Lucas' mother became caught up in the Nazi furor and excitement. She participated—fully at first and then with less and less enthusiasm. She tried to make an exit. After the war, she was pulled, strong-armed, maybe, into a Neo-Nazi group after the Russians took over. The murder of Lucas parents had something to do with all of this, but no one had ever figured out what. Or at least no one told me.

I looked the incident up, but little was said except that Lucas' parents were strong opponents of the East German regime. His father wrote underground articles. His mother made speeches.

A dispensation was made for the orphaned boy since he had no other family in the GDR—Lucas was allowed to emigrate to America to live with an aunt and uncle in Arizona.

I also told Erich what Eloise had told me that morning. Eloise said, in her shaking voice, that Mama had killed Lucas' parents. She hadn't set the bomb herself. She had given directions to others. Orders. Eloise told me that Mama was a senior figure in the Stasi.

I described the series of threatening notes that Mama had received. I told Erich about Mama's death. A slow-motion explosion was growing from it.

Erich asked me how the photo of his father came into the story. I told him what we knew of how the photos had come to Mama, how she had handed off five of them to Lucas after he had described to her his idea for composite photos that he was calling his *ghosts*. I described the addresses noted on each of the envelopes—in this case Erich's address on a side street in Stockholm.

I explained that it had been Lucas who wanted to uncover the identities of the people in the photos. He sought to learn why Mama had died. He thought the photos might help. He was desperately upset. His circle of friends closed in, as we always do, in part trying to shield him and in part trying to shield ourselves.

Then I began to talk about mysteries unraveling. I talked about hiding in my room as a little girl for whole afternoons, living in my imagination, avoiding my brother and my mother. I talked about keeping secrets. I talked about the way Germans learned not to say things, especially about the past. It's like the spaces between notes, the absences of color or texture in a painting or photograph. These voids speak.

I talked, dramatically, about the risks of waking the dead.

I may have been boring him, or he may have been reaching out, metaphorically, to lend a hand, since by that time I was floundering. We paused for a minute to listen to the music, to order second glasses of wine.

Erich asked me to tell him more about modeling. I sketched in a few corners. He told me that after he had moved to Stockholm, he had acquired clients in the fashion industry and thus had become interested in art photography. He had made a study of it. Being about the same age as I am, he remembered some of my pictures, and he remembered the Helmut Newton photos. It used to feel odd to me, maybe vaguely exciting, to sit with a man who was telling me that he'd seen me naked. Nothing is left of that now. It's all numb.

He asked about the circle of friends I'd mentioned. I described Frankie and Nik a little. I related their long and deep history with Lucas. I said that they all seemed to have expatriated to Berlin in order to transcend their pasts, if not hide from them.

I commented that, in my experience, most expatriates spend their time wearing their new homes like suits of fancy clothing, showing off for friends and relatives. But my three expatriate friends seemed to want the reverse. They wanted to withdraw into their new clothing—the streets of Berlin—as into vast cloaks.

Erich: "That's a compelling reason to expatriate. I understand this. This is why I'm in Stockholm."

Me: "I understand it, too. Berliners find themselves unable to hide from anything. We're all naked. Some of us remain in this condition and some do not."

We spoke a little of Berlin. It seemed to amuse him. I envied him that.

Erich: "You were a Wessi. I was an Ossi. We grew up only a stone's throw apart, we both spoke the same language, but we may as well have been on opposite sides of the earth. You were taught English in school. You were taught geography and history. I was taught to lie. We learned to speak one way at home, quietly, and another way at school. Any misstep could be reported. I was a Young Pioneer. Each day, our teachers would recite, 'For peace and socialism, be ready.' We would reply in unison, 'Always ready.'"

He talked of preparing for the exams that would determine his course when he finished school. He felt visceral fear of being pulled aside, of being denied a future. Although he didn't know of his father's secret life at the time, he intuited the risk. He told me of fleeing Berlin the week after the Wall came down, heading to Stockholm, never returning.

Me: "How did you know of Mama? Abbie Ingvall?"

Erich: "My mother told me that name once a few months after my father killed himself. It burned into my memory. I repeated it to myself at night. My mother told me never to speak it aloud.

"You see, the Stasi had been closing in on my father. He knew they knew all about him. He was paranoid and depressed. They understood this, and he knew they understood it. There was nothing he could do.

"Little clues would turn up every other day. We would come home and the beds, made before we left that morning, would be tousled. The phone rang at all hours, but there was never anyone on the line. He would fill the gas tank of his little car, but it would be empty the next morning. He found love notes apparently written by other men to my mother. The headlights of his car would mysteriously be left on and the battery would be dead. He would find holes in the pockets of his pants. He would hear his name being said by someone on the radio faintly screened behind music. These apparitions slowly filled a person's head.

"This, I later learned, was called *Zersetzung*. Decomposition. Rotting. The Stasi would cause a person's mind to rot from within. Always quiet and invisible. Deniable. The Staatssicherheitsdienst, the State Security Service, excelled in it.

"My mother told me that Abbie Ingvall was famous for Zersetzung among the whispering dissidents. She was a skilled practitioner of the art. My mother always felt that Abbie Ingvall —Mama, as she was known—used Zersetzung to kill, indirectly and discreetly, my unstable and terrified father."

The evening had grown into full night. Frost had settled on the cobbled streets outside. We finished our wine and sat for a while in silence. We both thought deeply in silence.

Then I pulled out my phone. I asked if I might take a photo of the two of us against the backdrop of the café. I swiveled and held the phone at arm's length and tapped the shutter.

"Unrelenting photographer," I said. He smiled.

Afterward, I brought up the photos stored on my phone and thumbed through them. On impulse, I stopped at the photo of the three of us that Frankie had taken at the dinner table in the restaurant a few nights previously. I studied it for a minute. I held the phone out for Erich.

"Is the woman on Lucas' right the person who visited you?" I asked.

"Yes, it is," Erich said. "How do you happen to have her photo?"

"She crashed our group recently. She seems to be getting around a lot. I need to go find out why."

On the frigid street, we shook hands. Then we hugged. He was still carrying his attaché. It bumped against my back when we hugged. The warmth with this person I had only met an hour ago formed a momentary deep and much-needed barrier against the loneliness.

It had begun to snow lightly. Crystals moved sideways through the street in the breeze coming up from the harbor, sparkling in window light. Across the obsidian water, stepped gables and church spires rose gracefully into the glowing dark.

"Don't worry about Lucas," Erich said. "It sounds to me like he will stick with you in every way. You've attracted strong things into your life. He is one of them."

I was crying just a bit as we parted and walked away. From nowhere, I remembered Matthias' words: *If we don't run, we're just ghosts of what might have been.*

PART THREE

TEXTURE. PATTERN. SPACE.

CHAPTER 26

The morning edition of *Bild* announces that the Berlin police are now looking for an individual in connection with the death of Staatsbibliotek archivist Abbie Ingvall. Surveillance cameras caught someone talking to Abbie Ingvall on a bridge over the river at the time she was estimated to have died. The police seek a woman who appeared in the video.

Under the article is a small black and white portrait photo of Abbie wearing a rounded hat and her eyepatch, the unscarred half of her mouth frowning, looking slightly ominous. Beside that photo is another, a very blurry nighttime photo from a high angle of what appears to be a woman in a long coat and a beret standing by a bridge parapet. Her arms gesture toward something out of the photo. She appears animated.

Lucas sees this small article on an inner page of a copy of the newspaper left splayed open on the counter when he comes down to the café to buy his morning croissant.

Lucas crosses Rosenthaler Platz on foot. Morning traffic has begun to slacken in the boulevards. Street pavements and tram rails shine wet, but the sidewalks still glower with ice.

On the building across the square, the enormous banner with the face of the sorrowful woman has developed long streaks of dirty rime. These descend vertically, striating her downcast expression, terminating along the hem in a row of dull icicles. The cloth of the banner hangs heavy, distorted. The face of the woman darkens as the streetlights go off.

Ahead of Lucas as he walks westward, a woman carries two shopping bags bulging with groceries. She is wide and heavy-legged and thickly-dressed against the cold and slow with her burden. Despite her low center of gravity, her booted feet jerk left and right on the ice as she steps across grates and ridges of snow. She falls.

Lucas runs to her and kneels. Her groceries have scattered across the sidewalk. Another woman cries out, and a man as well. Soon, a circle has formed around the fallen woman and Lucas.

Because of the time he spends helping her to her feet and collecting her belongings, he is late when he arrives at the flat in Lichtenberg occupied by Hannah Müller and the man she describes as not being her boyfriend.

Lucas has retrieved his car, which he stores in a parking garage many blocks from his building and seldom drives. It is a small, old Volkswagen Golf. It is dented and inconspicuous. But it starts and runs smoothly and navigates the slick streets.

He double-parks at a corner and hurries toward the building. Signs in windows along the block advertise vacancies. A man and a woman lean against the wall of a Waschsalon, smoking. Across the street, children in parkas and snowboots run and scream in a vacant lot where dry grasses protrude through the grey snow-crust.

A faded mural in sepia tones of a man shooting a handgun at a row of mannequins covers a brick wall fronting the park. Mannequins slump and fragment, frozen in mid-destruction. Along the base of the mural, a line reads *die Geheimnisse von Berlin*—the Secrets of Berlin. The children dash past the image again and again.

In the flat, the five framed photos lean against a wall of the bedroom Hannah shares with her friend. The photos face the wall. A blanket has been carefully spread over them, as if to hide. The bundle is large, the size of a mattress.

Lucas glances around the flat. Little decorates the walls but a few posters of socialist causes, current and antiquated. Hannah's friend, a man named Klaus, uncovers the framed photos. Klaus is dark-haired, bearded and perhaps ten years older than Hannah. He wears wire-rimmed glasses. The posture of his back and shoulders as he bends to lift the first of the photos, viewed from Lucas' angle, is recognizable to Lucas from the security video. He is careful with the photo, though it is wide and awkward. Lucas steps in to assist him, as does Hannah.

One by one, they carry the photos down four flights of stairs and load them into a Skoda van which used to be painted white. When they have finished, Klaus stops on the driveway and lights a cigarette. He glances frequently at Lucas, as if evaluating whether what he has been told will hold true. A siren calling from down the street causes him to jump.

Hannah climbs back to the flat a final time and returns with a small backpack.

"I don't own a suitcase," she tells Lucas.

Hannah wears bell-bottomed jeans and a belted plaid woolen coat with huge lapels. She wears a blue and ochre scarf of ratty silk. On her feet, she wears thick-heeled brown leather boots that lace high up her legs. Her blonde hair, as usual, is a mess, but evidently a deliberate mess.

She stuffs the pack into the van. Lucas glances around the now-silent street. The children have departed the vacant lot.

Before Klaus and Hannah climb into the van, Klaus turns and then approaches Lucas. He takes a postcard of Hollywood from one coat pocket and a pen from another.

"Can I get your autograph?" Klaus asks.

Hannah smirks from the door of the van. "You said you'd never even heard of him," she says to Klaus.

"I looked him up. It might be valuable someday."

Lucas follows the white van to Frankie's gallery, a slow drive through kilometers of bleary, wet streets. The van pulls into the alley beside the stone building, where presumably they had parked the previous visit, and Lucas pulls in behind them. Hannah and Klaus get out of the van. Klaus scans around with an expression suggesting he is expecting the police or other trickery.

Frankie's gallery manager, Hendrika, opens the side door for them. The glass of the window which had been broken has already been replaced.

Hendrika is tall, black-haired and wafer thin. She wears a slim black dress. Her arms, emerging from half-sleeves, display blue and yellow tattoos in sweeping designs. Dark eyes flash behind narrow glasses. She glares cautious fury at Klaus and Hannah, who both hunch as they silently begin to unload the photos.

In the gallery, two hired men wait to help Hendrika re-hang the photos. The unweighted and loosely coiling wires still dangle against blank walls above the name tags.

No words are spoken by anyone during the unloading process. Hendrika stands in the hallway in the draft of winter air from the open alleyway door, her decorated arms crossed against the cold and against the presence of the thieves. When all five photos have been moved into the gallery, Lucas escorts Hannah and Klaus outside.

Hannah retrieves her knapsack from the van. Lucas nods to Klaus and turns toward his vehicle. Hannah looks at Klaus briefly, offers an expression of parting, but says nothing. She quickly follows Lucas with her pack and climbs into his car.

"How much time before we have to be at the airport?" she asks him as he backs the Volkswagen into the street and proceeds toward Gendarmenmarkt.

He looks at his watch. "Three hours."

"Can we visit my mother? I've been wanting to."

Lucas drives back over the island past Berliner Dom and along Karl-Liebknechtstraße. Alexanderplatz drifts quietly by in thin morning haze, the smoke from currywurst vendors collecting along the avenue. Traffic on the boulevards moves slowly. Police direct cars around an accident. The Fernsehturm has lost its spherical head in the overcast.

As they travel through the somber cityscape, Lucas and Hannah do not talk. They both watch the familiar scenes unfolding, glimpses of monuments and stark parkland set against stone and wintry sky, framed between buildings which loom in dressings of sleet and concrete. Along a frozen field, a flock of black birds, swallows or starlings, cloud the branches of barren trees.

Lucas drives as he does many things: with sharp attention. Hannah slouches in her seat, but with tautness molded into carelessness, feline, a creature slack but alert. These two humans begin the process of sensing each other more fully.

Lucas turns easterly onto Alexanderstraße and rounds Strausberger Platz past its dead fountain. They drive back toward the south end of Lichtenberg, from where they came in separate vehicles an hour earlier. He taps on the car's radio. It plays an American song from the eighties. He turns off the radio.

Lucas parks in the small, almost-empty lot facing forested and sepulchral Zentralfriedhof Friedrichsfelde. Snow has begun to fall. The wind which clipped around walls and eaves earlier in the morning has died. As they enter the cemetery, the flurry of heavy flakes grows denser and quickly whitens the ground. They leave wide, wet footprints on the graveled walks. The cemetery is already quiet, but the snow erases the drifting residue of city sound.

"This way," Hannah says. Off to their right rises the blocky silhouette of the stone stele installed by the socialists with its raised steel lettering: *Die Toten Mahnen Uns*. The dead remind us.

Noticeable is the complete absence of bird cries among the barren trees, even for winter. Silence aches in their ears. They follow gently curving paths that slope almost imperceptibly uphill through trees and past rows of headstones. Figures and geometric shapes in eternal granite, little elements of architecture and agonized statuary, in rows and clusters, all wait under their temporal drapery of new snow, clutching Berlin, the 21st century, in cold, still arms.

They pass the Feierhalle.

"They held a very small service in there for my mother. Only a few people. Old friends. Abbie told me that she was there, but in the back. I didn't know her or notice her, but she later told me that she observed me, studied me. She knew who I was though she'd never met me," Hannah says. "It was just a few months later that she found me at my school to introduce herself."

In the northern reaches of the cemetery, she guides Lucas around a tree-lined curve of pathway to a cluster of graves. A few slim branches have broken from trees with the weight of new snow. She searches. She finds a headstone and beckons to him and he comes to stand beside her. Nearby, a small backhoe is parked by a mound of fresh, reddish earth. The snow is already three centimeters deep over everything.

Hannah stoops and brushes off the low, simple stone. It reads, *Ulrike Müller 1974 – 2015*. It offers no hint of the person's life other than a modest suggestion of her existence.

The two stand in silence side by side for a full minute. Hannah says, "I wish I had some flowers or something."

She looks around and then steps toward the nearest trees and picks up a broken branch. She taps off the snow and ice, a few dead leaves, on her pantleg. She unwraps her thread-bare blue and ochre scarf from her neck and carefully ties it around the stick. Then she bends and gently inserts the stick in the ground, like a prayer flag, beside her mother's headstone. When she straightens, she takes Lucas' arm tightly in one hand. With the other she wipes a quick tear. Snowflakes melt on the still-warm fabric of the scarf.

"I didn't see her for two years. I had to live with a foster family. Then they told me she had died," Hannah says.

Left of Ulrike Müller's grave, a new rectangular hole opens in the ground, dug within the past day with the nearby backhoe. Lucas glances to it and Hannah's gaze follows his. They both look into the hole. The soil of the hole's sides is chiseled into planes and dusted with frost. They consider its shadowed depth which, though only the height of a man, seems unfathomable.

"I bet that grave is for your grandmother," Lucas says. "She must have decided to be buried beside her daughter some time ago since there isn't much room here. She probably bought that space a while back. Maybe she bought both spaces. I imagine Eloise notified the cemetery a day or so ago about Mama."

Hannah takes in these speculations quietly, still looking into the hole.

"Abbie never told me much about her daughter. My mother. She barely acknowledged her. It's odd that she would change her mind," Hannah says.

Lucas considers this. "Maybe it wasn't so much a change of mind as a recognition. An acceptance."

Hannah nods. She says, "I think when my time comes this is where I will want to be, also."

—— CHAPTER 27 ——

They drive south in burgeoning rush hour traffic on slushy highways to Schönefeld airport to catch their evening plane to Tallinn. Their flight, it turns out, is delayed due to the weather. If it had been on time, Lucas might not have seen Nik's text when it arrived:

Met daughter of ghost #4—Man with Dog. He committed suicide. She says he was targeted by the Stasi. He knew Abbie Ingvall's name. Also, someone else was here asking about Mama last week.

Lucas texts back: *I'll call you from Tallinn.*

When they land in Tallinn, however, his call is to Heike.

"Hi."

"Hi. Where are you?"

"Tallinn airport. Just got here."

"Hannah is with you?"

"She's right here. We're heading for the rental cars."

"I have something to tell you. Actually, I have a lot to tell you, but just one thing for now. Do you remember the woman named Andrea who was at the gallery opening and who came to dinner with us?"

"Yes."

"She was here in Stockholm last week. She came to find the same person I came to find. By the way, I found him. He's the son of *Man with Seabag*."

"I know."

"You know?"

"I mean I guessed that. Based on what Nik said about the person in his photo."

"His name is Erich. We had a good talk."

"Did he say anything about Stasi?"

"He did. How did you know?"

"I have a lot to tell you, too."

The snow-laden front draped over Berlin, latest in a wave, has not reached northeast to Tallinn yet, or is spreading in a different direction. The highway into town from Lennujaam airport lies frigid and nearly vacant, stabbed occasionally by frosted knives of headlights. Lake Ülemiste is a frozen black expanse to the south.

Though the train into the city's center would have been faster, Lucas has rented a car because they need to search for the address on the photo in the morning. The rental process takes a long time owing to the sleepiness of the attendant, and it is past midnight when they arrive at the hotel Lucas has reserved in the Old Town, a slight, Gothic-doored edifice he remembers from visits years ago.

"But I reserved two rooms with one bed each. I called this morning." Lucas says this to a small and slanted man at the reception desk.

"There must have been a misunderstanding," says the man, using the passive voice in English. "One room with two beds has been reserved."

"Is another room available."

"The room you've reserved is all that is available. Perhaps the hotel across the street?"

Lucas shakes his head with fatigue. "We'll stay here."

The room is large and woody. The two beds of which the man at the front desk spoke are narrow but draped in soft blankets and heaped with pillows. The timbers of the building creak softly; outside, an occasional voice ripples as late-night pedestrians pass on the steep street.

Lying in her bed under down comforters, Hannah says into the dark, "You were a big movie star, weren't you?"

From the other bed comes Lucas' quiet laugh. "Where'd you hear that?"

"Abbie told me." Long silence. Then, "Was it fun?"

"Was what fun?"

"Being in the movies. All that stuff."

"It had its moments. Like everything. It was what I wanted for a while. But having what you want often kills what you want."

She mulls this for a minute. "Even so, I'd like to do something like that."

"Movies? It's a tough business. Very discouraging at times. But if you want to do something, you should try."

"I just mean something exciting."

"Ah. It's a big world. Lots of exciting, pleasurable, useful things going on out there. You have tons going for you, Hannah. I'm sure you'll find your way."

The two of them lie quietly for a while. Then Hannah says in a voice that quavers slightly as if with emotion or screwed-up courage, "Would you help me?"

Lucas says, "That's a very open-ended request, Hannah. If you mean help you get into my old line of work, I'm not sure that I can. I'm not well-connected anymore. I suppose I could send introductions to some old friends who are still in the business. But what would I say? I met an eighteen-year-old-girl, grand-daughter of a friend, limited English proficiency, no training or skills, who wants a job? No insult intended, but you realize that would be a tough sell."

A few more quiet minutes pass. "Lucas adds as if expand-ing to himself, "The falsity of Hollywood. We're all nothing but effigies. A thinking person must try to identify what is solid and what is transparent, what is solid and what is fixed. Like developing never-ending reels of film."

Hannah nods in the gray silence, perhaps suggesting she is precociously aware of this.

Then Lucas adds in a more concrete tone, "But I'll help you think through your options and advise you on paths for-ward. I'll do anything I can for you. Like I said, you have a lot on the ball. You're going to go far, I think. But your life is just beginning, you know. When you graduate from college, you'll be entering kindergarten. Again, not to be insulting."

Her voice smoother now, Hannah says, "I know. It's just exciting to be around someone who actually made it all happen."

Lucas' voice takes on a subtle edge. "Yeah. I made it all happen." He pauses as if to say more, but then rolls onto his side facing the wall.

Down the street, bells toll, possibly from St. Catherine's, reminding them of the short night remaining.

When the bells finish, Hannah gently pushes aside the covers and rises from her bed. She wears a set of men's under-wear in pale blue: t-shirt and boxer shorts. She steps through a scant patch of moonlight tossed across the floor and sits slowly on the edge of Lucas' bed. He lies with his back to her, but at this he rolls slowly to look at her. Neither person says anything for a minute. Then Hannah reaches a careful hand and caresses his hip.

Lucas draws a full breath. Then he sits up and scoots slowly backward so he reclines against the pile of pillows. He reaches and takes Hannah's hand in his own. His hand around hers is neither tender nor rough; his grip is more like a handshake.

"It's been an evening of small follies and misinterpretations, hasn't it? But let's see if we can get back on course now. I said I'd do anything for you. I'm sorry if that seemed like an open door. You're a very beautiful woman, and in the day and a half since I met you, I've come to care about you much. This though you did steal my property."

Through this, Hannah remains quiet, her hand in Lucas.' Her face, out of the moonlight, is a dark mask. She breathes softly through parted lips.

"There are a dozen reasons why we won't sleep together," he continues. "But let me tell you about only one." He pulls her hand and she leans beside him and turns. The two of them recline against the pillows side by side but a hands' breadth apart. Lucas gently tugs the comforter over them against the cool of the room. It is so quiet they can hear his antique Panerai wristwatch ticking on the nightstand. He speaks upward into the old rafters above.

"Heike is my life and breath. It's hard for me not to think about her—to avoid becoming glum and irritable—when I'm away from her. All this may seem odd from your vantage point. That old, grey-haired people should feel the way Heike and I do is perhaps surprising to you. I agree, it's uncommon. In the world of surfaces in which I've dwelt, she's a person of depth. And I think she, who was once only a mass of images herself, you know, sees the same in me. Alone, we are flat. Together we have dimension. I won an Oscar. But my partnership forged with Heike is the one thing in my life I can look back on and say to myself, *Well done*."

He falls silent. The two of them lie together, long lumps under the puffy comforter. After several minutes, Hannah slips the cover aside and steps back to her bed and climbs under her own blankets. Lucas still lies on his back, face upturned to the ceiling.

Lucas adds, "I hope one day you have someone as important to you as Heike is to me. And I hope he feels about you that way, too."

From her bed a few feet away, Hannah says softly, "Thank you."

A minute passes, and then she adds, "One other thing Abbie told me. A few weeks ago, she said to let you know, if anything happened to her, that she's sorry."

— CHAPTER 28 —

"The first speaking role I ever had was in a high school play. I was sixteen. The play was *Death of a Salesman*. I played Biff Loman, the older son of Willy Loman. I was thinking about this in the middle of the night, for some reason. I haven't thought about it in years."

Lucas and Hannah are walking cautiously down icy cobblestone streets from the hotel toward the carpark where Lucas left the rental car. Trails of dusty frost trace the spaces between the paving stones. They place their feet carefully. Both are bundled against the frigid, clear Tallinn morning.

Lucas continues, "I don't know why I'm telling you this. Just meandering around in my head. Biff Loman was a man of early promise with everything going for him who could never get it together. I remember some of my lines. *I tell ya, Hap, I don't know what the future is. I don't know what I'm supposed to want. And, I've always made a point of not wasting my life, and every time I come back here I know that all I've done is to waste my life.*"

They walk a distance in silence. Then Lucas adds, "And in Act Two: *Pop, I'm nothing. I'm nothing, Pop. Can't you understand that? There's no spite in it anymore. I'm just what I am.*"

Hannah looks up at him. Her gaze is calm but intense and unwavering. Her cheeks are red with the cold. She slows, and he slows with her.

"I want to preserve this moment forever," she says. "A famous actor quoting an old play, saying lines that cut into my soul. That character. That's exactly how I feel. How I'm afraid I'll feel."

Lucas smiles at her. He starts to say something but checks himself. He looks across the street.

"Let's get some breakfast."

They enter a café and order coffees and croissants. They stand at a marble counter along the front window.

"Can I see the photo again?" Hannah asks.

Lucas draws the photo they've named *Woman in Raincoat* from his coat's inner pocket and lays it on the counter facing Hannah. In the photo, a woman leans against a stone parapet. The background is apparently a ruined fortification with crenelated crests. Though the day appears clear, the woman wears a raincoat. It is a belted affair, slightly large for her. Her face is attentive, lips slightly parted as if she was about to smile. She holds a pair of sunglasses in her hand, her wrist flipped outward suggesting she'd just pulled off the glasses for the photo which came a bit too quickly. She wears pinstriped pants and narrow black shoes. Her long hair is straight and neatly brushed and tucked behind her ears. In the black and white photo, her hair is dark and shadows spill under her eyes.

Hannah studies the photo for several minutes.

"She looks happy," Hannah says. "But maybe a little nervous. Maybe she just didn't want to have her photo taken."

Lucas nods. "Or maybe she shares a secret with the person taking the photo, something that animates them both. Look at the way she looks at the camera. Snapshots can be mysteries.

That's why this one seemed so perfect for my photo project. And the others that Mama sent to me."

"Where's the address?"

"It's in a neighborhood south of the city."

"And you think the person there may be able to shed light on this photo?"

Lucas nods again. "I do think so. Heike and Nik have already told me that the people they found were related to the people in the photos. Frankie also, although she's interviewing her person this morning. And I think I may have been right that Mama wanted us to find these people."

The address is a house on a quiet sidestreet of bare trees and short, low fences in the Lilleküla district. Yards are tidy and snow-dressed. A few of the houses still display Christmas decorations, a simple wreath or straw-crafted angel, Estonian-style. Lucas and Hannah step through the gate and up to the varnished door.

A woman answers their ring. She wears workout clothing. Her damp face is deeply lined, her grey hair tied back. She breathes deeply. In the background, a television plays an exercise video. They converse in English.

She looks at the photo. An amused expression crosses her face.

"Where did you say you found this?" she asks. Lucas re-explains that the photo is from an archive in the Staatsbibliotek in Berlin.

The woman says, "I'm not sure, but I think this is my husband's sister. She looks like her. I've seen some old photos of her, but not this one."

"May we ask your husband about it?"

"He's at work. He'll be home at noon. May I take a photo of your photo?" she asks. She retrieves her phone from a bracket on an exercise bicycle and snaps a photo of the woman in the raincoat.

"I'll check with my husband. I think he'll talk to you. He's very private about his family, but he may be interested in this."

With almost three hours to spare before they can speak to the husband, Lucas and Hannah circle back to the city's historic rise and walk up to Old Town Square. Wan sunshine angles up southern-sloping streets, though the shade where lanes bend is arctic. A handful of pedestrians cross the square, heads down, aiming toward their jobs in offices and shops.

"No cruise ships in port. Saints be praised," Lucas comments to no one.

The two of them walk slowly and aimlessly, hands in pockets, close together. This sixty-year-old man and eighteen-year-old woman have bonded. He could be any grandfather out for a stroll with his granddaughter, except that when they step into a shop to look at engravings, a salt-and-pepper-haired woman behind the counter sizes him up, measures the cut of his distinctive face against the newsreels of her memory, and says in Estonian, "*Vabandage, kas teie olete Lucas Block?*" She catches herself and asks in English, "Excuse me. Are you Lucas Block?"

Hannah turns and grins at him happily.

They cross under Long Leg Gate. A lone guitar busker, knitted cap over wild hair, sits under the gate playing somber chords wearing fingerless gloves. In the cold air, his lugubrious notes ring and persist. His breath circles in thin clouds. His coin basket is empty; Lucas drops in a few Euros.

In the long, ascending canyon of stone-walled Pikk Jalg, Lucas says, "Thank you for accompanying me."

Hannah shrugs. "Not like I had anything else going on."

A few steps pass in silence. Then she appends, "Thank you for not having me arrested." She adds quietly, "And for being so nice."

Lucas says, "I apologize for the way I presented it. I think I said, 'You're coming with me.' How rude that was."

Hannah shrugs with deliberation.

"I was thrilled. At this point, with how complicated everything is, I would love to have someone simple and strong in my life. I would do anything." She says this the way young women typically say it to older men, with lax intonation and quick flick of the eyes, measuring.

Lucas' eyebrows knock about. "Simple, no doubt."

They crest past Nevski Katedral and wander through vacant and windswept Kuberneri Aed, the Governor's Garden, follow pathways through an open-air display of historical photos, blown-up large and layered in Lucite, forlorn in the snow, and stop at Pikk Hermann. The wind whips their scarves. Lucas stands looking up at the flag atop the rotund tower for a minute. "We've reached the top," Lucas comments to no one. Hannah stands beside him, her arms crossed, her coat clenched about her.

Lucas notices her shivering. "Let's get you inside somewhere," he says. They circle back down to Katariina Käik and take seats in a café by windows facing the narrow, sloping street of tall doorways and heavy-shuttered windows.

Lucas leans over his coffee cup and talks quietly to Hannah. "The reason I wanted to bring you along is that I had a sense you would be able to help me understand Mama a little better. You have a different and unique view of her. She came to you. An old woman who had never sought or seemingly even considered family connections changed when she encountered her granddaughter. That was only a year ago. Although I knew nothing of you until twenty-four hours ago—and apart from Eloise I was the closest friend Mama had, I think—I suddenly felt that you are an integral piece of some puzzle that I haven't yet even begun to perceive. Plus, I don't like to travel alone."

"I wish I could tell you more about her."

"Did your mother talk about her?"

Hannah shrugs. "Not much. My mother didn't like her mother. But she never said anything."

"What was she like? Your mother."

Hannah shrugs again, but this time purses her lips and shakes her head slightly, looking down into her cup.

"My mother didn't like anybody, I think. She never had any real friends. She would make friends with someone but then talk about her meanly, critically. Before long, the friend would disappear from her life. She brought men in occasionally. I always hoped one of them would stay, would be the one for us, for mother and me. They always seemed to be nice men. They tried hard, I think.

"I so much wanted someone there, someone to counterbalance my mother, someone to help me and lead me. My mother didn't let them succeed. One day the man would be gone, and my mother would throw out every trace of him, all the gifts he'd brought, all his leftover clothes. She seemed to get tired of everyone so quickly. She got tired of me eventually. I could sense this by the time I was ten.

"One day when I was fifteen, I just packed a bag. My mother stood there leaning against the wall and watched me. She smoked a half dozen cigarettes in the time it took me to pack. My mother smoked an immense amount. Abbie said it was the smoking that killed her. I don't smoke but not because it's unhealthy; I don't smoke because my mother did. Anyway, when I put on my coat, she gave me a little hug. There were tears on her face. But she never said a word. She had eyes like pebbles."

The two of them sit quietly for a minute. Stray walkers pass in the street outside the steamed windows.

"What were your parents like?" Hannah asks.

Lucas sips his coffee and clears his throat. "I lost my parents when I was young," he says, and smiles at her. "We lived in Germany at the time. In East Berlin, not too far from where you live, actually. Someone planted a bomb in their car when they went for a drive in the country one day. I was in school. I was ten years old."

Hannah breathes in deeply but says nothing. She just watches his face.

"I knew they had some enemies. My parents talked about it occasionally. I didn't know why they had enemies because they seemed nice and ordinary to me, like the other kids' parents. They were very cautious. I had to take special routes to school. My father always came and left by the back door of our building, that sort of thing. Then one day they were gone. I came home from school and I was alone in the world.

"I was put into a facility for a while, but then I was sent to live with my aunt and uncle in Arizona in the United States. They had moved there after the war. My mother's older sister and her husband. They were my only living relatives, and the GDR allowed them to come and get me."

Hannah smiles discreetly.

"What?" Lucas says.

"Nothing I was just thinking. We're both orphans."

Lucas nods. The observation hovers between them for a minute. A coffee grinder roars in the background.

"And you still don't know who killed your parents? Or why?"

This time, it's Lucas who shrugs. "My aunt and uncle apparently never seemed to want to know. When I moved back to Berlin, I made an attempt to look for information for a while.

"Nothing surfaced. A lot of time had passed, and Berlin had changed greatly. I was told that my parents, especially my mother, were Nazis. There are some records of their activities, some news stories. But that's all I know. Maybe that had something to do with it. The closest I came to learning something . . ." and at this Lucas stops. He sets down his cup.

Hannah still studies him. "What did you learn?" she asks softly in the café clank and chatter.

He composes himself for a minute, re-gathers his recollection. "I was talking to Mama one evening. Your grandmother. I had moved to Berlin not long before. We were at a social gathering, some sort of party. I had met Heike a few weeks earlier. She had introduced me to Mama. Mama had taken me in. She seemed to be sort of looking after me, and I needed looking after then. I had lost my wife not long previous."

Hannah nods. "Abbie told me about that." She whispers this.

"I thought you didn't know much about me."

"Abbie told me a few things. This was toward the end, when she was telling me to go to you for help."

Lucas continues. "That evening—this was more than a decade ago—I was telling Mama about my history in Berlin. I mentioned my parents. She got a strange look in her eye. Remember how she would turn her head to look at you with her one eye? She did that, but there was a difference. Her eye flared at me like a cornered animal's. Suddenly very tense.

"Then she said that she knew my parents. She didn't say she knew them; she said she knew *of* them. She said nothing else. That night she seemed to fall into one of her truly bad down periods. I didn't see her for several months afterward. I thought maybe she had just heard about my parents' demise back when it happened. Also, she was an archivist for the government, so I thought maybe she had run across them that way.

"I never asked her about it again. I was sort of afraid to. Afraid because of how she had behaved that night. And anyway, I'd decided after I'd been in Berlin for a while that I really didn't want to dig up my parents after all. Some things, some episodes, some transactions that formed us long ago are better left buried."

They sit for a while. Lucas consults his watch and then goes to the counter to order another coffee.

When he returns, Hannah says, "That's odd about your parents being Nazis. I stole your photos because I thought the people in the photos were Nazis. Leftover, underground Nazis still around in the seventies. Someone planted that idea in my head, one of Klaus' crazy friends, the night before I went to the gallery.

"I knew Abbie had given you the photos of the people, but when I saw them in the gallery, saw what you had done with them—light and airy and floating in modern spaces—I thought you were trying to make my grandmother look bad. Or maybe make fun of my grandmother. After all, you were the glamorous and powerful movie star. And I had no idea why you would have a photo of me among the others. I didn't know what you were up to. I was just afraid."

Lucas mulls through these comments in silence for a minute. "I don't think the people in the photos have anything to do with Nazis," he says. "I think they were just good, ordinary people."

Outside, scuffed-up snow lifts with sudden wind in the stony street. Weather closes in, darkening the midday. Lucas checks his watch once more. "If they cancel our flight home, we may have to take the bus all the way through Riga and Vilnius to Warsaw and then the train from there to Berlin. It will take forever. I've done that in the past. Lots of cows and forests."

He draws his phone from a coat pocket. He shakes his head sadly.

"It's almost dead again. And I think I left the cord in Berlin. I'm always doing that. I'm so bad about it."

Hannah says, "You can use mine. Although my plan is super-basic, so I'm not sure it will make calls here."

"We're a pair, aren't we?" Lucas says. This makes Hannah grin broadly.

Lucas stares at her face, at this momentary expression, her gleam of teeth, her sharp blue eyes under her intelligent forehead and febrile, detonating mass of blonde hair. To him, her face is, for a second, a one-off reflection of the face of the young woman in *ghost #5*, but somehow altered. Lucas evaluates the light, the tone, the angle, seeking the mechanical cause of the observable difference, an explanation rooted in settings and the passage of light through materials.

—————— **CHAPTER 29** ——————

They return to the parked rental car and then to the little house in the Lilleküla neighborhood. This time, a man comes to their knock at the polished front door. Like the woman, he is small and grey-haired. He wears a bent-knotted knit tie. The woman, still dressed in workout clothing, stands behind him.

"It's my older sister," the man says, looking at the photo. The group sits on a sofa in a front window of the house. The man has introduced himself as Carl Becker. They converse in German.

"Her name was Trudi. She was seven years older than I. I remember that raincoat. She wore it a lot when we lived in Berlin. I was just a boy. Trudi was in college. She committed suicide. I'd never seen this photo before last week. Maybe it was taken by her boyfriend. It's about the right age. She was in love when she was in college."

Carl sets the photo on his knee and removes his small, wire-rimmed glasses and wipes his left eye gently with a fingertip. He slowly replaces his glasses.

"I take it you mean East Berlin."

"Bergmannkiez. A little north of Tempelhof."

Lucas says, "Forgive me for prying, but for our project it's important to gather a few historical details. At the time of her death, do you know if she was targeted by the Stasi? Had she fallen into the disfavor of the government?"

Carl nods. "Trudi believed so. There was no way to prove it. My sister was a little unstable, but a person of profoundly strong beliefs. She spoke her mind, sometimes to strangers, which as you know could get a person into a lot of trouble. My mother said she broke under pressure because of her childhood. Our family had many problems. My father abused her when she was small. But I never believed that was the reason she died."

"You said you saw this photo last week. Did someone else show it to you?" Lucas asks.

"Yes. A blonde woman. She said her name was Andrea. She was very cryptic. She seemed nervous. She said that people were coming back from the dead. 'Don't worry. Your sister will visit again.' This she said to me before she left."

On their way to the airport in the rental car, Lucas and Hannah speak little. But at one point, Lucas utters quietly out of nowhere, "*We're free. We're free.*" Hannah turns and gazes at him.

"Biff Loman. *Death of a Salesman,*" Lucas explains. "I don't know why that just came to me. Something's afoot in here." He taps a finger on a temple.

Hannah turns her eyes back to the late-afternoon highway, the low-rise of misty black tree trunks scrabbling along the shore of the frozen lake.

"It can be terrible when things start to make sense," she says.

—— CHAPTER 30 ——

Due to storm-delayed flights followed by the long drive back into the city and the delivery of Hannah to her flat, he arrives home after midnight. When he arrives, Heike is in the bedroom. She is still awake, lying atop the comforter, arranged straight-legged and honest in that imposing, solid stance in which he first saw her in the Helmut Newton photos, a fallen statue.

Per habit, she is completely naked, save for her reading glasses. She was reading a book, but it has fallen at her side. The room is lit only by a small, green-shaded reading lamp, which casts undulating gleams and pockets of jade darkness down her long body, and a dim suffusion of light through the French doors from the square below.

Heike doesn't hear him come into the flat; she is not wearing her hearing aids. When she sees him enter the bedroom, she slowly reaches for a blanket and covers herself to the navel.

"It gets so hot in here. I can never seem to set the thermostat right."

He adjusts the thermostat and opens the French door a crack, admitting a slip of icy air and the ping and rumble of a late streetcar. He removes his clothes and lies beside her on his back. His body is hot and smells lightly of travel.

She turns and presses against him longitudinally, but stiff and with perhaps a touch of trepidation. Her upper leg does not drape over his. Her stomach remains tight and withdrawn and untouching. Her face is close against his shoulder, and tendrils of her hair slip gently across his skin. His chest bears the palm of her left hand. Her breathing softens the darkness.

After two minutes of silence in the shadowy and overheated room, she says, "We should talk."

He does not reply. But he reaches and places a hand on top of hers. This was a signal.

"I haven't been entirely forthcoming with you," she says. "Mama wasn't either."

This comment hovers, suspended in the quiet, for almost a minute. Then Lucas says, "I know."

He says it in English. He says it with an intonation devoid of chill or harshness. Like his hand on hers, it encourages.

So Heike relates to him two stories.

The first story she has known and kept to herself for twelve years. Prior to yesterday, only two or three people knew this story: Heike and Abbie, and perhaps Eloise. But yesterday Heike rehearsed it before the stranger she met in Stockholm. It was the story of the circumstances in which she and Lucas met.

Heike tells Lucas that she deceived him when she pretended that she didn't know who he was and had maintained the deception ever since, an accustomed costume, day by day as the episode slipped backward into memory. She describes how easy it was for her at the onset, for a woman adept at standing before cameras and faking passion, but how it had become very difficult.

She explains that Abbie had instructed her to meet Lucas. She describes her close-up view of the power Abbie had over people, her methods of manipulation, how she would grant a favor unasked and then request a favor in return, how she would plant ideas and then act as if the ideas were the recipient's, how she would balance chiding and praise and dismissiveness and attention, how she selectively shared secrets, how she always seemed to know what each person feared most.

Abbie was a master of manipulation, Heike says. She and Lucas had both been, at times, Abbie's subjects. Abbie wanted Heike to spy on Lucas, to learn what he knew, what he didn't know and was seeking.

She tells him how she scoured the TV program guide to find one of Lucas' movies, which used to be shown more frequently, and then had staged the evening, not long after they met, when the two of them stayed in to watch a film, how she had casually tuned to the channel with his movie and then how she pretended to be surprised to learn that he was the actor in the film.

She explains that she had been desperate to perform this episode, to get past pretending she didn't recognize him, even though Abbie had urged her to play her naïve role further.

They lie together in silence for a while.

"It was such a small thing. You could have told me," Lucas says.

"You were so honest with me. I was dishonest in return. I was like a willing Manchurian candidate. At this point, I don't know why, and it all seems so ugly and pointless."

Presently, he stands and walks to the French door and pulls it shut. He stands naked at the window for several minutes. Across the square, the giant poster of the downcast woman seems to float in the dimness above the streetlamps. The vertical streaks that had begun to descend her image two days earlier have deepened and darkened.

Lucas returns to the bed and lies again beside Heike. She again turns and presses against him, and he again places his hand on hers.

Then Heike tells him the story she had learned from Eloise the day before about Abbie Ingvall. She explains that she had just learned the real reason Abbie had assigned Heike to meet Lucas—that Abbie thought Lucas knew what Abbie had done.

Abbie thought that Lucas had come to Berlin to seek revenge. Abbie thought Lucas knew all along that Abbie had ordered the killing of his parents.

When Heike had finished, each of these two people lies on the bed in agony for a time. Agony is perhaps most acutely felt when the people feeling it are naked.

They lie on the hot, damp comforter, apart but locked together, sharing their nakedness, their pain, their disillusion, their distrust, their discouragement. They share this banquet of misery in silence.

"I'm sorry," Heike says eventually.

He reaches and touches her. "Yours are small offenses," Lucas says. "A lot of things are coming into focus for me now. It's as if Berlin is suddenly lit from within."

Side by side, they each consider the architecture of their own privations and complaints against existence. They review their own crimes. Perhaps they consider the nature of retribution, and what Nik might have called karma.

Eventually Heike adds an afterthought, one she had been unable to dismiss.

"Lucas, you didn't sleep with that girl, did you?"

She imbues this with a touch of levity, but as if casting about for material out of which to form a joke and finding only curtains of fear.

Lucas says, "Of course not."

A long minute later, Heike says, "I know." She shades this phrase the same way Lucas said it a half hour earlier.

But then, Lucas turned toward her, and this time takes her body in his hands and pulls her to him. She melts along the entire length of him. They are each perhaps surprised to find the other ready. But clifflike emotions can be indistinct and blend into odd conclusions about what the body needs and wants.

Heike gives a small, soft cry in the darkness. Lucas slides over her and she wraps him and urges him with her waist, her stomach, her long-fingered hands. Their fingers interlace and grip, a common motif for them. The room is still hot despite the brief ventilation it had received from the opening of the doors, and they glow.

When they finish, her gaze indicates that this time wasn't how it usually is for them; something old revisited on a wave of change and regret. Her skin shines, as does his. Two people both at or near six decades into life—in the final third—but lean and limber and smooth-skinned and supple, as confused as teenagers.

There is nothing to say now. They lie together and listen to the distant, occasional rumble of trams in the street. The pain and disillusion may have persisted, but it mingles now with a tiny illumination of purpose—an image beginning to appear and purify as if by magic as it develops in its bath. This purpose allows Lucas sparse rest through the small hours.

CHAPTER 31

Lucas leaves his building on Rosenthalerplatz in the morning, after Heike has left for her studio. In a long, black overcoat, green knit cap and scarf and black leather gloves, he walks through the vast, sepulchral city.

In Unter den Linden, a huge, outraged demonstration marches slowly west toward Brandenburger Tor. Many thousands of people glut the streets and Pariser Platz at the foot of Brandenburg Gate under the quadriga of four horsemen. Police in riot gear lounge against parked, black, windowless vans, watching.

Deep and rhythmic chants swell episodically among the crowds, rising in tone as people pick up on the words and synchronize their voices. Drums beat. Wet, cold air under a low cloud layer contains the sounds close to the ground, present and personal, dull and thunderous.

Lucas encounters this march accidentally by approaching the boulevard from Luisenstraße, from the north.

It is as if all of Berlin lies before him, all seething time and place, its knotted history and perpetual dissatisfaction and regret. Not revolution—guilt. The mass of melancholy, startled, placard-bearing humanity is Berlin: unsettled city of the dead and the dreaming.

In an effort to avoid anyone recognizing him, taking photographs and pressing him for his views about the demonstration, he diverts quickly away from the mass protest, cutting crosstown to navigate the Tiergarten.

As he walks, he pulls from a pocket of his coat the business card given to him by the blond woman who called herself Andrea when she joined the group for dinner a few nights earlier. The full name on the card is Andrea Hofstadter. She had said she worked for a large accounting firm, but the card is the sort privately printed, with a generic emblem and only a phone number. Lucas dials the number as he walks.

"Hello?"

"Hello. Is this Andrea?" he says in English.

A long pause follows. Lucas continues to walk. His feet crunch gravelly old snow as he crosses a curbstone.

"Yes. Who is this?"

"This is Lucas Block. Do you remember meeting me last Thursday evening at Denver Gallery? We went to dinner afterward."

"Certainly."

"I think it's time for us to talk. Don't you?"

Another long pause ensues. Then she says, "I do."

"Can you meet me tomorrow afternoon?"

"I can."

CHAPTER 32

Lucas then crosses Landwehr Canal and meanders along Böcklerpark and past Markthalle Neun and eventually Nikolaikirche. A few tourists hunch through the square toward the statue of St. George near the river. The vacant shops glow with hope.

Berlin wraps long, chilling fingers around a person walking its streets. The walker transects patches of exuberant noise and patches of quiet, muffled and dimmed like oblivion. The light everywhere can seem to reflect from no definite urfaces and to take on hues of a past which may only provisionally have occurred.

A pedestrian in this city can feel weighted, grasped, slowed, as if a million teeming and indiscernible souls adjoin and anchor. Destinations waver. Walking in Berlin can seem an endeavor to reach somewhere that does not exist.

At least, these are Lucas' perpetual impressions as he moves about, an inveterate early-morning and late-night walker of this old and new city's streets and squares, riverside paths and park trails. On this winter day, in the leftover and frayed cold of a grey-shouldered stormfront passed and depleted, he walks head down and hands in overcoat pockets. The sense that his destination may not survive the duration of his travels is heavy freight upon him.

He circles back to the neighborhood in which he lived as a boy, south of Boxhagener Platz. Now, it is an area thick with nightlife and clubs: Berghain, Raw-Gelände, Matrix, Suicide Circus. Lucas has seldom ventured here, though Nik is a frequent visitor.

A few residential streets, once socialist and uniform but now color-blocked stacks of flats, with brass nameplates by doors and Volvos in parking slots, radiate eastward. Lucas soon stands on the street, Oderstraße, across from the home where his family lived when his parents died. Bracketing him, leafless elms reach from circular sidewalk grates among tuffets of ice. He stands by a wrought-iron fence mounted on a low stone wall, hands still in pockets, and looks upward to the higher windows of the building, his former room on the left, overlooking a slim park. A yellow paper cutout of an animal, perhaps a cat, hangs against the glass inside the window.

***

People came to him here, strangers and a few
figures recognized from his parents' circle.
They crowded around him. They smelt of wet,
smoky wool clothing—a smell never forgotten.
They tried to explain. They blunted their terms.
The car. The explosion. His parents would not
have felt anything, he was told. His parents were
in a happy, peaceful place now, a woman stated
earnestly. Faces strained into elongated masks of
reassurance; he is cajoled to pack his little suitcase
and to follow the people in uniforms. Everything,
to him, disguised. Hands on his shoulders, steering.

The odor of the last meal he ate in the little sunflower-tiled kitchen lingering as he passed through: potatoes with bits of ham and mushrooms fried in butter.

***

All of this swirls suddenly around him again on this granite sidewalk by the distantly familiar iron fence. He remembers tracing his fingers along the rough curves and angles of the fence. He remembers individual paving blocks. He has not been in this exact place in a half-century. Memories avoided but suddenly unearthed render him weightless. He looks down to his feet on the ice. He looks around. Toward an entrance in the wall surrounding the little park, a woman leads a slender grey dog. The dog pauses its purposive stride to gaze at Lucas until the woman tugs it forward.

A few minutes earlier, walking to this street, Lucas had felt heavily burdened. Now he cannot touch the ground. Strung between these opposing sensations is the equivalent of waking from a disorienting dream.

—— CHAPTER 33 ——

Lucas walks a kilometer southeast to Karlshorst and to the home of Eloise Lawrens, the partner of Abbie Ingvall. He rings the bell at the building's entry. She buzzes him in, opens her door for him and hugs him gently. The side of her face, the sharp corner of her glasses, presses against his chest for a long moment. She smells, to him, of age. He has seldom hugged her before.

They sit on a sofa and an armchair facing each other in the small flat. Books fill the room. Leaning shelves lining two walls have long overflowed; stacks of books tower and slope everywhere, closing in on pathways between the furniture. A scent of dust and aged, crumbling paper pervades. Two cats curl in a window in a scant limb of sunshine.

Lucas removes and pockets his sunglasses. Eloise leans forward toward him. An elaborate black clip bridles her silver hair. With large, reddish hands, she pulls her argyle cardigan tighter around her ample torso, her pendulous form balanced in the chair's deep seat. Thick lenses in black frames enlarge her pale blue eyes in her round face. She wears an ankle-length knit skirt of black wool. Her feet in grey socks and old leather MaryJane's rest on a ribbed and gritty knotted rug between them; her feet are small below trunk-like ankles.

"Thank you for calling me," she says. "Thank you for coming here."

Lucas says, "I wish the circumstances were happier."

"I'm sorry," Eloise says. Her voice is papery. "She told me never to say anything about it. She said it was for the best. I believed her and did what she said."

Lucas nods slowly. "Everyone seems to know what's best for me."

"I'm sorry," Eloise says.

They sit together for a while in silence. From a nearby flat, music plays. It is baroque church music.

"Twenty years," Lucas says. "That's a long time, isn't it? Twenty years she kept that little nugget of information from me. I suppose I can see why she would. But everyone around me was keeping their mouths shut, too."

"Heike never knew anything about that part of it," Eloise says. "The before part. What Abbie had done in the past. Only Abbie and I knew. It happened during a very bad time for Abbie."

"Rather a bad time for my parents, also."

"Abbie's hands were tied. She had to do it. She had orders. The pressures were unbearable then. People did things they would never have dreamed of doing at other times. Things they only remember as nightmares afterward. Everyone was complicit."

"Not everyone, Eloise. You know that."

The woman's face slowly sinks. They sit in silence, as if awaiting a signal. Both of them start to speak again at once.

"We all were taught not to trust anyone . . ."

"All I ever wanted was to escape the past and start over . . ."

They pause. Lucas finishes his sentence.

". . . but the past seems to keep re-opening itself."

Eloise nods. "That it does," she says.

A flutter of wings sounds at the window and they both turn. A bird has landed on the narrow ledge and rests for a moment. Its tiny breath makes a spot of mist on the glass. Then it vanishes.

"Tell me what you know about how it happened" Lucas says.

Eloise draws a long breath. She twists a silver filigreed ring on her finger. She looks down at it, and then up at Lucas. She smiles slightly.

"Abbie gave me this ring," she says. "At one point we wanted to get married, you know." She slides the ring from her finger and lays it gently on a round end-table within the circle of light at the base of a copper-shaded lamp. She draws another slow breath and sighs this time. The air is dense with learned secrets and shadows and old heat.

"Abbie rose very high in the Stasi. She was fourth in command in Lichtenberg toward the end. They pulled her in after the Red Brigades fell apart. She walked eastward through Charlie carrying her old suitcase—you know the one, the ancient leather one she brought from Finland when she first came to Germany—and up to the Stasi offices and introduced herself. She did things like that, you know."

Eloise sits up straighter in her chair and draws in her sweater again.

"It goes back to her earliest years. Since she was a college girl in Helsinki, she had always been fierce of heart. An idealist, a communist at the deepest, deepest level. That's why she studied history, that endless search for cracks in the walls of capitalism. And that's why she moved to Berlin in 1970, eight years after she graduated. She never found many like-minded people in Finland, of course.

"But Berlin was another matter. Here, she promptly fell in with people connected to Baader-Meinhoff. She finagled. It took a couple of years, but she was part of the second wave. They trusted her and looked up to her. She was older than most of them, and frankly smarter. They called her Mama, you know, although I think that nickname goes way back to Finland.

"You remember how awful that gang of monsters could be. Robberies. Kidnappings. Even murders. I think she was intoxicated by all of it, the power, the dream of overthrowing everything, of starting a new civilization. It was a crazy time. The IRA in Belfast. The Basques in San Sebastian. Abbie and her friends wanted to change the world. They were all so excited, hypnotized by the prospect of a dream that was doomed from the beginning.

"Before long, Abbie became pregnant. The man's name was Müller. I never learned his first name; Abbie never mentioned it. She gave up the girl for adoption. Her daughter was the mother of the girl Hannah, whom I know you've met.

"After what they used to call German Autumn in, I think, 1977, Abbie fled to the east. She changed her name a couple of times. She maneuvered on forged documents. The Stasi drew her in. They'd been watching her. They saw her power. Capacity. Willingness. They took her on, as Baader-Meinhoff had done previously.

"She excelled. I loved her . . ." and at this Eloise stops talking for a full minute and looks with unseeing eyes back toward the window where the bird had visited. ". . . but I did not love what she did at that time, in the life she lived before I met her," she then continues, glancing back to Lucas.

"I met her after the collapse in 1989, after she had escaped a second time and melted back into society, again on forged papers to keep people from knowing who she was, that she was the same person who had assassinated people for the Stasi. Abbie Ingvall was the third or fourth name she had in her life. The only identity she had that stuck throughout was Mama."

Eloise rises and shuffles heavily into the kitchen. Lucas waits quietly. After some clanking and the hum of a microwave, she returns with two cups of instant coffee. They sit stirring their coffee for a few minutes.

"She changed, you know. After the fall of the communists, she transformed. She became a different person. It was as if there was a new creature inside a shell, a bird struggling to get out. A creature who protected and loved and nurtured. She was a complex human being.

"I think she lived two full lives, one after the other. The first life ended when the wall fell and she was burned in the fire. It was after she changed that I met her, of course, not long before you came to Berlin. We had fallen in love. I only saw the warm, positive side of her. I could hardly believe the stories she whispered to me about her earlier life.

"Then you showed up. For a long time, Abbie was very afraid. She thought you were here to find her. So eventually she sought you out. She was like that, you know. She kept her enemies close. She used Heike for that. Heike was almost as much a victim as you were. I felt bad for Heike. So young and broken and hopeful and beautiful. She didn't know why Abbie wanted you traced, but Heike would have done anything for Abbie then."

"Tell me what you know about how it happened."

"You mean your parents?"

Lucas nods.

"Lucas, do you really want to talk about that?"

"In one of the first conversations we ever had, Eloise, I told you that the reason I came to Berlin was to find out what happened to my parents."

"I guess we can't leave the dead buried."

"It's not we who unbury the dead. They exhume themselves. All of our history," he makes a sweeping gesture to the city or the world, "is an accumulation. It's not a library where we can just shelve the old books and forget about them. The library is alive. The old books—the old bones—dance among us."

Eloise says, "I don't know much. Abbie described it to me a few times, but never in detail. She was so ashamed of her former self. She died a little inside almost every day. This was after you had come to Berlin.

"There were articles in the magazines, chatter on the talk shows. You were an East German boy who had been taken to America, became a movie star, went to prison and then returned to our convulsive city. You were extravagantly interesting, for a while.

"The stories talked about the tragedy of your parents. I remembered hearing about their murder at the time. But then one night Abbie told me she had a connection to you. As a Stasi leader, she had targeted your parents for elimination. Your mother was part of an insurgency against the Stasi. Your mother pretended to be aligned with them, but she fooled them. She behaved as if the Stasi's control techniques, of which Abbie was the master, had worked on her.

"Your mother was a double agent, of sorts. She stole money that the Stasi was trying to funnel to certain groups in the west, neo-Nazi groups. It was all part of a scheme, a disruption, fomenting enemies of enemies. Your mother disrupted the disruption. She gave the Stasi's money to West German charities.

"So, they killed her. Abbie pulled the trigger. She didn't set the bomb—she never came out of the shadows. She just gave the order. The Stasi didn't kill that many people directly, you know. They ground people down and let them kill each other, and themselves. But your mother really got under their skin."

"All I've ever been able to find about my parents are some old newspaper articles. All other trace of them seems to have been erased. That was probably the Stasi's doing, also."

"I would be sure. Abbie was very good at her job. She tended to details."

Lucas says, "One thing I always wanted to know is whether my parents were Nazis. My uncle and aunt seemed to think maybe they were. But they were unclear. They had left Germany well before the war."

Eloise says, "Your aunt and uncle knew a lot more than they told you. From what Abbie said, your parents were not Nazis. That was a pose intended to throw the Stasi into turmoil, confuse them. Sonia and Rupert—especially your mother, Sonia—were almost as good at messing with people's minds as Abbie was."

Lucas sips his coffee and sets the cup on a low table. "Thank you for telling me all of this now," he says to Eloise. "I wish . . ." he starts but does not complete the sentence. Eloise nods. She seems to understand the wish.

"How did Abbie get burned?" Lucas eventually asks. "She never seemed willing to tell me. Perhaps now I can be allowed into the circle."

"You're still angry. You have a right to be. I'm sorry." Eloise says it first in German, *Es tut mir Leid,* and then repeats it in English softly.

Lucas clasps his hands in his lap and studies them and then unclasps them. He looks up at Eloise. "Angry. No. Maybe hopeful," he says. "My life has been a fog imposed by others. I hope the lens will clear."

Eloise says, "You were in America at the time, but I know you were paying close attention. It was fall, 1990. News was coming in so fast. The Soviet Union was collapsing. Erich Mielke resigned. Then the Wall fell. People started occupying government offices all over the country. The Peaceful Revolution, it was called. We were all so excited."

Eloise stops and straightens her sweater. She sips her tepid coffee.

"We learned over the next few weeks that the Stasi were destroying the records. They were shredding and burning them. All the information they had gathered on everyone over the years. The history of our society. At least the recent history of it. All going up in smoke. So, people stormed the Stasi headquarters.

"That was the second week of January in 1990. I didn't go that night—I wasn't as fervent about all of it as a lot of my friends. I went down to watch the Wall coming apart, things like that. But I was afraid of the nighttime protests, the violence.

"About two years after that night, I met a woman at a photography exhibit. She was small and had terrible burn scars across her face, only one working eye. She wore hats to hide a missing ear. But I found her enchanting and intriguing all the same. Smart, wry, deep, mysterious.

"It wasn't until much later that she told me that the day before the storming of the Stasi headquarters, she was burned trying to prevent her Stasi colleagues from dumping boxes of files on a bonfire in the courtyard of the complex on Normannenstraße. She was struggling to save some of the material she had been partially responsible for gathering. Material that would have incriminated her. She slipped and fell, or tripped, or maybe was pushed, into the flames.

"She hoped, I think, to have the truth become known. She intended to expose herself to the world. She was already then trying to emerge from the darkness in which she had spent her entire adult life. That night, the fire, the agony, completed the cleansing of her soul, though not her past.

"The Abbie I fell in love with, the Abbie you knew, and I think also loved—I think that Abbie was born that night. I know she loved me, and eventually you, as she had never loved anyone before."

Lucas stands and puts on his coat.

"I need to leave. I need to walk some more. I need to think."

"Lucas, please don't hate her. She did her best, after she realized how far she had fallen. That's all any of us can do. We all keep trying to atone."

"She was a brilliant woman," Lucas says. "She didn't consider that killing my parents and then lying to me about it for twenty years was wrong? That it hurt me? You didn't realize that contracting Heike to spy on me and then hiding that from me for twenty years was wrong? Atone? I went willingly to prison to atone. You all don't know the meaning of the word."

"We all keep trying."

He opens the door.

She calls to him, "Lucas."

He has stepped into the hallway, but he pauses when she says his name.

"At the Bibliotek, in the office where Abbie was working in the Archives, there's something saved for you. You should retrieve it."

CHAPTER 34

At the Staatsbibliotek zu Berlin, a young woman says to Lucas, "We're all so sorry about Abbie."

She leans toward him and touches his arm. She is tall and fragile-looking, thread-slender. A black clasp holds back her long, blonde hair. Her glasses are tortoiseshell. Her lipstick is wide and dark, as are the tattoos down her neck into the low collar of her blouse.

The two of them stand at the end of a long, wooden counter.

"We called her Mama. Did you know that was her nickname? When I first heard that, I thought it might be insulting, but I think she liked it. That's what everyone around here called her."

The woman describes herself as a graduate assistant. While working on her doctorate, she assisted Abbie in the Archives division of the library. Eloise had provided her name. Lucas asked for her when he arrived. It is Wednesday, the day after Lucas spoke with Eloise.

"She left a suitcase for you. An old suitcase?" the woman says. She phrases it like a question. As she talks to Lucas, she becomes increasingly excited and bouncy. "It has your name on it.

Mama brought it here before she died. I know because I saw her carrying it when she came to work, and asked her what it was, but she didn't reply. Later, after we heard the news, I saw the suitcase by her desk. Eloise called yesterday and told me to give it to you. I'll go get it."

She returns after a few minutes with a scuffed and worn leather suitcase. A paper tag is tied to the handle: *LUCAS BLOCK*, in Abbie Ingvall's printing.

The suitcase is small and light; inside, a few items shift about.

Lucas carries the suitcase down a curving hallway, heading toward the public reading rooms. He passes an open door leading into an empty and mostly dark auditorium with a low stage. Nothing prohibits him from entering, so he descends a sloping aisle and takes a seat in the first row. Dim illumination from exit signs glows among the seats. His kneecaps are inches from the stage. He looks to the stage for a moment, then glances around at what the view must be from the footlights. A line from *Death of a Salesman* comes to him and he whispers it: *The jungle is dark, but full of diamonds.*

From the hallway, a few disembodied voices pass, but the auditorium is quiet. He sets the suitcase on the carpeted edge of the low stage in front of him, gently, like placing a coffin on a bier. He clicks open the old brass latches and slowly raises the antique lid.

On the top of a small pile of items is a photo, which Lucas lifts and studies in the room's dim light. It is a print of the original photo he used to compose *ghost #5*. In the photo, a girl dressed in striped bellbottoms and a tight sweater and big, buckled shoes stands on her tiptoes, arms upraised, on a cobbled street which slopes upward away behind her. She is light-haired. She floats. She is weightless and brightly illuminated. The girl looks for all the world like the girl Hannah, as Lucas and Hannah herself and the rest of them had assumed all along. But Lucas holds a thumb over half of the face of the girl in the photo. Only a fragment of the face remains. He looks into her one bright eye.

"Mama," he says.

From behind his thumb, the half-face of the woman who came to be known as Abbie Ingvall, Hannah's grandmother, peeks out at Lucas and the world again, taken when Abbie was just a teenage girl, in some brighter time in some brighter city long before.

Lucas slowly rotates the photo. He holds it at arms' length to focus his aging eyes. On the back, in Abbie's tight script, is written: *Für Hannah mit all meiner liebe. Ich versuchte.* For Hannah with all my love. I tried.

Lucas sets the photo on the edge of the low stage in front of him. Lucas lifts the next photo, a larger print. He sits for a long time. He sets the photo on the stage and wipes his eyes with his sleeves. He picks the photo up again.

"Hello, Mom. Hello, Dad," he whispers.

In the photo, a couple in wedding clothes stand on the threshold of a church. The doorway of the church is open but dark. The man's arm is around the woman's waist. She holds her long, lacy dress off the cobbles with her free hand. The couple, having stepped down on the stones of the street, is slightly lower than a blurred, smiling group of people waiting behind them, in the obscure doorway, pausing for the photographer to snap the shutter, to capture the joyful pair, frozen in tableau.

On the reverse of the photo, in Abbie's handwriting: *Vergib mir.* Forgive me.

Lucas places the two photos he has examined back into the suitcase and lowers the lid. Both hands on the suitcase, he tenses as if to stand, as if his strength for this enterprise has dissolved. But after a long moment, he slides back into the seat. He breathes deeply and with deliberation. He opens the lid again. He lifts the two photos he has already examined and sets them on the edge of the stage. He reaches into the suitcase.

He removes a pair of eyeglasses. They are narrow and steel-framed reading glasses. He opens them and slips them onto his face, a perfect fit, as recognizable as a favorite pair of shoes which mysteriously vanished many years before and then suddenly, for no apparent reason, is re-found. He lifts a hand and studies the skin on the back of it through the reading glasses, the seams and sinews, the knuckles. He shakes his head.

Wearing the reading glasses, he picks up the two photos from the edge of the stage and studies them again, this time holding them closer.

Next is a snapshot of Nik. It is black and white. Nik sits at a café table, slouched back in his chair; on the round marble top, a magazine and coffee cup. Morning sunlight slants across. Nik offers the photographer a wry smirk. He has just taken off a pair of sunglasses. The photo is several years old, when Nik's hair was still salt and pepper. He wears a tuxedo. His tie is undone and his shirt-collar open. Fatigue pulls at his features, but gentle amusement lifts them. His gives the appearance of having been out all night, which, statistically, was likely the case.

Lucas' best friend. The man Lucas trusts most. The elegant comrade-in-arms since college.

On the back of the photo, another of Abbie's inscriptions: *Was weiß er? Was verbirgt er?* What does he know? What does he hide?

A photo of Frankie is next in the small stack. She sits on a couch holding a frosted martini glass. The couch is the one Lucas sat on the day before in Eloise's flat. Frankie wears a white coat, tight and slick. Around her neck, she wears a bristling choker of silver with darts of crystal. Her earrings match. Her face is melancholy, though she, like Nik in his photo, smiles at the camera. It is a beautiful woman's automatic smile of habit. It is unaccompanied by warmth in the eyes. She reclines slightly from the camera, perhaps from whatever is happening in the room.

Lucas pushes the reading glasses tighter onto the bridge of his nose. Frankie's face. So familiar. He's looked closely into her eyes a thousand times. So close. So frigid.

On the back, the same inscription as on the photo of Nik, but with feminine pronouns.

In a corner of the suitcase, a bright object blinks as Lucas tilts it to capture some of the auditorium's dim light. It is a silver ring. Lucas examines the ring. It matches the ring that Eloise removed from her finger the night before, when she and Lucas sat to talk. A piece of tape attached to the ring affixes a small note: *Sag ihr Eloise dass es mir leid tut. Sie hatte die ganze Zeit Recht.* Tell Eloise I'm sorry. She was right all along.

A few photos remain. The next that Lucas lifts and views is a photo of Heike with Lucas. The photo vibrates in his fingers. It generates waves of vivid recollections: the occasion, a birthday party at Heike's flat; the clothing they wore, the shoes; the smells and sounds of the evening, the remarkable or banal things people said, the laughter; Abbie taking the photo, looking at them through the viewfinder of her big Nikon, her face just a camera with a rounded hat on top. In the photo, Heike is laughing. Lucas looks pleased, as if it was he who made Heike laugh. They hold one another, each with both arms.

With trepidation, he turns the photo over. But there is no inscription, no clue.

But the next item causes Lucas to lean forward in his auditorium seat and then back again. He shivers.

"I was afraid of this," he whispers. The room has good acoustics, and his whisper moves through it. He looks around momentarily and then back to the item. "Why are you doing this to me?" he says, this time even more softly.

The artifact he has unfolded is a clipping from a magazine, a German lifestyle magazine from decades ago, *Der Spiegel* or *Stern* or *Bunte*. Its age is evident from the quality of the paper and the advertisement on the back of the large clipping.

He holds a photo of his wife, Katherine. She stands barefooted on a boat dock somewhere, wearing a pearly skin-tight dress which seems to lift in a vague breeze, along with the tails of her long, dark hair. Her arms are lank and relaxed at her sides. She is slightly turned, as she always preferred to stand for photographers.

The cutline states that Katherine Bridger, noted American actress and wife of award-winning German-American actor Lucas Block, would be attending the Berlinale that February.

She was promoting a just-released film with the production's German director. The film had been nominated for awards.

Lucas came with her on that trip. They stayed at the Adlon. Cameras flashed at them everywhere they went. Lucas had won an Academy Award the year prior. The world was a gentle haze, and smelled like quinine and fresh lime. At that time, Lucas would finish a fifth of gin by noon and a second by dinner. After dinner, he would drink in earnest. Always the best English gins.

The photo in the clipping is a publicity still, presumably provided to the magazine by Katherine's agency. Lucas could not remember. He squints for courage. He lifts the clipping toward the dim light from one of the room's exit signs. He observes his wife.

With the thinness of the magazine paper, an image shows through behind Katherine. The image is from an advertisement for Morgen cheeses, with a back-screened illustration of an eagle in flight, the logo of the company. The wings of the bird show through the frail paper. Standing on the dock in her party dress and bare feet, double-exposed like Lucas' *ghost* photo composites, floating and be-winged, Katherine appears to take flight.

In the suitcase is a man's wallet. It once held much, apparent from the rounded stretch of its waist. But now it contains only a single item, a snapshot in a yellowed window slot of the wallet. The photo is of three girls standing between two adults. The five of them face south into the sun on timbered fishing docks, recognizably the waterfront in Helsinki with unmistakable, narrow-shouldered Uspenki Katedral on the hill in the background.

Though the photo was clearly six decades old, the face of the girl in the middle bears every resemblance to Hannah—same posture, same features, same stare. She wears the same grey clothing as the girl in *ghost #5*. On the back of the photo, in dim script: *Das war ich.* This was me.

Lucas tilts the suitcase toward him. Only two items remain. He lifts one of them. It is a photo strapped with a rubber band around a tube-like brass and glass object. Lucas removes the rubber band. The tube-like item is a jeweler's loupe. The photo is a snapshot of him.

The photo was taken from a distance with, Lucas can tell, a long lens. Lucas sits alone at a café table. It is sunny. He wears Ray-Bans. His mouth is serious. He is in profile since he looks up the street or across the plaza, maybe in Berlin, though he could be anywhere in Europe, apparently unaware of the photographer, not posing. His age in the photo he can discern from the way he wore his hair and the cut of his slacks. This shot was taken at least two decades ago.

In the photo, a folded newspaper dangles from his hand. He had just been reading this newspaper when the photo was taken.

Lucas draws a breath, realizing. He removes the reading glasses and instead sights the photo through the loupe.

The headline of the article showing on the newspaper comes clear: *Ausgraben die Stasi.* Excavating the Stasi.

Only a single item now remains in the suitcase. Lucas picks it up with his fingernails. It is a key. It bears no markings or indications of any sort. It is an ordinary door key. Lucas re-examines the suitcase, but nothing remains.

Lucas takes the small pile of things from the edge of the stage, all but the key, and places them back in the suitcase. He closes and latches the lid. He stands and slips back into the aisle with the suitcase in one hand, a hunch-shouldered traveler in an antique land.

The key he slips into a pocket of his jeans.

CHAPTER 35

In the morning, as he makes his coffee, Lucas' phone rings.

"Block," he says into the phone, German-style.

Frankie says, "Lucas."

"Hi."

"Lucas," she repeats.

"Are you okay?"

A long pause follows. He hears her breathing. To him, the pause is recognizable. She is gathering herself.

"I need to talk to you. I have to tell you something," she says. "It's important. Not like anything I've ever told you before. Important."

"Okay."

"Not on the phone. I want to be with you."

"Okay."

"Where are you?"

"At home, Frankie. It's eight in the morning. Are you okay?"

"Are you alone?"

"Heike already left."

"Can I come over?"

"I'm in my bathrobe."

"No matter. Can I come over? Lucas, I'm sorry to be like

this. It takes a lot for me to get up the courage to talk about difficult things. You know that about me. I happen to have the courage right now. I woke up with the courage this morning. It's been decades since I had any courage."

"You can come over whenever you want. I'll be here. I'll put on some clothes. Have you had breakfast?"

"I don't eat breakfast."

"I'll cut up some fruit," Lucas says. "Frankie."

"Yes?"

"I don't know what you want to tell me, but I had a feeling you would be telling me something before long. Ever since Mama died, windows have been opening everywhere. It's as if old things are suddenly bathed in new light. I've always had a sense that I had more to learn from you. About you. Please come and talk to me. You can tell me anything. We'll be okay."

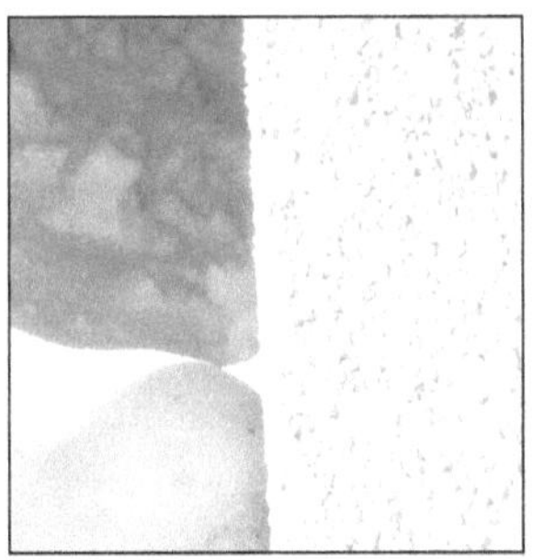

CHAPTER 36

In the early afternoon, Lucas' phone, lying on the table in his darkroom, rings. Lucas sets down the strip of negatives he is drying.

"Block, Guten Tag," Lucas says into the phone.

"Lucas, it's Nik."

"Hey."

"Can we get together?"

"Sure. When."

"I need to talk to you."

"Okay."

"Right now?"

"Okay. Where do you want to meet?"

"I don't know. Somewhere I can have a drink. A whole bottle of them."

"It's the middle of the day. You can come over here, but you'll have to bring your own bottle."

"I want to talk to you in private, but somewhere public. I need the presence of people. I want to hear voices and music."

"How about that bar up near Immanuelkirche? The one where we used to hang out sometimes years ago. I think it's still there."

Nik says. "Good. I have fond memories of that place. I would like to be somewhere we have happy memories but don't know anybody."

Lucas says, "Nik, Frankie came over for a while this morning and we talked. About old times. She had some very fascinating history to fill in for me, to bring me up to speed. I'd like to share that with you, too. You may find it interesting. She told me a secret she's been keeping since 1984."

"She did?"

"Were you going to tell me the same secret?"

"No. But I think I know the secret Frankie told you."

"Yes, she said you did."

"I have a different secret," Nik says. "A bigger one. Bigger and much more terrible. I'm trying to make whole again something I broke. Broke and then hid."

Lucas considers this for a moment, then says, "Mending is all we can hope for, isn't it? And nothing can be mended unless it was first broken. Torn apart, even."

Nik says, "Often, in the hope that sustains survival, we think we're through with the past, but it's never through with us."

CHAPTER 37

That evening, Lucas and Andrea meet under the bombed and destroyed Kaiser Wilhelm Church on the Ku'Damm side. In bleary winter sunset, the broken-tooth spire of the church casts its last craggy shadow of the day across the sidewalk and adjoining Budapester Straße. Traffic roars on the boulevards around them.

They cross to the north side of the church. Lucas looks around vaguely for somewhere to sit, a bench or raised planter. Instead, they stand, one on each side, of a jagged bronze fracture inset into the pavement near the names of people carved into the steps of the church, a memorial to terrorist attack victims at the Christmas market there. Haphazard groups of burned-out candles in little glass cups scatter near the carved names among stray, desiccated flowers.

They stand in a slice of late sunlight coming between the drum of the new church and the old, broken bell tower. They face each other.

Andrea wears a heavy tweed coat, light brown, with darker leather on the shoulders. Her scarf is thick, deep blue and wrapped tightly. On her head, she wears a matching blue beret pulled down over one ear. Her face, between the dense wrap of her scarf and her hat, is white. Her eye makeup is shadowy. Her blonde hair wavers in the indistinct wind.

Whereas the last time Lucas saw her, at dinner in the Italian restaurant after the gallery opening, she affected a demure and admiring expression, her face now is a galvanized mask with two slots through which her blue eyes glitter at him unblinking.

They must raise their voices. The noise of the evening rush hour from Kurfürstendamm and Breitscheid Platz rattles the air.

"Please tell me what's going on," Lucas says.

"I came to Berlin to find you," Andrea says. "I found more."

She looks down to her brown leather purse. She opens its zipper and reaches inside. When she looks up to him again, it is as if Lucas is looking into a mirror at his own face, for instance, when he looks up from the sink after shaving. The blue eyes, the cheekbones.

Andrea holds out a thin leather portfolio, half-sheet sized, closed with a snap.

"Here are your ghosts," she says.

Lucas takes the portfolio. He glances down at it and then back at her. Then he looks at the portfolio again and undoes its snap. Inside nest three sheets of paper clipped together and folded in half lengthwise. The paper is haggard with age and handling. He opens them.

A letterhead in discreet blue runs across the top: *Staatssicherheitsdienst Lichtenberg.*

Below, a typed heading leads the page: *Abbie Ingvall: Erfolgreiche Vorsätze.* Successful Resolutions.

Below that, a numbered list of names, in some cases pairs of names, runs onto the third page. Lucas flips slowly to the end of the list: 114 entries.

He returns to the first page and scans again, this time more slowly, running a finger down the list. His finger stops at the name Rainer Weiss. Lucas looks up at Andrea. She is watching him. Her expression is inscrutable save for an air about her eyes of witnessing an execution.

Rainer Weiss is familiar to Lucas. Nik met the daughter of this man in Edinburgh.

Lower on the list, he sees the name Gertrud Becker. The man that Hannah and Lucas met in Tallinn was named Carl Becker. His sister was named Trudi.

Lucas continues scanning. He spots Marie Kiel, the aunt of the woman Frankie met in Zermatt. A few names below that appears Gunther Goldschmidt, the father of the man Heike met in Stockholm.

Just before Lucas re-folds the papers, he sees a pair of names toward the bottom in position number 110: Sonia and Rupert Bloch. Bloch is spelled the way Lucas spelled his own name, the way his parents Sonia and Rupert spelled it, the way his family had spelled it for centuries, before he changed it to Block based on advice from his first theatrical agent.

Lucas closes the portfolio. He clears his throat.

"The existence of this list doesn't surprise me," he says to Andrea. "But where did you get it?"

"I took it from her."

"Who?"

"Your collaborator. Abbie Ingvall."

A pair of policemen in thick coats with revolvers in their belts sidle past on the north edge of the sidewalk. They glance at Lucas and Andrea standing face to face by the steps of the church. One policeman nudges the other, but they continue walking.

"My collaborator? What gave you that idea?"

"You said so yourself in the gallery and at dinner. She told me she was going to give it to you. I'm doing that for her."

"Why did she give you the list?"

"She didn't. I took it from her." Andrea says this and then stops. Her eyes waver as if cutting off a flow of other things she would like to have added.

Lucas draws a deep breath, as before stepping onto a stage. He looks around, to the traffic, to the buildings with their glassy fronts across the street, the reversed images of cars and pedestrians flashing in the windows.

"Why did you go back to the gallery the night the pictures were stolen? That was you, right? You went in and wrote on the wall."

"It was me. The night after the opening, I couldn't sleep. I wandered around. I passed the gallery and saw the pictures gone, the door standing open. There was no one around. I dared myself to go in and leave you a message."

Lucas considers this for a minute. He changes direction. "You chased down the relatives of the people in my photos all over northern Europe over the past two weeks. You must have had their addresses for a while. Where did you get the addresses?"

"Abbie Ingvall's granddaughter gave them to me." Andrea says this, again, with an air of accusation.

"Hannah didn't steal the folder of negatives with the addresses in it until two days ago."

Andrea waves a dismissive hand. "She had them before that. Her grandmother gave her the information when she first told the girl about your exhibit. I saw Abbie Ingvall talking to the girl in a restaurant near the zoo one day when I was following Abbie. I approached the girl later and told her I was writing a book about Abbie Ingvall. She told me everything she knew. She was proud of her grandmother." Andrea's face turns aside for a moment.

The two policemen emerge from the space between the old and new churches. They descend the steps near Lucas and Andrea. They casually study the pair as they pass behind Lucas.

"Why are you involving yourself in this? Who are you?" Lucas says to Andrea.

"I came to Berlin to find out."

"Why Berlin?"

"This is where the bodies are buried. And you're here."

A siren passes in the street. They wait to speak further until it has passed. In the space of that time, Andrea's mask of a face melts and quivers. Her visage is suddenly familiar to Lucas.

"You are my father." Andrea says this. It is not a declarative statement. It is not an accusation. It is instead an admission of some variety of guilt.

Lucas lifts his eyebrows. He nods. "That's possible. I had a rough run as a younger man."

"I came hoping to locate you," Andrea says. "To see you. To learn what you do and why. To find out about you, and therefore about myself. As you put it, to find out who I am. But I was wary because you are a murderer."

In a lull in traffic noise, she begins to speak in a rush. Her hands lift from her sides toward Lucas, into the space over the bronze fracture in the pavement between them.

"I read all the articles about you that I could find. I read the chapter about you in a biography of fallen movie stars. I came here unsure of what to expect.

"After I located where you lived, I was afraid to speak to you. I was afraid of what you might be like. I followed you around. I did research. I went to the library, the Staatsbibliotek. Talking to someone there, some chipper and talkative graduate student, I learned the name of Abbie Ingvall who also worked at the library. I was told she was a close friend of yours. I also learned the name of her partner, Eloise Lawrens.

"I found where they live. I approached Eloise Lawrens when Abbie Ingvall wasn't home. I told her I was writing an article about Abbie for a magazine and wanted outside viewpoints.

She happened to drop that Abbie had once worked for the East German government.

"Not just the government, I later found out. The Stasi. She was a handler and enforcer. She was responsible for the deaths of a lot of people. At least this many." She reaches out and taps the portfolio in Lucas' hands.

Andrea's galvanized mask has returned. She speaks over the racket of a cluster of young people on skateboards who approach on the sidewalk. They all suddenly stop and pick up and carry their skateboards when they see the two policemen, who stand on the steps not far from Lucas and Andrea.

"Abbie Ingvall thought she had managed to cover up her past life," Andrea says. "What she failed to understand is that a lot of people still remember. Underneath the crust of liberal, artsy, vibrant, peace-loving Berlin is an old, seething collective memory of a century of wrongdoing and legions of wrong-doers. Berliners seek to forget and move along. But that deep-rooted habit of never forgetting, that ancient training, doesn't let them. Ask around. You learn things that weren't supposed to be known.

"I came to Berlin to learn whether there was anything left for me to gather from you, my biological father. The seed from which I sprang, the blood in my veins.

"I learned that in addition to being a murderer, which everyone already knew, you were raised by Nazis and you were in partnership with a Stasi executioner. You playfully exhibited photos of Stasi victims. You challenged the world to say anything or do anything about it. No one was saying anything. So, I did. I spoke up first to Abbie Ingvall. Now I'm speaking up to you."

Andrea's hands, shaking in front of her, now suddenly drop. She stands like a lawyer whose closing argument has ended.

The two policemen have taken out their phones. They appear to be comparing images. They look back and forth repeatedly. One takes a surreptitious photo of Andrea over Lucas's shoulder. The other has dialed a number and has turned and is talking to someone in a low voice.

Lucas gazes directly into Andrea's eyes. His look is level, both in the sense that his glittering blue eyes do not waver and that she is exactly his height. She is tall, like Frankie.

Lucas says, "It's odd. The dead don't stay dead and the living are never fully alive." This elicits no response from Andrea, nor, perhaps was it so intended, since he states it in a whisper, as if wondering to himself.

Then he says more directly to her, "How do you know I am your father?"

"My adoptive parents told me so. It's in the adoption papers. They waited until I was eighteen. I think they were afraid of you because of your past. And it's taken twenty years for me to build up the resolve to come and find you. For a long time, I thought I didn't care. I told myself not to care."

Lucas says, "Who did they tell you your mother was?"

"I don't know. It wasn't in the records. My mother abandoned me. I've been left to make my own way in the world. To create myself. I started with going to school and learning a trade. I'm an accountant. I add things up. But to understand the sum of credits and debits, you must begin with a balance. In my case, that meant learning who my parents were. I've learned all I want to know about you. Next I have to unearth my mother."

Lucas says, "I think I might be able to help you with that. Unless there were other mystery children in my past, which is possible, I believe I know who your mother is. But first, there are three things you should know about your ancestors on my side."

He pauses. She pauses. The two of them stand together without speaking for a long moment. Then, by a slight change of posture, the carriage of her head, she seems to acquiesce.

Lucas counts on the fingers of his left hand as he speaks.

"First, your grandparents Sonia and Rupert, my parents, were not Nazis. They hated Nazis. They also hated the Stasi. They were rare heroes. They stuck their necks out. That's what got them killed.

"Second, Abbie Ingvall is guilty of everything you say. But she was also a—I won't say victim—a product of complicated history in the process of trying to redress her past. That's all anyone can ask of another. We're all products of history. Those photos of her victims that wound up in my exhibit were a part of that atonement, which I didn't understand when she gave them to me. I only learned the reality of Abbie Ingvall's life after her death. Buried in the earth, she is teaching me. Life's most powerful lessons spring from the ground, from the dark and the past. They are chthonic, like Greek gods. Abbie Ingvall's burns, received the night the Stasi fell, started a long, slow process which ended last week in the freezing river.

"Third—and this is the least important point—it turns out that I'm not a murderer. I learned this today from the only eyewitness. I had never been sure of the truth before. I couldn't remember through my haze, or chose not to.

"I always assumed I was guilty, and thus accepted my whipping willingly. I carry generations of guilt on my shoulders. Orphan's guilt. But in fact, in a clumsy, drunken, stupid effort, I tried to save my wife's life that night.

"Like you, Andrea, I sought to understand what had happened to me, and who I was. The only way forward is to embrace the ugliness of what happened before.

"If anyone ever tells you not to regret your past, they don't know what they're talking about. It's only through deep, fiery regret over the hurt we've caused others that we have any chance of improving our flawed and damaged selves in the short time we are given. The good sort of regret begets humility. One should value regret, not abhor and discard it.

"And if anyone suggests that you should hate the people who have hurt you, that it is right to do so, remember that there is no person who has not hurt and been badly hurt. We all limp slowly toward the fire."

"You sound like a priest," Andrea says, but not with rancor.

"I'm an atheist. And an ex-drunk."

"Was your wife Katherine my mother?"

"No. But I think I know who was. That's another thing I learned today. I can introduce you to her. She would like to meet you."

The two policemen have put away their phones. One draws his gun. The other unsheathes a pair of handcuffs. They descend the steps and approach Lucas and Andrea quickly.

"You've been electronically identified as a person of interest in a murder investigation," one of the policemen, the one with the gun, says loudly and with careful German enunciation. "We are placing you under arrest."

He says this to Andrea.

As they lead her away, she looks back at Lucas, nakedly. Her blue eyes, a reflection of his own, ask to hear the rest of the story.

PART FOUR

TWO TESTIMONIES

CHAPTER 38

Hannah Müller

I can't do anything right.

Everything I touch seems to fall apart in my hands. I wonder if this is the life I'm destined for. It wouldn't surprise me. My life got off to a weird start. It keeps getting weirder and weirder. The problem is, I don't know how to fix it. I don't know what to do.

I let Abbie down.

She told me to learn to trust people. She said this because she could tell how little I've ever trusted anyone. It took weeks before I would say three sentences in a row to her when we met for coffee. I've always felt that if I open my mouth, people will see who I really am. And who I really am is not anything anyone will appreciate seeing.

She told me to remember that people's motives are complex. She said this because I'm always talking about how everyone has only one goal, usually money or fame or sex. For some people, their goal is just happiness, or safety. All anyone wants from you is to squeeze as much of their goal out of you as they can. Then they discard you.

She told me to stay in school. I promptly dropped out.

She asked me to help her. I didn't understand. I don't think I tried. I couldn't imagine that an old person who had been through everything would need help, and certainly not from someone like me. I can't even help myself.

I let Lucas down. I stole his belongings. I hurt him. Then when he befriended me, I tried to sleep with him. What an ass I am. I've been on my own since I was fifteen, and sometimes I feel like I've seen and done everything, but I don't understand the first thing about how to be an adult. I was grateful that he let me down easy. The humiliation I felt that night was just the right amount. He understood that.

I disappointed my mother. With all her problems, I realized then and I realize now how much she did for me, how much she tried to do beyond what she was capable of doing. I never admitted it to her. I ran away from her. I'll never be as strong for my child as she was for me. I'll probably never have a child.

I even let Klaus down. Silly man. I got so wound up in resisting him, in acting like his girlfriend and then telling him I forgot my birth control pill, ignoring his lectures on socialism, neglecting to make his dinner when I made mine, borrowing his belongings, asking him for rides everywhere, asking him for money. But when I got frantic and asked him to commit a felony with me, he stepped up. Then I turned myself in and almost got him arrested. That man deserves at least an apology from me. If I ever see him again.

That strange woman Andrea started all of this. All the problems I caused recently. She came up to me one day out of nowhere and asked me if I was related to Abbie Ingvall. She said she was writing a book about Abbie. It sounded so grand.

She asked me if I had any information that I could share with her about Abbie's projects. It happened that I had a list of four addresses in my bag that Abbie had given me the day before. I told Andrea that the addresses had something to do with a photo project involving Lucas Block that Abbie had told me about. Andrea copied down the addresses.

Abbie had given the addresses to me as a backup because, as she put it, "Lucas may not notice what he's supposed to notice." She meant the addresses on the wrappers of the negatives that Lucas later found and showed us. If he hadn't seen them, I was supposed to give him the list.

Abbie didn't know if she would be able to do it herself. She told me this. That was one of the things that scared me so much. I thought it had something to do with Lucas' pictures. I thought someone was out to get Abbie.

I never realized it was Andrea.

I was doing my best to follow Abbie's advice—to believe in people's inherent good nature. I trusted Andrea because she seemed so earnest, so passionate. She seemed genuine.

The problem with trusting people is that they don't deserve it. Most people are image, with nothing but emptiness behind. Most people are outfits on mannikins in the windows of second-hand shops.

Me, for instance.

CHAPTER 39

Lucas Block

They led my daughter away in handcuffs.

I felt nothing at the time, of course. This unknown woman had accosted me and accused me and derided me. I think I felt a little flare of triumph at the moment she was arrested.

But the adrenaline of the encounter faded into that grainy substance that follows. Later, sensations deeper than anger began to unfold within me.

At least she might be my daughter. She might also be some crazy person making a claim. DNA tests seem to be in the offing. Back when I was in the movie business, we spoke of the risks constantly. Stories circulated among actors, in particular, about people coming out of the woodwork to sue for paternity and make a mess of things. And it happened not infrequently.

Though never to me. At least not until now.

But Andrea seemed somehow different; not like I would envision a gold-digger. Believable. In that conversation on the street, I couldn't shake the notion that she came off to me like a person whose feelings could be trusted. And, apart from looking a little like me and a little like Frankie, she seemed to resemble me in some odd, deeper ways.

Andrea had completed the work I'd set out to do when I came to this city.

As a child might do for a failed parent.

I had collapsed away from the task I'd set for myself of finding the truth about my parents, and by extrapolation rebuilding my view of myself. I'd touched upon the task shortly after arriving in Berlin. Immediately, I'd learned a few items about my family, especially the suggestions of their connection to Nazism. I wilted. After what I'd been through in Los Angeles, I needed to go upward instead of downward. I promptly deserted any quest for my past. Instead, I bought a Leica and started going for long walks at night, photographing street art in the shadows.

A fortress formed around me composed of Heike and Mama and then later my old buddies Nik and Frankie. No one spoke of the past. It was as if there was no past. We were nothing but the cool, colorful, jaded, sadly superior, aggressively self-satisfied environment we'd taken on as expatriates. It was as if we had become the city in which we lived.

Andrea blew the whole thing apart.

I didn't know how to tell Frankie that the child she'd told me about, the baby she had abandoned, had emerged like a vengeful specter from the tomb.

I didn't know how to reveal to her that this child of ours was probably going to prison for killing the person who murdered my parents.

Although I'd said nothing yet, it didn't seem as difficult to tell Heike about a mistake of youth. As if she didn't imagine that such things had happened. As if she hadn't begot a few complications of her own, that wild young farm girl running about Paris in the early eighties. But I wanted to find the right time. I wanted to tell the story properly.

I didn't want us to devolve into, "Guess what, I deceived you when we met," counter-balanced by, "Well guess what, I had a child with your best friend."

I wasn't sure what to say to Nik. In a way, I felt only numbness. I honestly didn't mind any more the fact that I'd spent six months in prison and watched my world destroyed. I embraced it. It was my cherished regret. Incarceration, humiliation and loss were overdue invoices for the good fortune I'd had in my life and the carelessness with which I'd spent that good fortune. Prison was my twelve steps.

But it would have been nice to know at the time what Nik had seen on the edge of that cliff. I certainly couldn't have said. In the fog of gin, I assumed the worst of myself. Un-countered, assumptions become beliefs and beliefs become reality.

Heike, Frankie, Nik and I—we had been a quadrangle arranged around a core. In the center of that square, Mama exerted gravity in four directions. She controlled us. She set us at each other quietly, meticulously and with great politeness. She was an artist. What she had once done for a government she had continued doing to protect herself. Manipulation wasn't just her job, it was Abbie Ingvall. In real life, through all the ups and downs, people seldom change personality or the survival tactics out of childhood.

Andrea, with Hannah's bumbling assistance, broke the delicate tension holding it together.

With Mama gone, the geometry was re-forming. I was now at the center. I would re-build us, our little coalition of aging, footloose, transgressive, interwoven souls. This is what I came to this city to do. It is my mission.

The task was there all along. It just took me a long time and a hard shove to get around to it.

PART FIVE

FOREGROUND. BACKGROUND.
VIEWPOINT.

<h1 style="text-align:center">CHAPTER 40</h1>

Lucas and Heike stand on the bridge called Friedrichsbrücke. The bridge crosses the Spree river from the east to Bodestraße on Museum Island.

The two of them lean against the old stone parapet. Together, they gaze down into the water. Lucas' arm is around her.

It is morning. The day came up clear and blue—the first in weeks. Scarves coil around their necks under the collars of their thick coats. Their breaths wrap clouds around their faces as they speak softly and lowly to each other.

"This is where they talked," Lucas says. He swivels and looks over Heike's shoulder and lifts his arm from her back to point.

"That's the camera that caught their discussion," he says. "Andrea was facing that direction, so the camera had a very good view of her face. That's how the police identified her.

"All Andrea and Mama did here was to argue. But then they moved that direction and out of the camera's view. The camera on the other side of the pillar was not working. That's when Andrea pushed her. It was three in the morning. There was no one around."

He is pointing now to a place lower on the curved bridge, closer to the street. Heike follows his gesture.

"The railing is so high," Heike says. "Abbie was tiny. If she was pushed, she wouldn't have fallen up and over the railing. Andrea must have picked her up and thrown her. Andrea is tall and strong. Like her mother."

"That's what the police think, also. But Andrea is saying she just pushed her. Not even pushed. Andrea is saying that as she was trying to pull the list from her hand, Mama just fell backward and over the edge."

A clot of cyclists on rental bikes ascend the gentle slope of the bridge to its center, where Lucas and Heike stand, and then slowly descend the other side and turn in under the arch toward the Pergamon.

Lucas continues, "But the physical movements surrounding her death may be more complicated. She did, after all, intend to bring about some sort of ending. The suitcase of things—that was essentially a suicide note."

"The list of people Abbie had killed." Heike looks out over the river again. She is simply musing to no one.

"That too. Mama was bringing the list to me," Lucas says. "It was to be one of her last acts. She was giving up. She was always badly depressed. The appearance of Andrea pushed her over the edge. Literally."

Neither smile. Instead, Heike asks, "How do you know this?"

"Andrea called me again this morning while you were in the shower. She's out on bail. She told me her version of what happened. That's why I wanted to come here. To see for myself."

"She called you, eh? Did she call you Dad?"

"Heike, cut her some slack. She's a mess."

"Someone died. None of this needed to happen."

"Nothing bad that happens ever needs to happen."

Heike turns to him and wraps her arms slowly around him. Sorrowed faces hidden, they stand like two casual lovers in the sunshine on the old bridge for a minute. Her face is against his neck and his face is buried in her long, waving blanket of brown hair streaked with gray. Her left hearing aid squeals slightly, as they do, when his head gets close to hers, but she doesn't pull away.

Lucas whispers to her. "In *Hamlet*, when the first ghost is departing, he cries, 'Stay, Illusion!' Hamlet doesn't want the past to vanish. It has so much to teach us."

They stand a while longer in the quiet and the cold.

"I love that about you," Heike says quietly.

"What?"

"Nothing in particular. Everything. I just love you." She stops for a few moments but then elaborates. "I love that you see a positive way forward. Even if it means walking though fire."

Her arms still around him, she pulls back her head a few inches. She looks into his face.

"Perhaps it's all for the best," she says. "Everything's exploded. But we can't run from ghosts forever."

Lucas smiles sadly at her and nods in slow agreement.

He says, "We run from ghosts, but we never escape. They belong to us. We possess them. Our ghosts are the things we hide and never say aloud."

— CHAPTER 41 —

An hour before sunrise, Lucas rises in his chilly flat and dresses in jeans, boots and thick overcoat. He wraps a scarf. He dons a driver's cap. He selects a camera from a collection in a glass-doored cabinet—his familiar old Zeiss Ikon with the fold-open lens carriage. He checks the film.

Leaving his building, he glances upward to gauge the sky. He notices the facade of the building across the square. The enormous banner of the young woman's downturned face is gone.

A golden sky, velvet with promise. A late winter day, clear horizon to horizon, though horizons are imagined in the city. The pleasure of cold; the limn of warmth to come.

He walks to the river. He crosses under the gate. He passes through Tiergarten. He circles to Potsdamer. He parallels the remnant of the Wall and eventually back into the heart of East Berlin.

He takes no photos. Instead, he holds the warm camera in his hand deep in his coat pocket as he walks and walks, kilometer after kilometer.

In the other pocket, in the palm of his other hand, he cradles the key found in the bottom of the suitcase. He does not know what this key might open. It came to him with no discernible history. But it must open something, and he may yet discover what.

At dawn, Berlin has an abandoned feeling, though there are always people about doing early-morning things. Berlin feels like a city that has been lost and then found again. There is nothing dead about Berlin at this hour.

This is Lucas' favorite time of day.

CHAPTER 42

Under its arched eyebrow of halogen lights, the left front window of Denver Gallery has received a new sign in the form of half-meter script letters applied to the glass. It now reads *travelers*.

A smaller sign in gold letters hangs over the gallery's hour-board displayed on the front door. It reads *grand re-opening*.

Inside, four of the original five composite photos the size of twin-bed mattresses hang in their previous positions. However, the name plates for these photos have changed.

The first reads *traveler #1: Trudi Becker*. The second reads *traveler #2: Gunther Goldschmidt*. The third reads *traveler #3: Rainer Weiss*. The fourth reads *traveler #4: Marie Kiel*.

The fifth photo on the transverse rear wall reads *travelers #5: Sonia and Rupert Bloch*. The shot, a vertical photo at their wedding, is clearly much older than the others. It has the clarity and air of the ancient and eternal—fine-grained film shot at high shutter-speed with an eye for the moment. The just-married couple emerges from the doorway of a gothic church. They stand on the paving stones. The portal enveloping the couple is sepulchral. The stone walls and ironwork of the church on either side of the doorway weep black and white detail.

This print, unlike the others, has not been artfully doctored into a composite. It is stark. It is root and kernel. It has been made large as life.

Gone is the horizontal image of a young Abbie Ingvall.

A substantial crowd, even more so than the last time, circulates in the gallery. Music plays; drinks flow.

Among the gathered are people that Lucas has flown in for the occasion from Stockholm, Edinburgh, Zermatt and Tallinn. Thérèse Hillyard chats with Erich Goldschmidt. Carl Becker and his wife converse with Camille Larsen and her husband. East German diaspora, they find they have much in common.

The front door opens and Hannah enters the gallery quietly, glancing about. She wears a typical outfit: flower-embroidered coat to her thighs, tight beige slacks with a river-wide belt, cracked and knurled knee-high boots of obvious mileage and years, round purple glasses in gold wire frames. Her hair, as always, is a deliberate and febrile mess. Women around the room turn and stare and absorb, even in an art gallery in Berlin.

Behind, Klaus enters the gallery shyly and nervously. He strokes his beard. He's worn an old corduroy blazer for the evening, a majestic gesture. He stands slightly adjacent, surveying. Hannah looks about for Lucas. Lucas detaches from a group and comes to her. Hannah glows.

Later, a group of four people—Nik, Frankie, Heike and Lucas—stand together on the raised area toward the rear of the gallery before the counter with its lone lamp. They have clung together for a moment of respite from the crowd and the noise.

"To restoration," Frankie says. They raise glasses, champagne flutes for Heike and Frankie, a whiskey glass for Nik, a bottle of mineral water for Lucas.

"Never mind the bollocks," Nik says, apropos of nothing.

The front door opens and with no fanfare a woman enters. She is blonde. She wears a red coat with chrome zippers.

"I can't believe she came here," whispers Nik.

Slowly, Lucas leans to Heike and says softly, "You see why I asked you to give that woman some slack. She has courage."

"She's your daughter," Heike says.

The woman in the red coat walks slowly over to the group of four. She stands before them. She watches Lucas unwaveringly, as if he possesses the key to her survival.

Lucas reaches out a hand to her. The woman steps forward. Lucas turns to Frankie.

"Frankie," he says, "allow me to introduce your daughter, Andrea."

At this moment, no one in the room is paying attention to this group except Hannah. Hannah draws her phone from her bag and snaps a quick photo of Lucas and Frankie with Andrea standing between them, Heike on Lucas' left and Nik on Frankie's right.

Five broken souls, each broken in his and her own way. Each glued back together. In Hannah's photo, the light from the little lamp on the table casts their splayed shadows across the floor.

Inveterate wanderer PETER ANDERSON has visited more than 60 countries, including extensive travels in all corners of Europe. His sharp observational skills bring depth to his writing about distant lands and keen insight about the people encountered along the way. Anderson studied English, Psychology, and Creative Writing at the Universities of Wyoming and Washington. He lives in eastern Idaho at the foot of the Grand Teton range amid a personal library of more than 7,500 volumes. His essays and non-fiction work have appeared in regional and national publications over the previous 40 years. *Viewfinder* is the second installment of the *Expatriate Trio*, published by Limberlost Press.

---------- ACKNOWLEDGMENTS ----------

My deep thanks go to Rick Ardinger, whose belief, assistance and friendship has been, for many years, one of the brightest elements of my life. Rick, master of the delicate art of letterpress printing and *maestro* of Beat literature, you're a star in the firmament of Idaho arts and letters.

To Meggan Laxalt Mackey, thank you for your dedication to your craft and to supporting writers and artists from the region. Combined with everything you do for the Basque community of Idaho, you're a significant element in the preservation and dissemination of Idaho history and arts. I'm forever pleased to call you friend.

Established in 1950 by the East German communist government, the Stasi (*Ministerium für Staatssicherheit*, or Ministry for State Security) was hated and feared by the East German people. At the outset, its principal role was to spy on the citizenry to identify malcontents and anti-communist individuals. However, over the span of its activity (until 1990), the Stasi also engaged in physical and psychological torture in its quest to quash dissent.

The psychological warfare practice called *Zersetzung* (literally: *decomposition*) grew in use by the Stasi after 1970 at which point physical torture had come to be viewed as too provocative and politically unsupportable. *Zersetzung* is, put simply, the art of surreptitiously driving a subject to the belief that he or she is insane. It was frequently focused by the Stasi on members of the public in the Eastern sector who had come to the attention of the communist government as being potential or actual dissenters.

The Stasi gathered personal information and kept secret files, often voluminous, on millions of East German citizens. During the collapse of communist East Germany in late 1989 and early 1990, a pivotal and significant event was the storming of the Stasi's Lichtenberg headquarters in an attempt to stop Stasi officials from destroying records. Many records were shredded or incinerated; however, millions of files survived. To this day, Germans continue to sift through the files hoping to uncover the information collected and wrongs committed by the Stasi to them and to their families, rebuilding pasts destroyed by the 20th Century's litany of terrible events.

FROM

LIMBERLOST PRESS

Gone in October
Last Reflections on Jack Kerouac

By John Clellon Holmes

> "He has awed me with his talents, enraged me with his stubbornness, educated me in my craft, hurt me through indifference, dogged my imagination, upset most of my notions, and generally enlarged me as a writer more than anyone else I know."
>
> *–John Clellon Holmes*
> from *"The Great Rememberer"*

On the July 4th weekend of 1948, John Clellon Holmes (1926-1988) met Jack Kerouac (1922-1969) in New York City for the first time, and the two became lifelong friends. As young, ambitious novelists, Holmes saw Kerouac as a mentor and comrade in a literary movement eventually known as the Beat Generation. They shared New England roots and the same birthday. They were characters in each other's novels, and they fed each other encouragement through letters and get-togethers at Holmes's home in Old Saybrook, Connecticut, until Kerouac's untimely death at 47, on October 21, 1969.

Originally published in a very limited edition by Limberlost Press in 1985, Holmes's essays/memoirs here reflect on Kerouac's burning innovation as a writer, on their New England heritage, on attending his funeral with poets Allen Ginsberg and Gregory Corso, and on the 1982 Naropa Institute celebration of the 25th anniversary of the publication of Kerouac's novel On the Road, a gathering which Holmes saw as a last hurrah with other movers and shakers of the Beat movement.

This new edition of *Gone in October*, newly designed and illustrated with more photographs, is a deeply heart-felt remembrance of literary friendship and personal loss, reprinted in commemoration of the 2022 Jack Kerouac centennial.

$17.95 (Plus $3 Media Mail shipping; Idaho orders please add 6% sales tax)
Purchase this and other books at **www.limberlostpress.com**, *or send check to:*
Limberlost Press, 17 Canyon Trail, Boise, Idaho 83716

LIMBERLOST PRESS

Rick and Rosemary Ardinger began Limberlost Press in the spring of 1976 with the publication of *The Limberlost Review*, (Edition No. 1), a magazine of poetry. The first issues of the magazine were quick-printed, collated, folded, and stapled and distributed like many other small press magazines of the 1960s and 1970s. In 1986, the Ardingers winched a couple of Chandler & Price platen presses into their garage and began to typeset and print the books themselves.

Limberlost Press is dedicated to publishing finely printed books of poetry, fiction, and non-fiction by both established and emerging writers. The Ardingers believe that fine work deserves to be presented and preserved on fine papers. Their poetry chap-books are letterpress printed on archival-quality papers and sewn by hand into limited editions for collectors and other discerning readers. They want readers to collect these books as heirlooms to pass along to the next generation.

Occasionally the press publishes books of longer length (stories, memoirs, and novels) via offset methods. Most man-uscripts are acquired by invitation; however, Limberlost Press welcomes submissions of quality poetry, fiction, and nonfiction by both new and established writers.

The press has published works by Allen Ginsberg, Sherman Alexie, Anne Waldman, Ed Dorn, Gary Snyder, John Haines, Gary Gildner, Robert Creeley, Keith Wilson, Hayden Carruth, Lawrence Ferlinghetti, and more. Limberlost Press is committed to publishing writers from the Mountain West, including William Studebaker, Margaret Aho, Sandy Anderson, Chris Dempsey, Ray Obermayr, Nancy Stringfellow, Alex Kuo, John Rember, Gerald Grimmett, Greg Keeler, Joy Passanante, David Beisley-Guiotto, Gino Sky, and others.

The Limberlost Review is an anthology that features some of the best writing from the Mountain West and beyond, including poetry, fiction, memoir, essay, translation, commentary about books we come back to again, interviews, artwork, and more.

To order the 2019, 2020, 2021, and 2022 editions of *The Limberlost Review*, or to purchase other items from Limberlost Press, contact:

Rick and Rosemary Ardinger
editors@limberlostpress.com
www.limberlostpress.com
17 Canyon Trail, Boise, Idaho 83716

Viewfinder is set in a classic serif typeface, *Goudy Old Style*. It was designed by Frederic W. Goudy for American Type Founders (ATF) in 1915. Goudy was a master of type design who led the field in the first half of the twentieth century in America.

Goudy Old Style was inspired by sixteenth-century Italian printing. Goudy added distinctive calligraphic elements to his typeface, including diamond-shaped dots, beautiful ligatures, and graceful italic letters. It is a classic typeface for fine books.

The *Viewfinder* cover and endsheet illustrations are by sisters Meghan and Kathleen Hanson, formerly from Driggs, Idaho, who now work and live in Stevensville, Montana.

The map illustration is by Erin Ann Jensen, a Boise native who now resides in Vancouver, Washington.

Author Peter Anderson is also a photographer. Each Part of *Viewfinder* is introduced with one of Peter's black-and-white photos. Each Chapter also begins with a smaller "snippet" from the primary photo for that part of the book, intended to encourage readers to look deeper into the photographs.

The Dedication and About the Author photographs are by Jeanne Anderson.

Meggan Laxalt Mackey (owner of Studio M Publications & Design in Boise, Idaho) is the book designer for both *Follower* and *Viewfinder*.

Viewfinder was published in 2023 by Rick and Rosemary Ardinger of the Limberlost Press, Boise, Idaho. *Viewfinder* is part of the *Expatriate Trio* by Peter Anderson. The group also includes the novels *Follower* and *Builder*.

HANSON

 LIMBERLOST PRESS